Scar Tissue

Scar Tissue

JUDITH CUTLER

This edition first published in Great Britain in 2005 by
Allison & Busby Limited
Bon Marche Centre
241-251 Ferndale Road
London SW9 8BJ
http://www.allisonandbusby.com

A catalogue record for this book is available from
the British Library.

10 9 8 7 6 5 4 3 2 1

ISBN 0 7490 8323 9

Printed and bound in Great Britain by
Bookmarque Ltd, Croydon, Surrey

JUDITH CUTLER began writing at an early age, and after studying English Literature she worked as a lecturer in Birmingham for many years. Her career as a writer began in earnest whilst recovering from chickenpox and her short stories have been widely published in magazines, anthologies and read on the radio. She is the author of two series set in the Birmingham area featuring Detective Kate Power and lecturer and amateur sleuth Sophie Rivers. *Scar Tissue* is her nineteenth novel.

For Kate Emans and the Paint Pot Girls,
who resemble Paula's Pots only in their enthusiasm
and professionalism

Chapter One

The July day was very bright, the window reflecting like a mirror, so I might have been mistaken. I blinked hard, shading my eyes with my free hand – there was no way I'd let go with the other, not this high off the ground – and peered again. It was a body on that bed, all right. A dead body, if the rope round the neck meant anything. It was our rope, too. Paula's Pots' rope. Some of the strong blue plastic stuff we use to hold back climbing plants and roses – especially roses – from parts we need to paint. The sort we use to tie the back of the van securely, or lash the ladders on top. I'd left a coil with our other gear, in a lock-up garage the owner let us decorators use. As luck would have it I was working on my own today – the others were over near Tenterden tackling a big urgent job that the July rain had delayed. I opened my mouth to let rip with a few appropriate words, the sort that Paula, the Boss, so disapproved of. Well, she wasn't anywhere round to hear.

But that wasn't the sort of thing ladies did round here, was it? Not nice well-brought up young ladies. Though that didn't apply to me, anyway. I was one of the Lower Orders, a working girl, paint all over my hands and trainers to prove it. And an accent that everyone down here had decided was pretty well foreign.

I came down my ladder rather quicker than I'd gone up, not easy with a brimming paint can in one hand and a brand new paintbrush in the other. I didn't want to put one in the other because that would mean I had to clean it. Paula was very keen on clean brushes. Halfway down I saw sense and shoved it in my bib for safe-keeping.

Damn it, a body on a bed wasn't the sort of thing you'd expect in the country. I mean, back where I used to work, up in Birmingham, where there were turf wars between drugs barons and battles between rival pimps, you got used to seeing the odd body that hadn't died of old age in its bed. I wiped my hands on my dungarees and fished out my mobile. Only to find we were in a black spot. That's the trouble with rural life. All those things you take for granted aren't there. Like mobile phone masts and round-the-clock supermarkets and big anonymous pubs. Well, anonymity in general. Which is how I knew that when I turned up at a police station with my big news they'd have heard a few rumours about me: someone's mother or cousin would have whispered to someone's father or nephew. So I'd be lost in the credibility stakes before I'd even started.

I always was a sucker for civic duty, though – a proper little Girl Guide without the uniform, me, and always had been. Litter, old ladies needing the far side of the road, motorists needing directions, old men needing a helping hand – that sort of good deed. I ran to the end of the road, still trying to provoke a spark of life from the moribund mobile, before realising this wasn't going to get me anywhere. So I ran back – not sensible in the summer sun, which in Kent can shine quite convincingly, especially at midday – and shoved my stuff in the lock-up garage. If I could get what Paula insisted on calling Trev, and I preferred to think of simply as the Transit, to start, I'd do my civic duty in person. For once he – or in my terms, it – coughed into life on the second try, and we bundled off down an archetypal leafy lane in the direction of Lavange, the nearest village of any size. I knew where the police house was – I'd driven past it a couple of times. And found it with only three false starts. You see, a city girl's used to big reflecting road signs, not discreet little finger-posts, readable only if you're going at the rate of a pony and trap, and though the Transit was never going to win at Le Mans, it wasn't that slow. Anyway, there it was – except it was no longer a police house, any old police house, that is, but Peel House, its architectural inadequacies hidden under bristling scaffolding. A chippy was just carrying his box through what would no doubt be turned into a noble false front aspect quadrupling its real estate value.

'Nah. Closed a few weeks ago. A couple of days after the post office and a month before the pub.'

'So where's the nearest cop shop?'

'You could try Halham: that's open during the week, I think.'

By now, what with the heat and the maze of roads going nowhere, I was thoroughly rattled. If I'd had any sense, of course, I'd have tried my mobile again. But I was now on a quest, a mission. And missions inevitably mean blinkers.

Half an hour later I found the police station at Halham. Someone had made an effort with hanging baskets and tubs, which made my heart sink – another spot of privatisation by the look of things. No. There was an official-looking front door, complete with entry phone. But not one to admit me. I was your hoi polloi, wasn't I? If I wanted to talk to the forces of Law and Order I could press a button or two and be put through to the main station in Ashford. I pressed. I pressed again. And nothing happened. I did the obvious thing. I banged the door and the adjoining window and yelled blue murder.

OK. A nod is as good as a wink to a blind man, as my gran used to say. It was clear I had to head for Ashford. I was on piecework, I had a house to paint in the brief interval of fine weather before the rain inevitably returned and here I was, driving to one of Kent's less inspired country towns. Another day I'd have gasped at the beauty of the Downs I was driving across. Another day I'd have thought it charming to be held up by a little train chugging slowly across the road by a quaint old pub called the Tickled Trout. Today I'd have swapped the lot for Spaghetti Junction. Not to mention a motorcycle patrolman in his gorgeous leathers to whom I could have poured out all my woes.

Ashford has an irritating ring-road, which always traps me in the wrong lane. It's got plenty of car parks, but you have to pay for those and I was parking simply as a helpful citizen, not as a mean shopper. There must be a spot for helpful Josephine Publics by the police station. There was. By the library. Jealously guarded by a parking warden, puce with the heat – or with anger: a motorist was just skidaddling out of the way. If I'd been in a linen dress in a Volvo, I might have got away with a smile and a nod and a point at the police station. Overalls and a Transit? Hardly. I ended up paying. Perhaps my honesty – OK, my cowardice – would stand me in good stead at the nick.

I've never felt comfortable in police stations – well, who does, apart, I suppose, from the folk who work there? But I squared my shoulders and breezed in, ready to confront an impregnable desk sergeant. Relief: the woman at the front desk was a civilian about my age and casual with it, at least about her mascara, some of which was melting into her sweat. She looked like those white-faced clowns I saw when I was very, very small and at my first and last circus. What was it the shrink on the detox programme had said: revisit your inner child? Well, there were flyers for a circus out Great Chart way early next week: I might take myself along if I have the time. I passed her a rather seedy Kleenex from my back pocket – in my panic I'd forgotten to peel my dungarees off, so I was even hotter than I needed to be. She rang through for an officer, and assured me, while I waited, that he was an absolute pussycat and I mustn't be put off by his fierce face. I'm glad she had, or I'd have been absolutely terrified, whatever he looked like. The Filth had that effect on me. But I mustn't think of the police as Filth or Busies or anything derogatory, I told myself, standing at best Girl Guide attention as he materialised on the far side of the desk.

'DS Marsh,' he said, his eyes a completely smile-free zone.

I nearly quipped that I knew his brother Romney, but thought better of it. It was his eyebrows that were the trouble: tangles of ginger, like Brillo pads left to rust on the draining-board. They were much thicker than his age suggested – brows apart, I wouldn't have put him at much more than forty, about five nine tall and weighing in at about ten and a half stone.

'Caffy Tyler,' I said. 'Except I'm not a Tyler, but a painter.'

'Caffy Tyler?' His brows quivered disapproval.

'When I was little I couldn't say "th",' I explained. 'The name stuck. What I'm here for, Sergeant,' I continued, thinking it was time I grabbed the initiative, 'is to report a body. The body of a man in his fifties, I'd say. Big, heavy – lots of rings. In the guest bedroom of the house I'm painting at the moment.'

You'd think he heard such announcements every day. 'And where might that be?' He almost yawned.

'Crabton Manor. Near Lavange.'

'Full address?'

'That is its address. It's a big house – doesn't need common things like a house number or a street. But it's not a proper manor.'

'No?' For a moment he seemed almost interested.

'No. Nothing medieval about it. Not like the one out Singleton way. Just a Victorian status symbol – you know the sort of thing: I can afford to waste more wood than you can afford to waste.'

'Lots of –?' His index finger described turrets and curlicues.

'All the better for my pay packet. Until this afternoon. I've already lost two hours' wages coming over here.'

Without meaning to, I had his entire attention: 'Do you mean to tell me you've taken two hours to report a death?'

I reflected on my epic journey and found my chin hardening. 'Not quite. But it'll take me at least half an hour to get back Now, would you like the details or not?'

The interview room he ushered me into wasn't too bad – I'd certainly seen far worse. And while I'd rather expected him to radio for an immediate investigation, he seemed quite keen to get the details down as quickly as possible. After a moment or two towering over me, just to establish who was boss, no doubt, he sat down opposite me.

'Now, the owner of this Crabton Manor is – '

'A Mr van der Poele,' I said, spelling the last bit. 'A South African gentleman, if he deserves the term.' He'd beaten Paula, my boss, down to a profit margin thinner than a coat of paint. 'He's not around much, which is good, because he's got these huge dogs he lets run free. He thinks it's funny if the ugly great brutes trap you up the ladder just when you need your pee-break.'

'Tea break?'

'You heard what I said. He has a lot of visitors, whether he's there or not – a lot of coming and going.'

'And where is he now?'

'He told my boss, that's Paula Farmer – she lives out Folkestone way.' I burrowed in my bib and produced one of her business cards. She was very keen on us handing out cards, was Paula. But she might not have wanted him to clean under his nails with it. 'He told Paula that he'd be in London for a couple of days. She may have his number.' She was very efficient on contact details, too.

'Women painters!' He wouldn't be asking for a quote for his house, would he? No, he inspected the proceeds of his ad hoc manicure and dropped the card on the table.

'Yes. We do all sorts of jobs, large and small. One week it'll be a pensioner's bungalow, the next a big place – not just the Manor, but we hope to get the contract for a proper restoration job down at Fullers. We're doing the outside at the moment.'

'That place on the Isle of Oxney? Hmm.' He nodded a

couple of times, and pulled himself to his feet. 'I'll get on to my colleagues, Miss Tyler.'

I decided not to remind those eyebrows I was a Ms.

'Would you like a cup of tea while you wait?'

Though I'd rather have had water, I was too astounded by the offer to tell him so. I'd never known policemen to be so generous with refreshments.

While I drank whatever he – or more likely, Melting Mascara – had brewed, he took a short statement asking me exactly what I'd seen and done. I was happy to tell him, especially as he hadn't shown any signs of asking why I'd left my home city and come to Kent to work. He was as affable as Mascara had said he'd be.

Until she called him out of the room for a moment, and he came back in, his face like thunder.

'I take it you've never heard of the offence known as wasting police time, Miss Tyler? I have to inform you that my colleagues have found no signs of the body you allege was at Crabton Manor. So would you like to tell me what kind of game you think you're playing?'

Chapter Two

That miserable bugger Marsh more or less booted me out. There was no way I'd let him see how he'd rattled me, any more than I'd ever let coppers see how upset I was. Coppers or anyone else. Whatever the situation I always presented the stiffest of upper lips. I beamed brightly at Messy Mascara. From under her desk, I got a cheery wave; she was also giving Marsh a number of fingers so small even he should have been able to count them. He might have caught her screwing her index finger into her forehead but she managed to convert that into a dab at her eye.

At least the parking warden homing in on the Transit hadn't seen any of this, so I managed to convince her that I'd been to report a crime and since the police had been so impressed by my news they'd given me a cup of tea, which had held me up. Since she'd not actually done more than prime her pen, she let me off. She looked hot enough to melt: why has no one in authority twigged that blue serge isn't good news on hot days?

I regretted feeling sorry for the representatives of law and order when another serge-clad figure, albeit in shirtsleeves, hove into view. This one was a police constable with a gleam in his eye that told me that he was going to spend an hour at least checking whether the van deserved its MOT. I knew it did; the garage knew it did. Starting system apart, Paula believed in properly maintained tools, whether as small as a bradawl or as big as a bus. But Paula also believed in minimalism when it came to the law and her wheels, so I leapt inside, praying it'd start first pull. It did. And not a single nasty particle coming from its exhaust, not that I could smell, anyway. Paula's Pots was an environmentally friendly firm.

I didn't think anyone would ambush me with a speed-gun on the ring-road, but there was a lot of opportunity for an unfriendly traffic cop to accuse you of changing lanes at the wrong place or wrong speed or whatever, so I peeled off as soon as I could, heading for a great oval shopping mall called the Designer Outlet. Much as I was tempted to go and pick up a bargain or two, my conscience and the heat combined to make me pass virtuously by – them and the CCTV cameras I was sure the police would take an unnatural interest in today. No, these days I wasn't usually this paranoid, but there was something about Marsh that reawakened all my former feelings about the police. I reckon it's only the middle classes who believe they're friendly, supportive individuals. Certainly people with my background don't: we see folk literally getting away with murder because they speak nicely and know the right people. So I turned resolutely from trendy tops and picked my way gently back. It was good to find that, little by little, my pulse rate returned to normal and the only reason my palms were sweating was the heat. At last, after a decorous drive down the motorway, I was happy to park the van in the shade of one of Mr van der Poele's mighty oaks. Well, it was actually a sycamore, but Trev wasn't complaining and van der Poele wouldn't have admitted to anything as vulgar as a sycamore on his patch. Did he have anything as vulgar as a new shallow grave at the bottom of his garden? It didn't take me long to establish that he hadn't.

And there I was, back up my ladder at Crabton Manor, seething and two hours adrift on my day's schedule. Now the sun had shifted round, it was easier to see through the window: no, there was nothing on the bed, not now, but you didn't need to be a forensic scientist or SOCO or whatever they were called these days to tell that something had once been there. It had lain long enough to make a dinge I thought I could still make out, and even my unscientific eyes had no difficulty seeing where the duvet had drifted on to the floor when someone had relieved it of the corpse's weight. No, it had definitely been lying on, not under the duvet – in this heat, under a duvet?

In any case, I demanded, how could the police possibly have checked? The ladders had been where I'd left them padlocked together – Paula insisted on that: she didn't want her ladders to be either victims or perpetrators of crime. Even though there was scaffolding climbing the gable ends you needed a twelve-foot ladder to get on to the first stage. Paula had a key to the outhouse that housed a loo, though I'd have been embarrassed to let anyone see, let alone use, so primitive a piece of plumbing with nowhere to wash your hands afterwards. But van der Poele had insisted that she give him advance notice when we needed access to the inside of the house itself to paint the tops and insides of window and doorframes. There'd be someone there to let her in and let her out, he declared. So the police wouldn't have been able to get hold of keys from Paula. They'd not broken down the door. How had they got in to see that all was well?

As I twisted to get a better angle to work at, a simpler explanation occurred to me: that the police had done nothing at all and were bluffing me, to save themselves hours of tedious paperwork. I wouldn't have blamed them, but there was no need for Marsh to have been so nasty to me. Maybe I'd give Messy Mascara a bell in the morning to see if he was usually like that or if he'd produced a special performance for me. Maybe it'd be safer not to bother.

I peered down at the tyre tracks crisscrossing the semicircular gravel drive in front of the house. Even if they'd been on snow or mud, I couldn't have made much of them. So I couldn't have swept back into Ashford police station demanding the head honcho to tell him one of his subordinates was a lazy, lying layabout and waving the photographic evidence under his eyes. But maybe I could photograph one thing. Paula insisted that we keep in the van glove-box one of those party cameras you use and throw away. People see big vans involved in road accidents and assume it's been driven by some testosterone-fuelled youth who'd ploughed it into innocent hapless family cars. Paula reckoned that if we could take photos before the vehicles were moved, we'd always be able to prove we were the innocent parties – which we damn well had better be. Maybe the camera worked like a rabbit's foot, or maybe we were too scared of Paula's response if we bent her Trev so much as a thou. out of true. So far, anyway, there'd been no need for the little gizmo.

I nipped down the ladder, retrieved the camera, small enough to tuck into my bib, and swarmed back up again. Just think, out there are thousands of women paying millions of pounds to their local gyms just for the privilege of doing an exercise I get to do for free every day.

I was sure there were all sorts of technical procedures for

photographing through glass, but I'd no idea what they might be. I tried pressing the lens right up to the glass, and holding it well away, straight on, diagonally across. And then I realised that the light was better than it had been all day for this particular bit of fascia board, so I applied my efforts to that.

It usually takes me about twenty minutes to do a section the size I was working on. Because I was on my own, and I didn't want to take unnecessary risks leaning to the side, I decided to quit after ten minutes to shift the ladder a little. I'd forgotten, as I always did, just how heavy it was. It'd be so easy to let it slip the tiniest bit and put one of the sides through the window. So very easy. And so very tempting. But before I could let my nosiness overcome my professional pride, I found another pair of hands was helping me. Paula's. And Paula's hands did not let ladders slip within half a mile of vulnerable glass.

'Working late,' she observed, treading on the bottom rung to plant the end firmly in the earth.

Paula didn't ask questions. She made statements. You had to respond to the statement.

'There was a little problem earlier,' I admitted. 'So I thought I'd put in a bit extra to finish off.'

She waited, unsmiling. Although she'd only be about ten or twelve years older me, mid to late thirties perhaps, she had this nasty habit of making me feel about thirteen again, having sneaked back into school for a bit and then being carpeted by my headteacher for not going more often and staying longer. Perhaps it was Paula's size: she was about five foot ten and strongly built. She dwarfed me, although I turned in at five-five and eight and a bit stone. To be fair, Paula had shown more kindness while I'd been with the Pots than the headmistress had the whole time I'd been technically in school. But I wouldn't push my luck.

'As a matter of fact, it's easier now – the sun's at a better angle.'

'Quite.' She still didn't smile. There was more to come. If not now, later.

I put my foot on the first rung.

'Client confidentiality, Caffy.'

Honestly, she made us sound like plastic surgeons or bank managers. I took a risk and shot upwards. Perhaps that'd be the sum total of my bollocking. Perhaps it wouldn't.

To be fair, she didn't leave me to tidy up on my own, but busied herself down below while I finished my section and rather more than made up the time I'd lost. Lost? Wasted? Used doing what I saw as my duty?

Risking a snub, when I was on terra firma again I asked, 'Fancy a drink? Down at the Hop Vine?'

She nodded. 'I'll meet you there.' She locked the garage, checking the padlock twice before she was satisfied, and set off in her hatchback.

Forgiven but not quite not forgotten. I, too, gave one last check round, then another, pressing my nose against the windows. There was something wrong somewhere, wasn't there? Surely? If only it showed.

To my amazement – she was usually slow getting to the bar – Paula had set up the drinks on one of the Hop Vine's outside tables, the one furthest, as it happened, from the children's play area. She even smiled as I straddled the bench.

'I didn't think you'd be able to wait for your Bishop's Finger,' she said, toasting me with her glass, which held her usual tipple, red wine. She claimed this had medicinal qualities.

I raised my glass and drank deep. The beer was just the right temperature.

'The trouble is,' she said, 'that mud-stirring sometimes means the stirrer gets splashed.' If she'd had spectacles she'd have looked over them, meaningfully.

She didn't need to. She was referring to my past, wasn't she?

'The police came to you and told you to shut me up.' I could make statements, too.

'They came for the house keys, originally,' she conceded. 'And then started talking about you and wondering whether I was employing the right sort of person. You were very brave not to change your name, Caffy.' She sounded as if she meant it.

'Or naïve. But then, who'd have thought I'd be doing anything that'd make the police want to look me up on their computer? I'm only painting up that ladder, you know.'

'Quite. And what interests me is that they knew all about you when they came to see me. Funny they should bother when you'd have thought they might be more interested in looking for this body of yours.'

'There was a body, Paula. Honestly. You don't imagine things like that, do you?'

'Tell me about it.'

I drew a little picture with my index finger in the pollen dust on the table. 'He'd be about your height, I'd say.'

'About five foot ten, then.'

'And built, as we used to say in Brum, like a brick sh – '

I bit back the expression. OK, it was the Bishop's Finger talking. Paula allowed her smooth brow to crumple in a wince. She had a broad forehead like the women in those paintings of Dutch living rooms, and an expression that was slow to change. Her eyes narrowed slightly in a further warning as she said, 'So it'd be hard work getting him off the bed and out of the house. Assuming that out of the house is where he's gone.'

'Rigor mortis,' I put in, eager to divert her from my vulgarity. 'Got to consider rigor mortis, too. Heavy and stiff: really tricky to shift. Plus he had some huge, chunky rings: big as knuckle-dusters. They might damage the wallpaper or paintwork.'

Paula nodded reflectively. 'Though I can hardly see van der Poele asking us to do any touching in.'

I hung my head. If the manor were as scruffy inside as it was outside, there'd have been rich pickings for Paula's Pots. Indoor work was better than outdoor, especially in the winter. As far as I knew, however, we were booked up nearly eight months in advance, thanks largely to Paula's meticulous working methods. And someone like van der Poele would no doubt be bringing in fancy London-based interior decorators. Not that Paula didn't have an interior decorator on her team. But Les Sprigg, cut it how you would, didn't sound remotely glamorous, and he worked not from a design studio, but from the back room of his flat.

I sank the last of my half-pint. We only ever had one drink, unless the whole team of us were gathering together and we'd draw straws to see who got to collect and return everyone at the end of the evening. 'Best be off then.'

'Eventually,' she nodded. She was fossicking in her dungarees pockets. At last she came up with a couple of keys on a ring, and a slip of paper. 'I thought we might try these out first.'

'In that case,' I said, digging in my own dungarees, 'we might try this again.'

'Van der Poele's agent slipped them to me,' Paula explained, releasing two locks on the back door. She'd made us strip off our dirty clothes, donning the sort of paper overalls that wouldn't have been out of place at an official crime scene but which she used when she'd got fine restoration work to do. And the overshoes might not have been forensically clean, but were brilliant when padding over valuable carpets to price jobs. 'He thought it'd be a terrible pain to be here every time we wanted to open a window. But he swore me to absolute secrecy. Seems the Boss Man likes people to jump when he tells them to, regardless of what other jobs he's also told them to do.'

'Is this how the police got in?'

'After we'd both told them we didn't have any?' Slipping on disposable gloves, she locked up behind her, a procedure I wasn't entirely happy with, I must say. When I've been in a tight spot, I've always liked at least one way out.

'What if –' I began.

'Trust me,' she said. 'Well, are you coming or not?'

I decided to trust her, and thrust my fingers into the clammy latex.

As I'd thought, the house was decidedly tatty. Rumour, pretty accurate in rural parts, I'd found, suggested he'd picked up the house and contents as a job lot. The kitchen still had an old range, supplemented by one of those microwaves that do everything, playing God Save the Queen while they do it. Some of the furniture was so ugly you couldn't imagine anyone having conceived it, let alone having spoilt good timber making it. Some of it was so sweetly light I wanted to pick it up and take it home with me. The carpets looked as smooth as silk, but were badly worn in doorways. Someone had replaced old velvet curtains with bright new ones, skewing the whole balance of otherwise interesting rooms. But Paula wouldn't let me dawdle, imaging things how I'd like them. She led me lickety-split up the main stairs and into one of the bedrooms with an incomparable view of our scaffolding. The sash windows came in a cluster of three, side by side. She opened the widest, the one in the middle. 'And if necessary, leave any talking to me,' she said.

I didn't argue. The heavy mahogany furniture didn't encourage arguing. I thought of countless ignorant young brides brought here and forced by this very fireplace into lying still and thinking of England.

The evening sun fell kindly in the rooms at the back of the house, the rosewood furniture glowing like fire.

'Worth a mint,' Paula said. 'Even this stuff, which is fake – see, the grain's been painted on.' Going round a house with her when she was preparing estimates was always an education. I particularly enjoyed it when a piece of furniture pernickety couples had claimed was a priceless antique was nothing more, according to Paula, than compressed paper, worth even less than they'd paid for it at some superstore. The thing was, she'd treat the tat as carefully as if it had been real Sheraton, and expect us to follow suit.

Next on our itinerary was the room I'd peered into. Not only was the duvet dragged sideways, there were a couple of what looked like blue rope fibres on the pillow. There was another halfway to the door. I took photos of the room itself, but doubted if the lens was up to taking details like the fibres. All the same, I tried.

'Something tied in our rope was here anyway,' she whispered. She picked up one, and wrapped it in a tissue before stowing in her pocket. And then she grabbed my wrist, touching a finger to her lips.

I heard it, too. The scrape of a key in a badly maintained lock. We were back like lightning into the room the window of which she'd prepared earlier, and out on to the scaffolding's top platform. We'd both had enough practice closing windows tightly and soundlessly. There was a ladder between our level and the next, where we stripped down to our summer shorts. Paula held out her hand for my overall and overshoes. She balled them tightly with hers, cramming everything into a space between the scaffolding and the planks it supported as if it were there to stop a bit of movement. Down the next ladder to the next level.

I gripped her wrist – I probably hurt her a lot. Because though I'd have trusted her to talk the hind legs off a donkey, if necessary, I couldn't see even an explanation that would con Mr van der Poele cutting any ice with his dogs. No wonder she was on her feet, screaming the place down.

Baying. That's what they were doing. Baying. I've always kept my own counsel about hunting and other countryside issues, never knowing whether my next client would be pro or anti-Countryside Alliance. But I tell you this, I was glad I'd been incarnated as a human, not a fox. There wasn't a hair on the nape of my neck that was lying flat: I was ready to wet myself with fright. And here was my boss on her hind legs drawing everyone's attention to our plight. She'd told me to let her do the talking – should I leave the screaming to her as well, or, as my instinct demanded, join in? Those animals must be jumping six feet into the air.

I decided to scream a bit too. Well, the scream more or less came out of its own accord.

'What the hell's going on?' He didn't say 'hell', actually – he used the sort of word that would have driven even Paula's eyebrows skywards.

A man with a bald patch strode in our direction. From here we could see the regular tufts where he'd had hair implanted. Not that his grooming was our immediate concern.

'You – you two up there! What the hell are you doing?'

The anger in his voice raised the dogs to new paroxysms of baying. I'll swear you could hear the snap of their teeth as they bit furiously at thin air they'd much rather have had thickened with a nice bit of my flesh.

I also heard the snap of the whip as he cuffed them back into simmering, resentful silence, legs braced for another attack.

Paula stepped forward to the edge of our platform. A quick flap of her hand meant I was to stay out of sight. I obeyed. 'Good evening, Mr van der Poele,' she said, as if greeting the vicar at the beetle drive.

'Miss Farmer, is it? Would you care to explain what the hell you think you're doing on my property?'

She gave him one of her bland, unfurrowed stares. 'Painting it, Mr van der Poele. Or I was earlier and will be tomorrow. I was just going over tomorrow's schedule with my employee, here, when we were set on by your dogs. I thought after the last incident you were going to keep them under proper control.'

So she'd complained to him without telling us, had she? Good for her.

'I'm entitled to set my animals on trespassers,' he said. 'Without warning.'

'Fine. But not on my staff. I have an employer's duty of care, as I said the other day.'

Van der Poele snarled an order, reinforcing its message with the whip. The dogs whimpered and lay down.

Paula made another of her statements. 'When you've confined them, we will come down and leave you in peace. By the way, did you know that one of your windows isn't properly fastened? I found it unlocked when I was discussing tomorrow's work.'

Van der Poele barked an order. Another man appeared, leashed the dogs and dragged them off to the outhouse housing our loo. I hoped they wouldn't stay there – I'd rather wee behind the bushes than brave them.

For security's sake, there was no ladder from here down to the ground. 'So how do we get down?' I muttered. 'It's too far to jump.' It was dusk, too – and goodness knew what lurked to break an unwary ankle.

We'd often teased Paula about the little rucksack she always carried. She pointed out – rightly – it was high fashion and we could get our own from that nice shop in the Outlet. We didn't dispute that, merely pointing out that torches and plumb lines weren't your average fashion accessories. Nor would we wear ours up ladders. To be honest, where she lived the torch might well have been useful: there were no pavements and no streetlights. Just to add to the fun there were no speed restrictions either, so if you didn't want to be squashed as flat as a hedgehog, it was either dress like a traffic cone or flash a strong beam at any oncoming speedster. Anyway, my camera was safely stowed, and Paula's torch was already in her hand, its beam illuminating bolts making easy hand and foot holds. When I was down she dropped the torch neatly into my outstretched hands and followed suit.

The van welcomed us phlegmatically enough, starting third go – just enough hesitation to set the dogs off again – and we set off sedately through the lanes. Paula said nothing till I dropped her back at the Hop Vine. I could rather have used another drink, but all she said, as she headed to her car, was, 'You join the others on the Tenterden job tomorrow. I'll work on van der Poele's place myself.'

I opened my mouth to protest – you get attached to a project, and I'd have liked to be able to point at the newly-painted eaves and say, 'All my own work.' But I thought better of it and simply waved her goodnight.

On the way home I saw bats and a badger, and felt very glad to be alive to see them. But then I came across a lifeless pheasant, its brave tail stuck up like a signal of surrender: life wasn't all roses, even out here.

Chapter Three

'You don't want to worry, Caffy,' Meg said kindly, first thing the following morning. 'We've all got phobias. I can't go up ladders the way you do, and mention a bat to Helen here and she'll go all hysterical on you. And those dogs would put anyone off.'

Meg was the oldest of the team, forty at least, and tended to mother us all. Her dark hair was streaked with grey, not from age but from where she'd run distracted painty hands through it when we worried her. Helen, her pale, blonde niece, was the youngest, eighteen or nineteen, and thin to the point where I was worried about anorexia. We all kept an eye on her, making sure she ate well while she was working. On the quiet, I watched to make sure she couldn't wander off and make herself vomit. But she stayed thin. Perhaps she was just blessed with skinny genes, and when we sank into tubby, waistless middle age, we'd be full of envy, not anxiety.

We were all in Trev, since he lived on the road outside my flat. I'd picked them up from Kingsnorth, once separate from Ashford, but now being swallowed rapidly by the dormitory estates the government seemed obsessed with building. I stuck to country roads as far as High Halden, because I was totally unable to resist the crossroads known as Cuckold's Corner. Then I joined what claimed to be an A-road, but was really a glorified lane, with nowhere to overtake the heavy lorry that might just reach thirty if the driver sold his soul. I saw a chance to change the subject.

'I thought the South East was supposed to be rich,' I

chuntered. 'And yet – motorways apart – it doesn't seem to have a single decent road. Haven't you ever heard of dual-carriageways?'

'It isn't as though we haven't asked for them,' Meg protested.

Good: with a bit of luck I could keep her on roads and off dogs until she'd forgotten she was supposed to be feeling sorry for me. While I've never minded lying my way out of a spot, it's always seemed to me easier to stick to the truth if possible, probably because it's easier to remember. Since in general I had a very happy relationship with canines, I wasn't too sure about Paula's reason for my no-show at Crabton Manor. Still, she had to say something, and after yesterday I owed her.

'A lot of very rich people do live down here, it's true,' Meg was saying. I must have missed a bit. She ran off the names of several former and current pop stars. 'But they don't shop locally – I mean, can you imagine someone like Mick Jagger popping into Paula's mum's salon and asking for highlights and a trim?'

I was hard put to imagine anyone popping into Paula's mum's salon – even Paula wriggled out of that.

'And some incomers certainly can't be described as assets to the community,' she continued, warming to her theme. 'There was that supermarket shooting last year – the gangland vendetta?'

I watched in my side mirrors the frantic attempts of the Jag – yes, latest series – to overtake me. Or perhaps he was just trying to hitch up on the tow bar.

'That's the one. Imagine being at the checkout when a

murderer pushes his basket ahead of you.' Helen supplied a satisfactory shudder, like a heroine in a silent movie.

I just sat very firmly on memories of the sort of things that happened in gangland vendettas.

'And, of course, there was that kidnap at the hotel near Tenterden. But perhaps that doesn't count, since the gang came down from London...'

And had been pretty incompetent, as I recalled. Even so, reducing such a vile thing to a matter for gossip made me feel uncomfortable. 'You'll have to remind me of the turn,' I said. 'It's a while since I was here, and you know how hopeless I am with roads.'

'If Paula heard you saying that, she'd be furious,' Meg said. 'You know how she hates people putting themselves down.'

Helen said languidly, 'I wouldn't mind going into Tenterden. I forgot to get myself any lunch.'

If ever there were a green signal, that was it. The van headed purposefully for the Waitrose car park, disgorging Helen and Meg – and then, yes, me too. Tenterden is one of those pretty little towns that I can't resist. While the others went into the supermarket, I drifted to the High Street. I knew the shops were geared for the tourist market – a steam engine from the preserved railway whistled even as I locked the van's doors – but I loved the wide village street, the quaint (and stupendously expensive) houses, and the immensely solid church, which looked as if you really could find sanctuary, if not solace, there. It wasn't nine o'clock yet, and though Paula liked us to be at work by then, we could clip a bit off our lunch break to make up. Just to walk up and down made me feel more comfortable than I could ever remember feeling back in Brum. OK. I exaggerate. Like a lot of people I didn't have an idyllic childhood, and in my later teens I was constantly looking over my shoulder. Me, and a lot of my friends. Here, though, the sun was shining, there was enough wind to blow a hint of the engine's coal smoke into the town, and a wonderful sense of contentment and well-being. Maybe I even started to hum as I ambled along.

If I did, the music choked in my throat. Over by a swish dress shop was – No, I couldn't, mustn't believe it was – .

Gasping for breath, I leant a second against the nearest shop window. Antiques. The owner came out, ready to shoo me away, but was soon fussing round asking if I was all right. Half of me wanted to hug her, the other half wished she'd go away and leave me alone, lest her mother-hen act attracted the attention of that man. Even the shop itself might – he liked fine things.

It was him. Had to be. You don't sleep with a man for nearly three years without recognising certain gestures, certain movements of the head. All that talk about criminals, and who should be almost within earshot but Clive Granville.

Gabbling my thanks to the shopkeeper, I pulled myself clear and dived into a newsagent's. If I grabbed a paper I could put my head down in that and hope he'd not notice me. And I could buy things, not just the paper I was already queuing for. It was patchily damp from where I'd touched it.

I broke away from the queue, nipping to a stand of sun specs and another of baseball caps. Camouflage. That was better. Retreating to the back of the shop, as a final touch I rolled up my dungaree legs: now I looked like a rather shabby all-American girl (if that isn't a contradiction in terms!) with my tan and perkily cut sunbleached hair. I was sure, however, that no cheerleader had ever gone for Joseph's coat trainers like mine, dappled with a hundred odd colours.

The others would be waiting for me. What if they came looking for me, yelling my name? Not a lot of Caffys in Tenterden. They'd lead him straight to me; and I'd have led him straight to them. More potential victims. I'd left Birmingham not just to save myself but also to protect the few friends I had left. Now I had a brand new group of friends, family, more like, and he could sniff them out and punish them simply for befriending me. I couldn't bear to think about what I ought to do – except that, in the short term, I'd better get back to them. So I paid up, and slipped gently from the shop into a waxing tide of elderly ladies. It was their shopping hour, just as it had been their shopping hour since William the Bastard had landed not all that far down the road. On one of my free weekends I'd actually walked to the site of Harold's battle. Poor guy, it had probably been an old lady's walking stick that had polished him off, not an arrow at all. Or being hacked with huge, heavy swords. I didn't envy poor Edith Swan Neck, his mistress, her job of identifying him. I'd had to do it once or twice for friends, if not lovers, in the clinical privacy of a morgue, with the relevant bits sanitised as far as forensic medicine could accomplish. It wasn't pleasant.

And I wanted to make damned sure no one had to do it for me. Which meant staying very much in one piece. It was hard to walk along trying not to have eye contact with anyone but making sure I saw Clive well before he saw me. I nipped sharply into the pedestrian way leading to the car park and was ready to heave a sigh of relief. But who should be looking into the very smart ladies' shoe shop (come on, Caffy, is there any other sort in Tenterden?) but Clive himself. He and his female companion, a woman rather younger and even slimmer than I'd been when he selected me, were engrossed in a row of sexy sandals. I scuttered past, hoping, indeed praying, that Helen and Meg didn't take it into their heads to yell greetings at me as I approached. Yes, they were turning towards me, and yes, their mouths were forming great round O's. Perhaps I could convince them I wasn't me. At least I had the paper to shield my face – I hadn't meant to buy the *Guardian*, but that was what I'd picked up. It would have been Taz's natural choice. But I mustn't think about Taz now. I must think about quietly and unobtrusively weaving round the car park and returning to the van by the most circuitous route possible: once anyone identified me with it I'd had it, it was so easily identifiable.

'Just say nothing, pretend not to be with me and go and open up,' I told Meg, flipping her the keys.

She took one look at me and caught them, bundling me in ahead of her.

'Don't ask. Just start and drive off.'

I was halfway under a dustsheet already.

The bloody van wouldn't start. Maybe that's why Paula insisted the damned thing was a he, it was so sodding temperamental. Shit. Not like me to swear these days. Neither Meg nor Paula approved.

'It's no use,' Meg almost wept, 'I can't do it. You'll have to try, Caffy.'

If it didn't start soon, it'd be under the bonnet time for me. Not where you want to be when you don't want to draw attention to yourself. Not when Granville prided himself there was no motor he couldn't tame. Motor or, of course, woman. By whatever means.

Just as kindly people were gathering round to help, I got it to fire. I should have handed over to Meg, of course. But I was so intent on keeping the engine ticking over, I stayed in the driving seat. And as I crept out of the car park, my eyes met, as if it had all been staged, the disbelieving eyes of Clive Granville. Despite the shades, he knew me.

I almost threw up. There was only one thing to do. Make sure he didn't catch up with us.

I ruthlessly carved a Mercedes, driven, by its octogenarian owner, more in the fashion of a Reliant Robin, took to every side street I could find, and finally found myself going in exactly opposite the direction to the one I wanted. It was only after I'd completed a lumbering U-turn that Meg spoke.

'Sorry,' she said.

'Not your fault,' I said, truthfully. 'I know Paula thinks it's a bit cute to have a van only I can start, but it really isn't funny. I can't think why she doesn't get the sodding ignition system sorted. Fucking stupid not to. She bosses us: why doesn't she boss the garage?'

'I know you're upset, Caffy, but all the same ...' Meg sighed, because I'd sworn, I suppose. 'And we don't criticise Paula, remember, not behind her back, do we?'

'Just shut it, Meg! Please!' These were my friends. I should be yelling at fate, not them. I took several deep breaths.

'Sorry.' Another breath. If I talked normally maybe I'd feel a bit more normal. 'Did you get some lunch, Helen?'

'I didn't fancy anything there,' she whined.

'But,' Meg declared, 'she can have my egg sandwiches – I've bought a baguette to replace them.' Despite her increasing pudge, Meg wouldn't miss lunch. Or fail to notice where the speedo needle was. 'Careful, it's that very sharp bend coming up.'

She was right. If I wasn't careful I would roll the van and kill us all and save Granville the job. And no, I wasn't exaggerating.

The place we were titivating was what looked like a Georgian farmhouse but was probably much older, a medieval manor with a false front, on a rise of ground called the Isle of Oxney. Maybe it had been an island once, when the marshes were still sea. Certainly the land to the southeast dropped away in what looked like old cliffs. From the house you could see Rye to the south and the vast spread of Romney Marsh to the east. Vast to me, at any rate, after my city upbringing (some might think updragging a better term), when the local park was terrifying because there weren't any houses in it. Even on a perfect day like this there was a strong wind. The roof bore signs of very recent major repairs by someone who knew his job, there were new gutters and there had been a great deal of repointing. Someone had injected a damp-course. Not surprisingly, the paintwork had weathered badly, especially where it had to endure the combined attack of wind, rain and sun. My job would be to go up the ladder and strip and fill where necessary. Some of the windows would have to be removed and reputtied. Certainly the whole lot would need a fungicidal wash and very careful priming. I loaded pockets and pouches with the necessary and with Meg's help hoisted the ladder. But I didn't go up straightaway – I sloped off to tuck the van further under the trees. I didn't think anyone could see it from the road now.

'You expecting a hot day or something?' Meg asked, puzzled, as I walked back.

'A scorcher – didn't you hear the forecast?' Painters and decorators are as keen on weather forecasts as sailors and farmers are. Paula admitted, if pressed, to having an unrequited passion for TV weatherman Rob McElwee.

She drifted me away from Helen. 'What's really the trouble? Something really upset you back there, I could see that, but I didn't want to say too much and worry Helen.'

'I saw someone I don't want to see ever again.'

'Easy – tell him to push off.' Meg thought that not swearing set her kids a good example. They'd confided in me that they thought she was pathetic not knowing the real words and wondered whether they ought to teach her.

'Not so easy.'

'Three of us!' The way she lifted her chin you could imagine sparring with a bully's mother in the playground – but not, of course, verbally.

'Even with the whole of Duke William's army behind me,' I said miserably. But I couldn't cough it all up, not now. Not now. Though I knew I'd have to say something about it all soon. I braced my shoulders. 'Anyway, time to get up that ladder.'

If Clive had really clocked me, I'd have to leave Paula's Pots. I didn't want him to find me, for a start, and I certainly didn't want to expose them to any danger. Being pressured by a drug baron wouldn't faze either Paula or Meg, of course. Not in theory. Not until they learnt what being pressured meant. Helen would make a natural target. And there were Meg's children. I had to go, there was no doubt about it. But I didn't want simply to do a flit. I owed them some explanation. Paula had taken me on not on the basis of my personal CV, as she said with a mild smile, but because I'd been top of my college course and because she recognised a good worker when she saw one. I insisted she told the others in confidence about my past, all of it, but no one ever mentioned it, not even Helen producing so much as a feeble snigger. And I'd shown my gratitude by working every minute of every hour Paula paid me for, by reading all the trade mags and introducing any new techniques that looked useful, and signing up for courses in restoration, so I'd be able to assist Paula in her specialist work. I'd turned Paula's Pots into my new family, and was far more loyal to them than my own folk had ever been to me.

And into this happy new life walks Clive Granville. Possibly. The more I smoothed in filler, moulded putty, the more I thought I'd been over-reacting. He couldn't have recognised me. Not with my cap and new haircut and colour and the sunspecs. And he certainly wouldn't have got more than a glimpse of me. He'd obviously got a new bird now. So even if he had clocked me he'd let me be. Surely he would. After all, he didn't need me if he'd got a new woman. Perhaps he was just down for a holiday. Perhaps he didn't plan to join fellow cons in what was once the garden of England and now seemed more like a hothouse for crime.

It was no good. I knew Granville better than that. I had to find the loo.

This owner had had whoever did the building repairs make sure the outside loo was not just operational but clean, with a water heater over a new washbasin. When you're throwing up, it's nice to do it in civilised surroundings. I blessed him, whoever he was, as I rinsed my mouth and told myself that letting go wasn't going to help.

Paula always insisted we took proper breaks, however busy we might be. The only exception was if foul weather were promised, and missing our lunch would guarantee we could complete a job before it arrived.

In turn, Meg always demanded that we listen to the one o'clock news on her battered trannie as we had our lunch. 'We may be labourers, but we can be educated labourers,' she said. 'Besides, it means I can help my kids with their home-work,' she added more honestly.

So even when the three of us were gathered together with our mugs and sarnies, we didn't have the discussion I feared was on its way, from the way Meg kept looking at me. Before we started again, she said, almost as if she'd caught me out doing a Helen, 'You're very pale.'

'Tummy bug,' I lied briefly, heading up the ladder.

We didn't have our group talk till much later, when we were packing up, in fact, by which time Paula had parked up by the Transit and was inspecting the day's efforts. And I started it, as I knew I ought.

'I'm going to have to disappear,' I said. 'No, not just leave promptly. I mean, vanish.'

'It's to do with the man who saw you this morning. When I couldn't start Trev. Oh, Caffy, I'm so sorry.'

'He saw me when I pulled out of the car park – nothing to do with you at all, Meg. Really, truly.'

'Forget about blame,' Paula said. 'Tell us about this man and why you're so afraid of him.'

I said baldly, 'I told you about me and drugs. It was him who got me hooked. It took me a long time to get off.'

'And he was the one who got you back on them after rehab?'

'Tried.'

'That's not all, is it? Because we all know you won't start again on cocaine or heroin or whatever.'

It was strange to hear them referred to by their polite names.

'Of course not.'

'Well, then? Had he threatened you in some way? He has, hasn't he?'

I looked round them seeing not just their faces but those of Taz, my social worker, and his colleagues, and of the staff at the rehab centre. 'Not just me. My friends. People he finds me with.'

'Threats!' Meg started dismissively, as if putting backbone in her kids.

Paula said warningly, 'It depends what sort of threats.'

For answer, I unclipped my dungarees and lifted my T-shirt. Maybe I should have done this when they first let me join them.

There.

CG. He'd carved the letters himself. Once they'd been

raw and bloody. I touched the scars, flattening and only pink, with little sideways marks in places where they'd had to put stitches in.

I heard the others gasp; Helen cried out, but covered her mouth. As if she were protecting a kid watching a nasty movie, Meg pulled her face on to her shoulder.

The silence was awful. Perhaps I shouldn't have shown them. But how else would they get the message? I made myself say, 'He said he'd do it to my face next time he saw me. And fill me so full of h – of heroin,' I added, 'that I'd die.'

Chapter Four

'In that case,' Paula said, trying to sound brisk, 'you can't possibly run away. You need us. Doesn't she, girls?'

I shook my head. 'No.' It came out so husky they might not have heard. So I added, 'I'm not putting anyone at risk.'

'We'll be putting ourselves at risk,' Paula said, naïve for probably the first time ever. 'Nothing to do with you.'

Meg pulled a doubtful face. 'My kids. And Helen's not much more than a kid.'

'Quite. Now – ' I began.

Helen, who had been chewing her hair – better than nothing, I tried to tell myself – stamped her foot. 'I'm old enough to make my own mind up. Caffy never said a word about it being my fault we were in Tenterden in the first place this morning, and it was. If I'd been sensible and packed myself some lunch we wouldn't have had to go there at all. Would we, Caffy?' Her eyes looked larger than ever in her thin face.

Trying to sound firm and calm, I said, 'No, but we did and it's nothing to do with being in Tenterden, it's to do with my past. I can't wipe it away any more than I can wipe these scars away.' I touched my stomach. It was horrible, as usual – feeling those tender ridges where there should have been ordinary skin.

Meg pulled Helen's face closer. I couldn't read her own expression.

Why ever hadn't I shown them before? Then we wouldn't have become mates on false pretences.

Suddenly Helen pulled away. 'You've looked after me: I'll look after you,' she said, sidling up to me.

'And the school holidays are starting this weekend: I suppose it wouldn't hurt my kids to go and spend an extra week with their dad,' Meg reflected. Hell, she couldn't let Helen's sentimentality sway her! 'Time he pulled his weight. It isn't as if he wasn't always moaning about access.'

'No,' I said, trying not to show how hard I wanted to say 'yes'. 'It's my life and I'm not living it with the knowledge I've put anyone at risk.'

'That's always good to hear,' said a male voice. We jumped as one, me hitching my dungarees swiftly. 'I'd rather no one took any risk on my property, thank you very much.'

As the rest of us swung round to see who was speaking, Paula stepped forward like the bride's mother ready to greet the vicar. 'Mr – I mean, er – Todd,' she said, 'I don't think you've met all my team.' She introduced us one by one to Todd, who was about sixty, with a very trim figure but a face that looked as if it had seen more of life than most. Not all of it good, either. There was something vaguely familiar about him, but it would have been rude to stare. 'Ladies, this is Todd Dawes, who owns the house. Caffy's been working on the higher-level stuff,' she added, somehow separating me from the others and walking Dawes and me towards my ladder. She hadn't had management classes for nothing: she was tactfully leaving the others to discuss the problem of what to do about me. 'As you can see, she's had to replace the putty on all those windows there, which is why progress has been slow with the painting.'

He looked from the window to the ground to me and back again. 'You're happy working up there?'

'No reason not to be,' I said.

'I can think of lots!' He had a smile that compressed his wrinkles and could have made him look rather like a tortoise. But it didn't.

I'd had it with elderly men looking at me appraisingly. But Todd Dawes didn't appear to be wondering how many perversions I would manage for a minimum fee. So I wouldn't be rude, even though my question was abrupt. 'Tell me, a draughty place like this, stuck up high and asking every wind there is inside – why didn't you whip the windows out and install double glazing? Mind you, it would have cost a week's pocket money, I suppose.'

I rather thought he and Paula exchanged looks.

'Good question,' he said. It was as if someone were raking through ashes – his voice was both gravelly and pleasantly warm. 'The thing is, this is a conservation area, which is pretty restricting.'

'True. You can't blow your nose unless you've got the right colour hanky,' I nodded.

'So,' he grinned, 'I'm forking out a month's pocket money to have the sort of secondary glazing everyone approves.' He looked up at the house with an expression of love – the sort most men reserve for their cars or their children. I recognised the feeling immediately: it was one of the things that had brought me into this line of trade.

'It deserves it,' I said, whether in response to my thought or to his comment I wasn't sure.

'Yes, it does. A couple of other people thought so, but I managed to outbid them. Have you seen inside yet?' God, the man even had dimples. If only I'd had a dad like that.

Swallowing, I shook my head.

'Would you like to?'

It was clear he wanted to show it off, and who was I to spoil a man's innocent fun? 'Do witches charm warts?' I asked.

'I'll take that as a yes, shall I?'

Paula coughed. 'We need to get Meg back to her children, and if you ask me Helen's got a date. You won't want to be driving Trev – that's our van, Todd – on your own, will you?' she added meaningfully.

Dawes looked at me almost sternly. 'I wouldn't have put you down as the sort of woman who couldn't drive a van.'

'It's a long story,' I said. 'But Paula's right – I ought to go with the others. No one else understands the van's starter motor like I do.' Mistake.

And he picked it up immediately. 'So it's the "on your own" bit, not the van driving bit.'

I scuffed my trainers in his overlong grass.

'Look, Caffy, where do you live?'

'The other side of Ashford.' There, that'd fix him. No one in his right mind would offer to run me home.

'Well, I'm meeting my wife at the International Station at seven-fifteen. It looks as if you have a lift – provided you want one.'

Try as I might, I couldn't see him having any predatory designs on me. My hair was wind-dried and wind-blown, not in a sexy Brigitte Bardot way (sister, did she do tousled well!) but in the before half of a conditioner advertisement sort of way. My dungarees stank of white spirit and paint. My feet were in those ancient trainers. No high heels, no basque, just a working-class girl with mates who knew where she was.

And I didn't get the bad vibes. That was what clinched it.

'If you're sure you don't mind… And provided we can persuade the van to start with Meg at the wheel.'

Entering the house was like stepping into Sleeping Beauty's palace – if she had one, that is. I was never very hot on fairy-tales. There was no furniture, no carpets or curtains – just these wonderful rooms waiting for us to breathe new life into them with our paint and wallpaper.

'You should have seen it at its worst: damp, rising and from blocked gutters. Broken windows. Wisteria thrusting blind growth between the sash windows and their frames and crawling over bedroom walls. You know, it was actually quite frightening.'

I nodded. Blind will in any form is scary.

'But we still fell in love with it.' That loving smile again.

Fell in love with it. Well, that made three of us. I'd have to be terribly careful I didn't fall in love with him too. Perhaps if I just treated him in the off-hand way I'd seen girls treat their deeply-loved parents… But despite my urgent check on my emotions, I couldn't help gasping, 'You will let us do it, won't you?'

'I'd thought some specialised firm – ' he began, awkward-ly. 'After all – you see, Caffy, it's only ours in trust. Don't shout it from the rooftops but we've left it to English Heritage in our will.'

Which meant they'd have to leave a lot of money to main-tain it. But he didn't seem to be boasting about his money, so much as apologising for wanting everything right. I liked him more and more each moment.

'Paula's fully-trained in restoration work. ' I said. 'And I'm booked in for a residential course at the end of August.' I wasn't just taking a week of my annual leave, I'd scraped together enough savings to pay for it too. I wanted to reach out and hug the place. 'Todd, it's all so wonderful. Look at that fanlight,' I said. Without any encouragement from me, my hands spread and clasped, as if I were some camp art expert. 'And that stair-rail.' It had been rubbed smooth by countless generations of hands.

'It makes you feel as if you've come home, doesn't it?' he asked, laughing as if he were embarrassed by his flight of fancy. 'Mind you, I daresay when it was at its grandest I wouldn't have made it to be under-butler.'

'I wouldn't have minded being a chambermaid. Provided they didn't have *droit de seigneur*,' I added. I knew a lot about *droit de seigneur*, after all. As Clive Granville could have told you.

I must have sounded more bitter than I'd meant. He gave me another one of his glances, and led me in silence through the other rooms, stopping from time to time to show me original shutters or an example of particularly lovely plaster-work filled up by generations of the wrong sort of paint. I'd have to use dental burrs to sort it out.

We were in the servants' dormitory when he looked at his watch. 'My God, we shall have to scarper,' he said. 'Mustn't keep my wife waiting.'

He drove an ordinary middle-aged Range Rover complete with tow bar, not the flash job I'd rather have expected. But then, if he'd sunk as much as I imagined into this new place, and was prepared to restore and presumably furnish it in an appropriate style, he might have had to make economies somewhere. He also drove more slowly than I'd have done, despite his haste to reach Ashford. Come to think of it, it was odd for a woman owning half a house like that to be reduced to travelling by Connex South-East, with its old-fashioned slam-door carriages.

But she'd come in on Eurostar, hadn't she, as I found out when she got into the Range Rover. We'd been too late for him to drop me off and then come back, so the poor woman found this scruff-bag sitting in her place.

If she was surprised, so was I. Lots of men his age turn in the old wife for a younger model – the old my wife doesn't understand me line. But Mrs Dawes, though rather better preserved than he, was no spring chicken.

I leapt out and helped load her case in the back. 'Paris. I've been shopping,' she said, as if she needed to. 'Not clothes. Lots of samples of fabric for the house.'

'You'll have to check that Caffy here approves,' Todd said. 'She's one of the restoration team.'

'You've settled on someone already!' Her voice was pretty chilly: it was clear that he should have discussed it with her first.

'You could say they've already settled on us,' he said dryly.

From my new place on a back seat I caught the glance between the two. My instincts had been right. If ever a couple looked together the Daweses did. His explanation – half-mocking, half-exasperated with not just me but also himself – brought a reluctant smile to her face. He clinched the deal with a comment I didn't understand. 'No pink bedroom for this one either.'

She bit her lip, but was smiling by the time she looked

back over her shoulder at me, nodding in agreement with something that hadn't been said. Not aloud, anyway.

I directed him to my flat, out in Kennington, quite a mixed suburb of Ashford. My bit was especially mixed, but in a town where cheap accommodation was at a premium, everyone apparently wanting an executive four-bedroom residence with en suite and downstairs cloaks, I wasn't going to argue.

I hopped out, swinging my bag after me.

'See you tomorrow,' she said, smiling and waving. Yes, she and I were old friends now, just like me and Todd.

That was what clinched it. As the bag brushed my stomach, I said, 'No. I can't work for you any more.'

Fine exit line. Pity I spoiled it by bursting into tears.

I was so angry with myself. Tears weren't something I did. I did tough and funky and baseball caps and dungarees, not great sobs that wracked my chest. The Daweses insisted on coming in with me, she sending him into my kitchen while she tried to calm me down. My tears weren't having any, though. The nicer she was, the harder they came. It was as if I were sitting outside myself, watching it happen. I'd no more control over the situation than over a tragic news shot on TV.

At last the tea someone had made – it must have been him – started to work, though by that time I'd run out of tissues and was reduced to sniffing into toilet roll. And yes, the kitchen and bathroom were up to visitors: it was something I'd learned that gave me pride in myself during rehab: the importance of clean private places.

While she sat beside me, holding my hand, he stationed himself on the chair opposite.

'Tell me, Caffy,' he began. And then he stopped. 'When I drove up, you'd pulled down your dungarees and were showing your mates your tum. I heard them cry out. They sounded really shocked, Jan,' he told his wife. 'Then you tucked yourself in and had some sort of argument with them – about putting them at risk. Which is where I came in, Jan. I said I didn't want anyone risking their neck on my property.'

She nodded. 'Quite right.'

'We talk about the house, which you've obviously fallen in love with just as we have, and then you say you can't work for us any more. What's going on? I'd really like to know.'

Well, maybe I could tell them about Granville and the drugs. Nothing else, though. Not nice people like this. Not friends I'd technically known a couple of hours but who already seemed closer than people I'd known all my life. Very weird, this love business, when you weren't used to it, and particularly when they offered it just as freely as I did, and with just as few strings. If I'd been a romantic, I'd have said I was like the Prodigal Son, simply walking back into their lives and being welcomed without recrimination for my years away.

'You had a take-away with Todd Dawes!' Meg squeaked. 'Todd Dawes, the delectable, sexy, Todd Dawes.'

The generation gap was yawning to the width of the Channel. I just managed to stop myself saying that former pop star though he might be, he still was old enough to be my grandfather. We were friends and colleagues, after all, and I didn't wish to insult her. But it was true, and though she may have creamed her knickers over him when she was my age, he was almost certainly Train Pass Man now. And not Dirty Old Train Pass Man either.

Helen said, 'You always told me to watch older men. Only want one thing, you said.'

I shook my head emphatically. 'He's never once, for so much as an instant, made me feel like a single woman in the company of a single man.'

'Which is all the more to his credit,' Meg conceded, 'since he must have had countless women thrusting themselves at him.' She looked at me shrewdly. 'You're sure he's not just being nice when he's with his wife?'

'Todd and his wife are both very nice to me,' I insisted, rather primly. 'He really wasn't on the pull.' Time to divert her. 'You didn't really fancy him, did you?'

'Did? Still do! It's the first thing on my Christmas list every year, his new album. Mind you, his voice is cracking a bit these days.'

'I thought that was only boys,' Helen said. 'You know, like Aled Jones.'

'More, wearing out,' I explained, not altogether kindly come to think of it.

'So what did you talk about?' Meg demanded. 'You and him?'

'And his wife. About the house. Their plans for it: they're thinking of having different rooms done in different styles – you know, reflecting the different periods of the house's growth.' Push me how she would, I wouldn't split. Well, keeping schtum about what people said had been part of my job, hadn't it? Client confidentiality, Paula might have called it.

Helen talked a bit about the spot she was growing on her chin: it certainly sounded like pre-date anxiety to me, so last night must have gone all right. I drove, following country lanes all the way this time and keeping an eye on the mirror all the time. Meg hummed what she claimed were his greatest hits.

Paula was waiting when we arrived. 'A word,' she mouthed at me, half-lifting a wallet of photos from her rucksack. Out loud she said brightly, 'You've decided to stay, then. Isn't that great, girls! Caffy?'

I nodded, silently. Sure I wanted to stay. But what I feared more than anything was that by succumbing to temptation I'd exposed to danger even more people that I cared for.

As if discussing my day's tasks with me, Paula took me on one side. 'I've sent copies of these to my bank,' she said, tapping the photos. 'Just in case. Do you want to keep a set too?'

I wrinkled my nose, 'Nowhere to hide them in my place. And my bank doesn't have vaults and things – it's a phone account.'

'OK. What shall we do with them then? Send them to a different police station and try again?'

'You keep them. You don't think the old jungle drums have been beating nineteen to the dozen about my inconvenient find? Oh, and my convenient past.'

'But the police – you know – '

'I can tell you've always been a law-abiding woman, Paula. The police are a corrupt load of bastards. OK, some police are a corrupt load of bastards. And if ever one stank of corruption it was my friend DS Marsh. The only thing that surprises me is that he hasn't tried to pin the murder on me.'

We laughed heartily, though I hadn't been joking. Not one scrap.

Chapter Five

The next day, on the grounds that if I was thoroughly busy I wouldn't have time to worry, I put in a good hard day's work on the most inaccessible bits of the Daweses' house. We had a minor triumph. Over the porch Meg and I found a name and a date: Fullers, 1502. OK, it was painted out with many coats of whitewash but we could fix that easily enough. We were all as pleased as if we owned the place ourselves. Fullers. I was glad we'd found the origin of its name.

But it wasn't the excitement of other restoration work there that kept me awake that night, though it certainly figured in the endless calculations I kept doing in my head. It was simple fear. The nightmares had been bad enough. My favourite, if that's the right term, had me yelling blue murder as usual – one reason I couldn't ever consider sharing a flat, however much money it would have saved. But being awake – lying there, remembering Granville's threats that he wouldn't just carve my face, he'd slice into my stomach deep enough for me to see my own insides – was worse, far worse. I knew he'd relish the chance. Enjoy the feel of the knife going in; enjoy the sight of my face. He'd told me, more than once, his favourite war story, about this man staggering into the field hospital with his guts looped over his arm so he could carry them. That was how he wanted me to turn up in A and E.

By six, sleep and I completely gave up on each other. So it seemed a good idea to get up and take a load in the van to the laundrette before anyone else got there. Although it was going to be another glorious day, I didn't have anywhere to dry so much laundry – sheets, towels, T-shirts – so I forked out for the dryer, too. I took care folding, as I always did, and piled everything neatly into the wicker basket I'd bought at a craft fair in Canterbury. And then I picked my way towards my flat. It couldn't have been eight, because some man on the *Today* programme – Meg had got her sticky fingers on this radio too – was just introducing the weather forecast. And I was thinking how this was one day we didn't need a forecast when I saw Arthur the Postie pushing his bike into the street. I waved. He waved. He dug in his bag and fished out a package, which he brandished at me. Then there was an almighty bang and there was no packet and no bike and no Arthur.

No. There was an Arthur. An Arthur screaming like people scream on war movies because their hands aren't there any more. OK, only one of Arthur's hands wasn't there any more. The other was grasping at his face, which also wasn't there any more. I had to stop the blood spurting. I had to find my mobile and I had to stop my hands shaking long enough to dial 999.

Somehow I must have managed, because very soon the street was full of emergency vehicles and a paramedic was congratulating me on my first aid with the clean towels. I'd almost certainly saved his life, he was saying. Though what life there was to save if you'd only one hand and no face I didn't know.

I didn't ask to go in the ambulance with him. I was too much of a coward. I just stood in the road watching it drive away. So did lots of other people. We all liked Arthur, even if he mostly brought us bills. But I was the only one herded into a police car.

My brain started working again. 'I have to call my boss,' I said. 'I'm responsible for driving the van to pick up the rest of the team.'

'You won't want to drive that van for a bit,' observed the young PC who'd shoe-horned me into the car. It seemed he'd been detailed to stick with me – there were plenty of other uniforms milling round by now, making nuisances of themselves with police tape just when people needed to get their cars out to go to work, but none of them took any notice of me.

'It's got all our gear in it. Everything. So even if your scene of crime guys need to look at it – '

'"Even"! You said "even"! What planet are you on, miss?'

For the first time I noticed he'd got ginger hair and white eyelashes. I loathe white eyelashes. 'I'm going to be sick,' I announced. It was a ploy I'd had to use countless times. Never failed. The only difference was that this time I was sick. Very. Like the other day at Fuller's. Even if I'd had no breakfast, there was bile.

But at least I was out of the police car and had my mobile in my hand. Paula answered first ring.

I explained about the van as best I could. My brain seemed to have deserted me, along with the contents of my stomach, and I'd only managed to stutter a couple of sentences when Paula announced she was coming over. I passed the handset over to the young man. He made various protests – 'We have to – we need – you'll be able – '. – that kind of thing, but he soon switched off, defeated, to judge by the expression on his face. 'She says to wait here,' he said, as if for one moment he needed to.

The breathing space had given me time to get my brain back into gear. 'I need to wash and change,' I said.

'I'm under orders to see you don't,' he muttered.

'You're going to arrest me if I wash a dying man's blood off my hands?' I asked, loudly enough for the neighbours to hear.

There was a murmur of sympathy. Someone stepped forward with an old counterpane – we none of us earned much, and no doubt she couldn't afford to ruin a good duvet – to wrap round me. 'You poor girl,' she said, smoothing the hair from my forehead. 'And brave, too. You should get a medal. Shouldn't she?' she rallied the rest of the women.

Someone produced a mug of tea.

'I'll get a bath running for you now, sweetheart,' another said. 'And if you give me your keys I'll get you a change of clothes.'

That was one offer I wouldn't be accepting. Everyone knew Sal's kids were the biggest thieves on the estate, and Sal the biggest fence. But according to her lights it was a kind offer. And it produced an escort of women to my own front door. The constable was literally biting his nails with worry.

Tough.

Paula's hatchback suddenly screeched to a halt – goodness knows how many speed tickets she had picked up. When she emerged, however, her manner was as serenely unflappable as ever, and she greeted the constable as if he were a ray of daylight in an especially dark cave. At the same time she scooped me from my doorstep into the tiny hall: we all have keys to each other's homes, in case one of us goes home with something vital. When the constable muttered something sounding like 'forensic evidence' she snatched a bin liner from a roll in my cupboard and thrust it at me. 'Clothes in there. Now, about my van –' she began.

I beat it to the bathroom.

The sight of Arthur's blood sluicing down the drain made me sick again. But at least I knew I was clean now.

No towels, of course. I'd wrapped my bath towel round the stump of his arm and covered the little left of his face with the other. In a well-regulated household there are probably lots of spare towels. When you're on not much more than the national minimum wage, and Paula really, truly couldn't afford to pay any more than she did – she'd shown us the books – you don't have spare anything.

I used the bath mat.

Whatever Paula and the constable had been saying to each other, it had kept Paula from passing fresh clothes into the bathroom. I found I couldn't put on anything I'd put on clean only a couple of hours ago. And of course they were supposed to be put in that bag for the policeman.

You'd think, after all these years, I wouldn't be embarrassed about men seeing my body. But that was then. Now I was a private citizen, entitled to as much bodily decency as the next woman. And I could no more have walked naked in front of that young man than I could have flown to the moon. Holding the bathmat in front of me, I opened the door a crack and hollered.

'If I can't stop you coming with me,' I told Paula – and to be honest, I hadn't tried very hard – 'you must at least call van der Poele and Todd and tell them you're held up.' Van der Poele would be furious to know that his work was being delayed; Todd Dawes would be horrified by the reason. There'd be some sort of action, from one of them, for better or worse.

'You're right. If,' she added, sarcasm running in beads along her tongue, 'it's OK by you, Constable?'

I had a funny idea that it wasn't, but since his partner, a young woman who'd turned up while I was in the shower, was mouthing vigorously at him, he simply nodded and started looking at my books.

I could almost hear Detective Sergeant Marsh sneering, 'Read a lot for someone of your sort, don't you?'

And the funny thing was that that was exactly what he did say, half an hour later, when we were in an interview room, together with a totally silent WPC, back at Ashford nick.

'I don't see what my reading habits have to do with the death of a decent, kindly old man,' I said.

'Who said he was dead?'

'Oh, for God's sake, copper, a man loses a hand and most of his face. Is he really going to survive?'

'As a matter of fact,' he said, sounding like a ten-year-old contradicting his mum, 'he just might. He's in intensive care and it's touch and go.'

What could I say? Most people in that situation might prefer to die. Perhaps Marsh thought the same. A little silence, less hostile, grew between us.

He broke it. 'So why should anyone want to kill Arthur?'

He wasn't catching me that way. We both knew that

Arthur must have activated a parcel bomb meant for someone else, didn't we? But I'd let him tell me. I shook my head. 'He was a very nice, friendly, decent man.' Not a bad epitaph, come to think of it.

'But someone tried to kill him.'

I shook my head sadly, like some philosopher shocked at the evil man can perpetrate. Evil in the abstract, that is. Man in general. I had to do something with my face, after all: I wasn't going to let Marsh have the pleasure of seeing me weep, or even throw up.

'Who tried to kill him, Cathy?'

I didn't correct his pronunciation.

'You must know who tried to kill him, Cathy. After all, the parcel that exploded was addressed to you.' It came out like a vicious accusation.

The policewoman gasped. I didn't blame her. I'd have gasped if I hadn't sussed that out the moment the first splatter of blood hit my windscreen. But I'd rather he didn't know that, or know that my brain had been on overtime ever since trying to prove to myself that I didn't know who'd sent it when I obviously did. When I'd moved to Kent, I'd been so naïve, naïve to the point of stupid, hadn't I? As if Ashford wasn't just three short motorway hours from Birmingham (OK, M25 permitting it was three). I'd done my civic duty and registered as an elector; I was in the phone book; the household bills were in my name.

It wouldn't have taken Clive Granville long to find me, not if he'd put his mind and the minds of his minions to it. An hour? A day at the very most. And he would have been on the phone to order the package as soon as he knew where to send it. When he told the bomb-maker to make sure it would get delivered the next day, he'd be obeyed. It was only because Arthur, kindly old Arthur, had raised the package in the air to show me my bounty that he'd been the victim. Except that that didn't sound like the work of one of Granville's usual henchmen. If it was, in fact, Granville would be furious – raging, ranting furious – that anyone had produced such an unstable device. He'd boasted once that when one of his hit-men had shot someone in the stomach, leaving the victim to die a hideous lingering death, he'd killed the hit man the same way, just to teach him a lesson. He knew a great deal about pain and pain thresholds did Granville – perhaps there was some truth in the persistent rumour that he was an ex-medic. No one ever accused him of being a professor of logic.

It would have been such a relief to pour all this out. If I'd been talking to that nice woman sergeant on *The Bill* I would have done. She'd have written it all down and got me police protection and the baddies would have been found and taken to court without being able to threaten the witnesses – and they'd have gone to a jail where they couldn't tell their accomplices on the outside whom to punish. But I wasn't talking to a nice TV cop. I was talking to Detective Sergeant Marsh, the man who had almost certainly connived in the moving of a body – a body tied up with our own blue rope.

I'd better get angry. I could do anger quite well. I'd practised so I could do it without yelling or swearing or bursting into tears. Unless I had to, of course. So I slammed my palms flat on the table. If they'd had the tape-recorder running –

and come to think of it, why didn't they? – I might have joggled the tape off its spools.

'Listen,' I said not loudly, but very clearly, 'you're treating me –'

Someone tapped on the door and opened it.

I carried on louder, clearer, '– like the villain, not the victim. Being a victim's never appealed, but being a villain certainly doesn't.' I wanted to tell him to stop dissing me, but maybe the language of black kids hadn't reached this far south yet. In any case, the idea wasn't to give him language lessons, but to get me out of here.

It's a good job there wasn't a tape recorder because it would have almost certainly have fused at the number of blue words March shot off when he saw Messy Mascara's face appear.

'Ms Tyler's legal representative is here,' she announced, not so much flinching as raising her eyes in boredom at Marsh's language.

'What's she doing with a legal representative? We're not charging her with anything.'

I should hope not. Even Marsh couldn't be that stupid. Not when he'd just admitted the parcel was meant for me. He stomped off, slamming the door behind him. Pity the effect was spoiled by the constable who opened it immediately and peered in. It was White Eyelashes, of course, the one who'd been so user-unfriendly at what even I might describe as the scene of the crime. Yes, it was easier to call it that than personalise it by thinking of it as the place where Arthur was blown up. Poor Arthur: after years of being almost toothless, he'd recently saved up for a full set of dentures, which had been giving him all sorts of trouble. And now he didn't have a mouth to put them in.

I mustn't cry. I mustn't cry. Because if I did I'd have to admit I didn't know who I was crying for, him or me.

I must think about who my legal representative might be and how he or she had got there. And who was going to pay. I'd never been the proud possessor of such an exalted person before. I'd known about the duty solicitor whose miserable job it was to represent anyone unfortunate enough to be hauled in for questioning who'd asked for legal support. I'd even met a few, with greyish, sagging suits – and for all I knew, greyish, sagging brains to match. But 'Ms Tyler's legal representative' sounded a good deal more professional than that. I looked forward to meeting a very sharp suit indeed. The only question was who was paying for the suit – not to mention the brain inside. I certainly couldn't afford to. I hoped to God the Pots hadn't clubbed together – they had no cash to throw around.

What if it wasn't a legal eagle? What if it was a particularly devious move by Clive Granville to get hold of me? But even I didn't think he could get away with murdering me in a police station, no matter how much I distrusted Marsh. Except getting away with wasn't exactly the same thing as murdering, was it?

The silence was broken by the re-entry of Marsh. With his thumb – a remarkably straight, uncurly thumb, the cuticles bloody fringes where he chewed them – he gestured me out of the room.

I followed the direction of Marsh's unyielding digit.

Had I given the matter any thought, I'd have supposed

that my legal representative would have been allocated a halfway decent room and that I'd have been discreetly ushered into it. I didn't expect to be decanted into the public waiting area, full of those posters alerting me to rabies and other interesting conditions. And I didn't expect to see Jan Dawes sitting on a plastic seat, wearing one of those linen suits that crease in the right places, with an ultra-smart briefcase on her knee. Although there was a folded *Guardian* on the case, she was staring at the same posters. I might have had a stare, too – you never knew when you might need to know about the Colorado beetle – but I found myself yelling, 'Jan,' and letting her enfold me in her expensive linen arms. Her case and the paper slid disregarded to the floor.

Jan turned in outrage towards the door where Marsh should have been. In his rapid absence, she had to content herself with turning on Mascara.

Before either could say much, I stepped between them, holding up a peace-making hand. 'Hang on, hang on. She isn't paid enough to be shouted at. It's people higher up you want to skin alive.'

'Indeed,' Jan said, her voice having a steely edge I'd never heard before. In a marginally less frightening but still icy voice she continued, 'Please tell the officer in charge that I do not intend to discuss private matters with my client in a public waiting area. If your colleagues can't provide me with a suitable interview room I shall have no hesitation removing my client to other premises. Should they wish to speak to her again, they can do so via my office. Here is my card.'

And we were out of the building before you could say 'parcel bomb'.

'I've got to get away from Ashford,' I said. 'I'll go back to Brum or even stop off in London.'

Jan, occupied by reversing out of her parking space, merely grunted. But she headed in the general direction of my flat, so I assumed she wasn't going to argue.

'I didn't know you were a lawyer,' I ventured, when the traffic thinned.

'Oh, yes. That was how I met Todd. I like to keep my hand in. But I prefer choosing curtains. Now, you go and get your things together, and I'll run you to the station.' Her voice was pretty cold. I shot a look but her face gave nothing away. Had I caused some sort of row – had what I thought was a quip about curtains been a sign that she'd really not been happy with the descent of Paula's Pots on her property? She certainly wasn't behaving like the woman in whose arms I'd cried in my flat.

She stopped at the end of my street. There was still a lot of police activity, a couple of TV vans and some ominous sheets of plastic sheeting around. 'I'll wait here. Go and get as much as you can comfortably carry and leave the rest. And don't hang about, Caffy – you've got a train to catch.'

I didn't argue, couldn't, really, the way my lower lip was trembling. So I slipped out of the car, and headed by a back route to what I'd come to think of as home. No one stopped me. My key slid into the lock I'd always kept well-oiled and there I was. I didn't have all that much in the way of clothes, so it wasn't hard to cram them into my holiday rucksack. The rest went into a holdall. Cosmetics, ditto. All those books, though. How could I leave them behind? They weren't what you'd call collectors' items, of course – none had cost much more than 50 pence from charity shops – but they'd been the education I should have had at school. There was only room for a handful in my holdall. I waved the rest a sad farewell. But as I reached the door I turned back. It was one thing leaving sheets behind, but not my old friends. Grabbing a couple of supermarket carriers, I crammed in as many as I could: I'd ask Jan to stow them in some corner of Fullers.

'I thought for one crazy minute you were going to try to take them with you,' she declared, relief replacing exasperation as I explained. 'Come on. I reckon we shall just make the ten-fifty.' She put the car into gear with an expression that didn't invite conversation.

I couldn't blame her. She must know that by giving me so much as a lift she might be making herself vulnerable.

As we rounded the last island to the station – Ashford has more islands than any town I know – she asked, 'Have you enough money?'

Enough for what? A single to wherever, plus a couple of nights in a seedy bedsit?

'Plenty,' I lied. Perhaps it wasn't as bad as that. Paula owed me for this week, and I'd trust her to pop it into my bank account on time. I might get another job quite easily. But I'd made myself unemployed, so if I didn't, I wouldn't be entitled to social security unemployment benefit for literally weeks.

'Where will you go? You know I have to be able to tell the police.'

'I'll phone as soon as I've decided.' It'd cost a lot more to get to Brum, but accommodation would be cheaper there. And like buggery I'd phone.

'I'll park and meet you on the platform,' she said.

So she was going to make sure I went, was she? I slung my rucksack over my shoulder and picked up my holdall as defiantly as I could – heavens, how many books had I decided I couldn't sacrifice? – and made my way to the booking hall.

'You'll have to book the Birmingham ticket when you get to Euston,' the clerk said.

'For God's sake, whatever happened to integrated rail travel?' I exploded. Then I remembered he probably wasn't paid any more than I was – certainly not enough to have to take the stick for my misery – so I mumbled an apology. We exchanged a half-smile. But to my horror, when he asked me if I wanted single or return, two huge tears dropped on to the notes I was passing him. More would follow any moment.

'Single,' I said, grabbing the ticket for Charing Cross and running.

The train was already pulling in as I staggered up the steps. Jan seemed to be in some sort of dispute with the woman serving in the Lemon Tree café and I had to go and interrupt, almost dragging her on to the platform, now empty apart from a couple of women with pushchairs who'd got off the train. The guard was about to wave the train off. Jan pushed me into the last carriage, slamming the door behind me. As she did so, she thrust an envelope through the window. 'Read this now!' she said. 'Immediately.' She managed such a half-hearted wave I hardly wanted to.

But I did. 'GET OUT AT PLUCKLEY. J. And make sure you bring this note too,' she'd added in ordinary writing.

I stowed it in my deepest pocket. What the hell was going

on? But the ticket inspector was here already, stamping the ticket, and now the guy with the miserable job of pushing the refreshment trolley backwards and forwards all day was asking me what I wanted. Suddenly sure that Jan would want me to draw attention to myself, I asked him for crisps, arguing about the flavour. He'd remember such an awkward customer, if anyone asked.

I slipped off the train – not easy to slip at all with my baggage – at the very last minute. Straight into the arms of Paula.

Chapter Six

'Quick! Into the Ladies'!' Paula said, thrusting a Marks and Sparks carrier bag at me and grabbing my holdall.

There wasn't a single cubicle that locked, of course. But I wedged the rucksack against the door and, despite the huge – but empty – loo roll holder, transformed myself into a rather frilly young lady, complete with strappy sandals, a floppy sunhat and wrap-around sunspecs. Pity they'd left the price tag on the sunhat – but one bite sorted that. No, mustn't drop it. I'm always pretty Green about litter – with Paula who'd dare be anything else? – but today I was meticulous. No evidence. Not with my DNA on it. If Granville wanted me badly enough he'd even get that checked.

Paula walked unhurriedly towards me as I emerged, tucking her arm into mine as if we were heading for a girlie day out – though I'd have said that in Pluckley, your quintessential commuter village, the opportunities for two women on the loose were pretty limited, shopwise. She let me into a car I'd not seen before, a nondescript old Astra on trade-plates.

'From my brother's workshop,' she said briefly. 'I shall stop round the corner and you'll get in the back of the car parked there and lie down. No, leave your bags.'

I did as I was told, diving into the back of a Focus driven by a tall blond young man with the same broad serene face as Paula, her no doubt long-suffering brother. I covered myself with a travelling rug for good measure. I could quite get into this cloak and dagger stuff – if it hadn't had the vicious hand of Clive Granville behind it.

And if it hadn't been so hot. Kent does hot quite well when it decides not to rain, and today it had decided to go for very hot. Some kind person had tucked a bottle of water beside me – one of those with a clever sort of teat, so it wouldn't spill. But what goes in has to come out, and goodness knows how many hours it would be before I could use a loo. All the same… So to feel the car slowing and stopping and have the door flung open was like being released from the fiery furnace into heaven, especially when I discovered where we were. We were parked right by the back door of Fullers, and all the gang – Helen, Paula, Meg – were there cheering and ready to hug me, as were the Daweses. The champagne Todd produced as soon as the Focus was out of sight was nice but a bit OTT, I thought, given the fact that Clive Granville might not have bought my escape to Brum story.

'Oh, yes, he will,' Jan said, when I voiced my doubts. She gave me another in what was becoming a series of hugs, before she topped up my glass. 'If he checks up, he'll learn that you looked like death warmed up when you were buying your ticket. Yes, the guy on the desk remembered you – '

'How –?'

'I went to buy a ticket for myself – one of these annual saver jobs – and asked if he knew what was wrong with this girl I'd seen crying. He didn't know of course, but said you were so upset he thought someone must have died.' She squeezed my hand. 'Then there was that woman in the Lemon Tree – '

'And the ticket collector and refreshment guy might remember me too. But they may have missed me later,' I added dubiously.

'Come and see where you'll be staying,' Jan said, taking me by the shoulders and drawing me into the cool of the old kitchen. 'Caffy, I hated being so nasty to you, but I didn't know how well you could act and I really wanted everyone to see an unhappy young woman.'

'Sounds as if I was more like a dying duck in a thunderstorm,' I said. But I wouldn't have wanted to go through that bleak half hour again. Being miserable on my own was one thing. I was quite used to it. But being miserable because someone I had thought liked me as much as I liked her had rejected me, was another. Liked? Jan had never been quite as warm as Todd, but if I'd ever had a choice about replacing my mother, she'd have been my number one candidate. And numbers two, three, four and five. I didn't mind sternness in women, not if I respected them. Without being gushy, she'd been warmer than Paula, who was the next best candidate for surrogate mum.

'You were entitled to be as miserable as a wet Monday.' Todd had followed us in. The rest of Paula's Pots got on with doing what they did best: applying paint.

'We didn't know where was safest for you,' Todd said. 'And then we saw this.' He put an arm round my shoulder to turn me round, then pointed. Not that he needed to – the huge mobile home spoke very well for itself. How on earth had they organised it so quickly? I could only suppose that their money had talked loud and clear.

'You mean I sleep in – ' I could scarcely keep the awe from my voice: it was about three times the size of my flat and –

'No. That's where we sleep.' He tried to hug away my

damned fool disappointment. How dared I expect anything like that? 'Sorry: I didn't mean to raise your hopes. We actually bought it with the intention of installing you in it and staying on in our hotel. But Jan said you'd be too vulnerable. And I'm afraid she's right.'

I nodded, trying not to look as crestfallen as I still felt. Maybe I was just tired: I usually had my hopes under better control than this. Maybe it was a case of them giving me a yard and my wanting a mile. I wasn't pleased with myself.

'So we're going to sleep there and you, Caffy, are going to sleep – well, somewhere else. Not the Ritz, I'm afraid, nothing like it – though you will be mistress of Fullers. I hope you're not claustrophobic?' Still talking, he led the way upstairs. His hand trailed on the banister rail – he turned and smiled when he saw mine doing the same.

He took me through the servants' quarters under the eaves, pushing into a big walk-in cupboard. As he demonstrated, it locked inside and out. There was just enough room for a sleeping bag.

'The trouble is, there's no window, so you'd bake if you had to stay here long. But we thought you could sleep up here in the ordinary bedroom area and retreat if you got nervous.'

Jan had been right. It was altogether safer than the caravan. So I meant it when I said, 'This is perfect. Just perfect. Look, if we push a couple of trestles and some dustsheets over by the door I could just scramble over them and maybe no one would notice it was there.'

He smiled and patted my shoulder, as if to tell me I was trying too hard and I didn't need to bother. I bet he'd have been great with his kids' scraped knees and first hangovers. Hang on: he'd never mentioned kids. Perhaps I was their substitute child, just as they were my replacement parents. Only I'd be nicer to them than their real child would ever have been.

'I hope and pray it doesn't get that far.' He returned to the main room, leaning his head against the dormer window and looking down at what would one day no doubt become a wonderful garden.

I swallowed hard. I had to say it, after all – couldn't live with myself if I didn't. 'You don't have to do this, you and Jan. You could pop me in your car and just drop me off somewhere where there's a big floating population, like Brighton, and I could disappear.'

He turned to look me straight in the eye; the trouble was, because the light streaming in was so bright I couldn't see his face at all. 'How would you survive?' His voice told me how anxious he was.

What I wanted to do was yell, 'I couldn't! Don't let me even try!' What I actually said, quite quietly, was, 'I could find some casual work. Waitressing, that sort of thing.' I didn't know why I hadn't thought of that before. I lie. I had thought of it before. And with it the thought had flitted through what passes for my brain that I could even earn a few bob on the game. I suppose I'd been so anxious to suppress that idea that I'd closed down the other little brain cells too.

I'd have bet a pound that Todd had read my mind, at least some of it. 'The other Pots want to keep an eye on you. Jan and I want to keep an eye on you. As part of our refurbishment here we're having all sorts of surveillance equipment installed – they start putting it in tomorrow. You've already done the hard bit – leaving your home as if you were on the run. And doing a very convincing imitation of being on the run. If whoever …' He tailed off.

'Sent me the bomb,' I supplied, keeping my voice as matter-of-fact as I could.

'Quite. He'll hear on the radio or TV that he got the wrong person, so he'll come looking for you – we've all worked that out. If he asks questions, he'll learn you've gone to London. But you've got other hard bits to do too.'

'Like not communicating with anyone except through me,' Jan said, stepping into the room. 'Even the police don't know where you've gone, remember.'

'And a bloody good job that is too!' I explained.

They wore twin masks of disbelief. 'But this is England,' Todd said stupidly.

My eyebrow went up of its own accord, telling them how innocent they were. A short account of my encounters with Sergeant Marsh had them literally tearing their hair.

'But this is England!' Todd repeated when I'd finished. 'We must do something. We must contact the media – get someone to do an exposé!'

'More realistically,' Jan overrode him, 'we get my old law firm to provide a representative to accompany Caffy when she makes a formal complaint at another police station.'

'Of course!' Todd was already digging in his pocket for his mobile.

'Hang on,' I said. 'That means revealing my whereabouts. Being seen, at the very least. Corrupt officers know some pretty nasty criminals – it wouldn't surprise me if Granville was on Marsh's Christmas card list.'

'No! Honestly, you'd get police protection and –'

'For the time being I'm happier here with your protection,' I said firmly. 'I know I've got to do something but I need a bit of time to think things through.'

They exchanged glances. Could I trust them? I didn't for one moment think they'd deliberately harm me – I had plenty of evidence that they really cared for me – but sometimes people think they know best. And in my experience they don't. Not when they're dabbling with criminals, who don't play by the rules that *Guardian* readers observe. If I dabbled with criminals, I'd make damn sure I was playing by their rules, not mine.

Jan might have had the presence of mind to claim to be my lawyer and flash her card at Mascara, but her idea of an unobtrusive lunch was to lay a trestle table in front of the mobile home complete with table cloth, carafe of wine and a selection of greenish recycled wine glasses. We were all to sit down together, employers and employees in one happy family.

Any other day, I'd have loved them for their openheartedness: today their naïvety almost made me swear. Fortunately Todd gave a discreet cough.

'Are you sure people swarming up ladders should touch any more alcohol?' he enquired, putting his arm round her. 'I think you should consult Paula.' As Jan toddled off, he turned to me, raising an eyebrow. There were a couple of white hairs sprouting eccentrically from each. I'd have trimmed or plucked them for him if I'd been Jan – they made him look much older than the rest of him suggested.

'It's very kind of you,' I said. 'More than kind. Like you've been all along. I don't deserve – ' Hell, why did kindness always prick my eyes? His too, by the speed with which he popped on his sunglasses. 'But the less attention we attract the better. I'd have thought Paula would want them to stick to their usual routine: we always gather round a radio and eat our sarnies listening to the one o'clock news. Yes, honestly! It helps Meg's kids' homework.'

He took a moment to work that out, but at last he grinned and nodded. 'So it would be better if anyone passing just saw the three of them, gloomily speculating, no doubt, on where you'd gone.'

'Quite. And you and Jan should do whatever you usually do for lunch. You wouldn't normally eat with the lower orders, would you?'

He winced. 'I told you, I'd have been very much below stairs when this place was at its best.'

'But you're not now, Todd. And however much you'd like to muck in with us, and us with you, of course, to an out-sider it'd look dead odd.'

'And the last thing we want is to do anything that'd attract anyone's attention: right?'

'Right.'

'OK. That's all of us accounted for,' he said. 'But what about you? You need to eat.'

'I'll do what I usually do if I'm working on my own: get a book and read while I eat. Only trouble is,' I added, as Jan returned, shaking her head with disappointment, 'I don't have any books and I don't have any food.' Hell! Little Nell on a bad day! God knows why I said that. Technically it might have been true. But Jan had my bags with books in them, and the rucksack and holdall would be around somewhere. As for food, they'd expected to feed six, not just the two of them. It wasn't like me to indulge in self-pity. But I couldn't switch it off. 'So I might as well get my overalls on and start work on part of the house where no one'll see me.' Bugger it, I really was going for broke, wasn't I?

'Not until you've eaten,' Jan declared, confirming that the others were already gathered round the radio. 'And I've got not just the books you gave me earlier but some of my own. Plus, I should imagine, some in that bag that weighed a ton! So come and choose something while I put a plate of food together for you.' She held open the door of their temporary palace, putting a motherly arm round me.

Now I could have guilted for Europe – might even have made it to be captain of the team.

Wide-eyed, I looked about me. I suppressed a grin: they were too kind to deserve it. But while they might have moved in here to guard me no one could accuse them of stinting themselves. Come on: in their place I wouldn't have either. According to the bill lying open on the pristine kitchen work surface, they'd been staying at Eastwell Manor. Had they meant to stay there as long as it took us to restore the house? I've never even speculated on how much it would cost to eat there, let alone stay, but several people we've worked for have celebrated big anniversaries or major promotions there and come back sucking their teeth at the cost. Everyone's always said it was worth it, however, for the service and sheer luxury. So Todd and Jan had given up the comforts of one of the region's chicest hotels just to come and look after me. That was bad enough, but what if they'd gone all hair-shirt and stayed in the sort of caravan my great aunt Gladys used to own in Weston-super-Mare? I'd have cringed with guilt every time I'd seen it. And believe me, a bit of old-fashioned envy is better than cringing with guilt.

Envy? Did I say envy? Well, I wouldn't have been human if I hadn't felt a twinge. Although this was just a mobile home, it was fixed, and on a fairly level site. So it felt more like a well-planned bungalow. Since they'd just taken possession – I'd have loved to see the traffic jams its delivery caused – everything was brand new, and smelt that way. The lunch Jan had been offering was still in a hamper. Goodness knew how they'd accumulated so much so quickly, but perhaps it was something to do with having a great deal in your bank you were prepared to slosh around. I didn't penetrate into the living area, of course, but I'd be ready to bet that everything was beautifully equipped.

Todd joined us in the kitchen, hefting a nice old-fashioned cardboard box, which proved to be full of books. 'Just some of the collection without which Jan just won't travel,' he grunted, dropping it on to the work surface next to the bill. 'Help yourself.'

'Not the Peter Carey, if you don't mind – I'm in the middle of that!' Jan said, over her shoulder as she unpacked the hamper.

That was all right: I'd had enough of villains recently not to want to read about Ned Kelly. In fact I didn't want to read about crime at all – not even fictional crime, which put about half the books out of court. I'd just finished *Persuasion*, you know, the one where the heroine claims that women love longest even when all hope is gone, and these days couldn't fancy the psychotic goings-on of Mr Rochester, so I was still picking round when Todd leaned over and pulled out *Dubliners*. 'Have you ever read any Joyce?'

'I couldn't make head nor tail of *Finnegans Wake*,' I said, without thinking. I prefer people not to know my love of books. I prefer people not to know of any of my loves, actually – it gives them power over me. But this was Todd, and the books Jan's. I had to let them in, not fend them off. Wherever would I have been if they'd not been openness itself?

I felt rather than saw them exchange glances.

'Try it, then. Unless you'd prefer a Fanny Burney?'

I took *Evelina* from his outstretched hand. In for a penny, in for a pound. 'She was the one who had a breast removed without anaesthetic, wasn't she? I've always meant to read her.' So I took the two. And a plate that Jan presented me with. Smoked salmon. Green salad. Some of the best bread I've ever tasted. And a glass of freshly squeezed orange juice.

'But we'd much rather you stayed and picnicked with us, in the cool of the van here, then went off and had a read afterwards, while we blitz the shops,' Jan said. 'Pillows, sheets, towels, china, saucepans, microwave – we've got to get busy the moment we've swallowed the last crumb. Come on, tuck in both of you.'

We did. 'Tell me, Todd,' I asked awkwardly at last, 'it isn't as if yours isn't a pretty well-known face – '

'To people Meg's age, maybe! You didn't recognise me, did you?'

'Sorry.'

He slung an arm round me. Weird how physical he could be, but not in a predatory or even remotely sexual way. 'No: don't dare apologise. It's great not being recognised. It used to be a problem, when my face was in the papers all the time: I even had to have a minder, then. But my fanbase has got older, and now I do hardly any live gigs, so generally we can be Mr and Ms Incognito. Jan's kept her maiden name and if anyone looks as if they've clocked us, she pays with her card. Which I can see she's dying to flex even as we speak. OK, love, I'm ready!' And he was gone.

'You ate with Todd? Again?' Meg demanded, as I went to check in with Paula and collect sugar soap and sponge. 'What did you talk about?'

'This and that. Their plans for this place, mostly.' I didn't let on about the books, or the fact that he'd taken an Open University degree about ten years ago, just for interest's sake. Just like that. Would I ever have the guts to try? Or the money, Caffy – even the OU has to charge fees. 'But they're off for the rest of the afternoon, and I'm reporting for duty.' I'd save the books for this evening.

We all worked a bit late to make up for the time we'd lost during the day, but eventually the other Pots left for home. Todd and Jan hadn't returned from their shopping trip – they must be shopping for England, for heaven's sake – and for the first time in a few hours I felt scared. As well I might. I was totally vulnerable. The Daweses had locked their caravan and though I had the key to Fullers, anyone with a mind to getting in would have found the old and brittle glass a cinch to smash their way through. I'd resolved not to use my phone, lest it give away my whereabouts. Of course, it was there for the direst of emergencies, but if I summoned the police, I might just get my old friend Sergeant Marsh. Better, then, to elude any predators than have to escape them.

The other thing I didn't have, of course, was any supper. What if Jan and Todd did what they must think would be the obvious thing and ate out? I thought longingly of the choccie biccies we always kept in the van for dire emergencies like this. Even melted choccie biccies would have been nice.

Enough, already! I was alive. I'd had the best lunch for years. I was cared for. And the sun was shining. I could bask in the garden completely for free.

The trouble is that basking, unlike painting, leaves the mind free to wander. What I'd have liked was a long drink, a long bath and maybe even quite a long cry. I sat up quickly. Well, I might not have those, but before the two best people in the world returned I had ahead of me a lovely long summer's evening and, in *Evelina*, a lovely long book.

Chapter Seven

The evening light was just getting too weak to read by when Todd and Jan returned, the car laden with shopping but also aromatic with the smell of curry.

Singing for my supper was beyond me, but the very least I could do was help in any way that seemed best. When Jan started wringing her hands over the unwashed state of the new china – a complete set, as if they were planning to feed the five thousand – I simply took it and washed it, stacking it on the brand new drainer until she could find tea-towels. Bedmaking, unpacking their cases; we did everything together. Todd produced a powerful lantern torch for me, with enough life in the battery, he promised, for me to read in bed. They'd also run to earth an electronic whistle in case I was scared in the night and, as if he was playing the lead in some Secret Seven book, a reel of black thread which he promised to tie between their front door and mine. There was also an inflatable mattress. It was probably too hot for the sleeping bag they presented me with, but there was a blanket, too. Luxury. The only thing they didn't offer – never had, come to think of it – was a place for my airbed in their caravan. But the glances I intercepted from time to time over the curry reheated in their state-of-the-art microwave implied nocturnal activities that the presence of a spare pair of ears might inhibit. And with all their precautions, including the thread, I felt quite safe and happy when at last I collapsed in my new bedroom. And very tired. Tired enough – despite all the things I ought to be worrying about, not least how I could ever possibly repay them for everything – to fall asleep almost immediately, lulled by the creaks of the old house settling around me.

One thing people never tell you about the country is how noisy it is. It was far quieter in suburban Ashford than here. The birds set their alarm clocks remarkably early, and they weren't the sort that turn off when you slam them, either. I'm a great one for early morning stretches – with a job like mine you can't let your muscles even dream of going stiff – but my avian friends went in for clog-dancing on the roof just above me. So I woke when they did. And started to think, something I'd tried to avoid the previous day. But even that little hamster of worry that twirls its wheel relentlessly in the grey early hours accepted as a given that I'd be staying here, not bolting to the coast or anywhere else.

In the midst of all the Arthur business – and how was he? Had he survived? – I'd forgotten the little matter of my Crabton Manor corpse. Mr van der Poele's visitor's corpse. It seemed that Paula might have done, too – but knowing her, she'd have stashed the blue fibres we found in the bedroom there as safely as she'd stashed the photos she'd had developed. She'd be waiting for a suitable opportunity to discuss our next move with me. Which would, come to think of it, be a real act of bravery on my part – a visit to her mother's hairdressing salon. The great and good around here might never venture into it – I should imagine Jan went to a very nifty cutter indeed – but its very awfulness made it the place for me. A poor perm turning my mop to frizz was just what I needed, though I hoped Paula's mum would do a good colour. I'd also get hold of some self-tanning stuff and hope it made my already deep tan even darker. Then I could get out and about if I needed to. As for clothes, I was down by one outfit, but as long as the weather lasted I could wash out and wear. Of course, I was as sure as I was breathing that if I asked Jan or Todd for a loan to buy more they'd press fistfuls of fivers on me. But they'd done so much for me already I'd be embarrassed to do an Oliver Twist – even if I knew they wouldn't do a Beadle back.

Hmm. Van der Poele and Granville, both in the same area. Two villains too many. And Marsh certainly in van der Poele's pocket, and probably in Granville's. Did they know they shared a bent policeman? And would they be happy if they did? It depended whether they were rivals or complemented each other. I'd give my teeth to find out. Unbidden, a grin crept across my face. I'd once read a play where these three vile people had to share a tiny room together forever. It seemed hell wasn't a matter of toasting forks and devils but of other people. Wouldn't it be nice to have all three villains banged up in the same cell for the rest of their natural lives?

The thought got me off the airbed and doing my stretches. It was still cool enough to warrant a few clothes so I slipped on a tracksuit. I needed that anyway – and the guarantee of a towel – before I headed for what I thought was the nearest shower. We knew there was still running water. OK, it would be cold, but that was life.

Life was also a dead mouse and a variety of defunct insects and no sign of a towel: perhaps personal cleanliness could wait till I'd cleaned the room thoroughly. Or perhaps other bathrooms would be in a better state – when I'd looked at them I'd appraised them with a decorator's eye, not a potential bather's. Yes, I remembered the mahogany fittings and the huge expanses of white enamel, many ruined by limescale, Kent having the hardest water I'd ever come across – a particular shock after dear old Brum's soft stuff. And no, I'd forgotten the collections of dead bugs.

It was still only six. If I started work it might disturb my hosts. I'd find a windowsill in the sun and do a bit more thinking.

One thing I'd have to acquire was a new mobile phone, since my existing one could be traced. But agreements for those involve all sorts of embarrassing details like ID and proof of residence using utility bills. Provided I did the paying, however, I was sure one of the Pots would sort that for me. Helen, perhaps – it wasn't dangerous, and she might even enjoy it. So long as she didn't offer to do it in her lunchtime…

Once I was back on the airwaves then I'd have a little talk with Messy Mascara. She'd given me the idea that she didn't like Marsh any more than I did. But splitting on him – even spying on him – was another matter altogether. I'd have to play it by ear – literally – since I wouldn't be able to see her face. I wasn't going to indulge in one of those clever phones sending pictures!

Except – my God! – I'd give my teeth for one right now. The window I'd chosen didn't face due east, but more south-east, so I had a lovely view across the Marsh – Romney, not Sergeant. The trees, the sheep, cast long shadows. So did a little band of men working their way surreptitiously amongst the reeds on the far side of what looked like a canal, though not the sort we get in the Midlands, with their built-up towpaths. Perhaps this was just a river, with its steep sides. Whatever it was, my first thought was that they were Granville's men, hunting me. My paranoia – yes, I really was about to bolt downstairs to yell to Jan and Todd for help – was soon replaced by simple interest. The men didn't want to be seen, not because they were heading towards Fullers, but because they were heading inland via the least populous route. Over to the west – I could just pick it out between the trees – was a removal van. As they saw it, they broke into a ragged run. Many seemed too weak to manage more than a stagger.

Kent used to be famous for its Free Traders, the glamorous name for smugglers of wine and spirits. Now it has a name as an access point for the worst sort of smugglers – traders in people. Call them refugees or asylum seekers or economic migrants, those poor devils didn't look as if they were heading for a New Jerusalem. They looked cold and tired and hungry. Terrified, not terrorists. But someone ought to do something about them. Someone like me, on the run herself? Half of me wanted to turn the blindest of eyes – people who've been at the bottom end of society ought to stick together, Robin Hood stealing from only the rich, that sort of thing. But the other half was revolted by the thought that unscrupulous people should make money out of bringing them in and probably out of any wages they managed to scrape; pimping not prostitutes, but the poorest of the poor.

Seething, I ran downstairs – yes, I marked which room I'd been using, since there were so many and when the police came I wanted them to see exactly the same view as I'd seen – and despite the hour banged on the caravan door. I was gobsmacked to have it opened by Jan, swathed in a towel and rubbing her hair dry.

'Damned birds,' she said by way of a greeting.

Todd, sporting a towel and an excellent torso for a man of his age, peered over her shoulder. 'What's the problem?'

'Illegal immigrants – I think. Trailing across the Marsh, just over there.' I pointed in the vague direction of the sun. 'I saw them from up there.' Another point.

Managing an ungainly run in his towelling flip-flops, Todd headed for the house. Jan called me back, thrusting her mobile phone into my hands, before pushing me gently off after Todd. I overtook him on the stairs. 'Third door on your left,' I yelled. As I reached the window and pointed, the back of the removal van was just being raised. 'They came from those reeds. Along that canal thing.'

'That'll be the Royal Military Canal,' Todd said. 'Built to protect us from a more organised form of invasion. Napoleon's.'

I'd ask him all about it another day. 'I'm afraid we've missed them.'

'That might be a good thing,' Jan observed, coming up behind us in a gorgeous wrap, black silk embroidered with gold birds. 'Unless you really want to talk to the police again?'

'It would probably be the Immigration people,' Todd observed. 'And in any case it wouldn't be the same policeman. I still cling to the belief,' he said, grinning ruefully, 'that the vast majority of the police force – '

'Police service,' Jan corrected him.

' – are decent men and women doing the best they can.'

'I'm sure you're right,' I agreed, though with less conviction. 'Trouble is, I've got no evidence. If I'd only had a film in my camera!' I couldn't afford one, which is why I hadn't made a mad dash for the camera, but he didn't need to know that.

'You'd need something with a powerful lens to do any real good,' he said. I knew as clearly as if he'd said it aloud that as soon as the shops opened he'd be banging on the doors of the nearest photographic shop.

So did Jan. She and I exchanged the sort of tolerant, conspiratorial look I'd seen mothers and daughters give when Dad found a need for some new toy.

'They might have been some farm workers waiting for a lift to pick more fruit or vegetables,' Jan said, the words meaning one thing, the tone telling him not to waste his money.

What would he say next? 'But I've always wanted a tele-photo lens?' or 'I've always meant to get one of these digital jobs?'

No; he was a bit more sophisticated than that. And a bit more truthful. 'Pity we've left the bird-spotting gear back in the West Indies. We could have used the binoculars, too.'

As one, we turned from the window, and headed for the stairs. It was only then that Jan broke away, peering into one room after another. Exchanging a tolerant father/daughter shrug, we pulled twin puzzled faces as we heard water running.

'Fancied another shower, did you?' Todd asked as she returned, shaking water from her hand.

'You didn't tell me the bathrooms were as filthy as that. And I'd forgotten there was no hot water. Get your towel, Caffy – we've got no bugs and the dearest little shower you've ever seen. What have I said?'

Hell, why did this keep happening? I'd always tried to keep my upper lip pretty ever since I'd learnt that my parents didn't like crying, and here it was, wobbling away, almost as uncontrollably as the lower one. 'I was just thinking about Arthur,' I said, not untruthfully, the memory of what had happened to my only towels bringing the emotions I'd been trying to suppress surging to the surface.

'Well, as soon as you've had a shower and some breakfast, we'll phone the hospital. No reason why Jan shouldn't be his legal adviser as well,' Todd observed.

We were now by their caravan door, and I was back in control of myself. More or less. Until Jan's shrewd look and the pressure into my hand of the fattest, fluffiest towel I'd ever held, set my lips trembling again. At least I made it into the shower before I had my blub.

'It's as good as France,' Todd observed, spreading apricot conserve on his toast. They'd put up a picnic table between the caravan and the house and we were basking in the already warm sun.

'Which is why we bought Fullers,' Jan said. 'So we could do this whenever we wanted. A nice quiet retirement.' She smiled, without any irony that I could see.

Instead of which they'd got me and my adventures. 'I'm sorry.' I hung my head.

'Don't be. Everyone should do their bit for society,' Jan

said, 'and this beats working in a charity shop.' She took my hand and seemed about to say something else. In the end, she compromised and gave a kind smile. 'Ah! Is that your van?'

It was. Rob McElwee and his weather forecast must have encouraged them to make an early start in case it got too hot later. Paula pulled it over into the shade and they all got out. Todd waved them over. Meg lagged behind till her brilliant blush had subsided.

'Time,' he announced, 'for your second breakfast and a council of war.'

'In conclusion,' Jan said, some half an hour later, 'we all agree that we need a straight policeman.'

'And we're not talking sexuality here,' Todd added impishly.

'So where do we find one?'

I'd not mentioned him to anyone for four? – five? – years. I'd buried him so deep in my heart I scarcely thought about him. What I wanted to say was, 'I know one. His name's Taz. He's with the Met.' He was the social worker to whom I owed everything. The ex-social worker. The pay and conditions and public hostility had at last got to him so badly he'd gone off to university with the avowed aim of making some money, but student loans and a lingering need to interfere in people's lives had driven him to the police, where he was now one of those fast-tracked cops. He'd known I'd been head over heels in love with him, of course, and had gently but firmly backed out of my life. He'd not been able to breach his professional code when I was his client; but, even if he had, I don't think that deep down he'd ever come to terms with my previous lifestyle. Much as I knew he was attracted to me, he saw me as a car with a dreadful track record, far too many previous owners, and a rather battered logbook. The only way he showed any feelings at all was with Christmas and birthday cards, which always carried his latest address and his phone number. Oh, yes, each year I memorised that number. I could do it now, leave a message saying, 'I'm in deep trouble: come and help.'

But even amongst all these dear friends I remained resolutely silent. And I didn't know why.

Chapter Eight

I soon set off for the easy part of the campaign – the transformation of Caffy. Paula's mum, a tall, broad lady called Stell, was so delighted with the prospect of a customer that she agreed to open the shop specially, an added bonus as only she would see how I looked as I went in and how I looked as I went out. You couldn't miss the gleam in her eye as I walked in: she'd wanted to get her hands on my blonde bob ever since she'd first seen me. Well, anyone's bob, really. True, she wasn't at all happy about turning me brunette, any more than at bottom I was, but she remembered dimly, she said, my stomach sinking, how she could tint my eyebrows and eyelashes to match, provided I wasn't allergic. There wasn't time to do patch tests now, so I'd just have to hope and pray.

'You shouldn't really colour and perm in the same day,' Stell fussed, 'not with hair this fine. And it's ever so dry – you girls really ought to use more conditioner and moisturising serum. Now, while all the hair colour takes, why don't I slap on this suntan stuff for you – it's ever so hard to do it yourself.'

Well, I have spent better half hours than the one in her loo, stripped to bra and pants, a polythene bag on my head to help the colour take and tanning mousse everywhere my underwear wasn't. I just hoped I wouldn't turn out like well-cooked streaky bacon. I couldn't look, of course, because I had to keep my eyes shut while the lash colour took.

In fact I was so pleased – or so appalled – with the result, I hadn't the heart to turn her down when she offered me a pedicure and manicure on the house, though I loathed nail varnish wherever it was painted. 'Then you'll be really transformed,' she said kindly.

And I was. Of course, I could only see the top half of myself, and I saw a much older woman, with a harder face than I could have imagined. Scary stuff – was this me ten years down the road? I'd have to make damn sure it wasn't. I paid her with my last remaining cash and scuttled out – I'd plenty of time before Paula came to collect me and needed to buy a few things.

Folkestone may house a lot of people, but it isn't your actual metropolis, so my shopping options would have been pretty limited even if I'd had the sort of plastic I suspected Jan flexed. But there was a sale at Debenhams and I managed to get a couple of towels at a reasonable price. I fingered them: though they weren't anything like the cuddly monsters that had engulfed me this morning, they were respectably fluffy. And although I had all Jan's library at my disposal, and went into the Oxfam shop for a shirt, I came out with a couple more books. You'd think I'd have got used to other people's cast-offs by now, but it had to be something I really needed or quite special to make me buy. Often I ended up with raggy stuff from a market, which lost its shape and colour as soon as you looked at it, and it wasn't any comfort at all knowing it had probably been made by poor bastards in India on slave labour rates.

Still with time to spare, I wandered over to the cliff path that leads steeply down to a defunct hotel and some rather sad amusement rides. If I looked farther afield, across a dazzling blue sea not yet dimmed by heat-haze, I could just make out the coast of France. Now that was tempting. As was the thought of simply nipping over the railings and jumping. That'd solve everyone's problems. The trouble was, even as I contemplated the act, I knew I'd never carry it off, not because of me, but because of the people I'd leave behind. One of my mates in the bad old days had topped herself without warning. It turned out she was HIV positive and couldn't face the future, but we were so hurt and angry with her for not trusting us to help. I couldn't inflict that on Paula and Co, or on the Daweses.

As I peered, I realised I wasn't alone. This bloke in a virtually fluorescent shirt and orange Bermuda shorts was sidling up to me. Forty-odd, weighing far more than he ought, with a beer-gut almost guaranteeing an early grave. And the ugliest legs I'd ever seen. I moved.

He sidled some more. And then, leaning closer, asked, 'Are you workin', darlin'?'

So that was what my transformation had done! I took a deep breath, smiled, and stepped towards him. 'As a matter of fact I am. Undercover. For the Vice Squad.'

That one never failed, did it? As I reached for my bag, apparently to produce ID or something, he spluttered, blushed and scarpered. In whichever order.

To my dismay, there was no sign of Paula's car when I got back to Stell's shop. But a young man was there. Stell didn't seem pleased to see him. Perhaps it was because he was spotty and smelt of sweat. 'This is Dean. He says our Derek's busy, but he'll take you back.'

'Derek and the others need a good run today while the weather lasts,' he said, flapping a not very respectful hand at

Stell as he opened the door and walked out. As I caught up, he added, 'So he asked me to do the business. I've got to go and look at a motor in Hastings, see.'

We didn't talk much on the way back; the encounter with the would-be punter had ruffled me and in any case he was so busy showing off his driving skills I wouldn't have wanted to disturb his concentration. I might not like my face much this new way, but it was better than it being reorganised by a trip through his windscreen.

At last he slowed, took a turn off the A-road, and started to weave through country lanes, much as I'd have done, if that been the most direct route. But it struck me that he was actually taking us away from our target. When he pulled into a gateway overhung by a heavy tree and cut the engine, I suspected why. When he unzipped his flies, I knew.

'How about a French job?'

Reeling at my betrayal I was out of the car, shopping and all, before you could say 'condom'.

The bugger followed me. It wasn't easy for me to stride out in strappy sandals, but it was temporarily harder for him, since he was trying to adjust his dress, you might say, at the time. At last, as he got close, I turned. 'Look here, Sunshine,' I said, 'I know plenty of ways of stopping men like you in their tracks. If you want me to bring tears to your eyes, I will. But if I were you I'd get back in that lustmobile of yours fast. And count yourself lucky if I don't tell the police.'

'What about – what about Paula? And Derek? He'd kill me.' He sounded like a three-year-old.

I smiled, not kindly. 'You'll just have to wait and see, won't you? Now – get lost.'

He didn't argue.

Striding out of the question, I might as well stroll through the lanes back to Fullers, which, irritatingly, I could see but not see a road to. Take to the fields in these shoes? Not bloody likely. So I teetered on, reminding myself horribly of that busty woman from those *Carry On* films, whose wiggle was supposed to provide innocent male amusement. Don't think I wasn't aware of the bitter irony of the situation. I was. I seethed with pain and anger. After my past, here I was, a decent qualified painter and decorator, changing my appearance and ending up looking and being treated like a hooker. I felt cheap – not just because of the sexual advances those bastards had made to me, but because I'd always thought myself as somehow different. I'd survived, not quite by thinking of myself as a foundling dropped into the wrong family. I looked too much like the few photos of my father and my voice was the same as my mother's. I was genetically theirs, all right. But something had always driven me. Even when I was at rock bottom, hooked and, to put it bluntly and in terms the *News of the World* would relish, Granville's sex slave, I believed I could do better. And if you sneer and think that earning your living slapping paint on other people's walls isn't much cop, then you should have seen what I started from. I'd never paint the Sistine Chapel ceiling, but I'd sure as hell paint Joe Public's ceilings better than anyone else. And the chance of working on Fullers had made another goal a possibility – what if I could become a specialist restorer, working on lovely National Trust or English Heritage properties?

There, I felt better already. Don't allow negative thoughts, the therapist had said. She'd even given us each a rubber band to slip round our wrists. Every time we had a negative thought we were supposed to ping it. I know some didn't bother, but my wrist was blue with tiny bruises for a few days. And even now I was with the Pots, there were some days I'd slip one on, just to remind myself. Actually, I needed a quick ping right this minute: I hadn't yet told Todd and Jan the full details of my past. They knew I'd been a drug addict and in thrall to my supplier, who'd carved his initials on my stomach, but they didn't know quite what I'd been doing when I said I'd worked in a hotel. I'd let them assume I was a chambermaid.

It wasn't that I wanted to deceive them, not actively. There just hadn't been the right moment. Actually, none of us had talked much about our pasts. I guessed that they didn't want to embarrass me by talking about artistic and professional achievements – not to mention the financial results – reaching heights beyond my imagination. I didn't want to embarrass them by talking about the depths I'd crawled from, worse than anything they could dream. Soon. Very soon. I owed them that. Come to think of it I owed them everything. And it galled me that the only thing I could do to even things up was to apply exceptionally smooth top coats.

I pressed on, constantly orientating myself by the hill Fullers topped. I couldn't be all that far from where the removal lorry had waited for its human cargo. I started looking carefully at the verge. If I'd known what I was looking for it would have helped. I know a bit from the wrong side about criminal law but not a lot about forensic evidence. Tyre tracks? In weather as hot and dry as this? Nonetheless, I walked very slowly, my eyes scanning the verge. A couple of hundred yards further on, it was clear even to my inexperienced eye that a large and heavy lorry had parked for some time – the grass was flattened and it had dripped some oil of some sort. Better still, one of the poor devils must have had a hole in his pockets: there was a scattering of French Euros. I picked some up, but left the rest, marking the place with a little heap of stones, as if starring in some children's adventure.

So I was hot but triumphant when I finally reach the top of Fuller's hill. Todd and Jan were reading the *Guardian* and *Times* respectively, over a mug of what smelt like excellent coffee. I braced myself – if I didn't like what I'd seen of myself, I didn't think they would, either. Though their eyes spoke volumes, neither said a word about my appearance, not until I too had a cup of coffee and a seat in the sun.

At last Jan spoke. She sounded just like my mate's mother when she had her first tattoo: primly approving in her words, but inwardly howling. 'You certainly look very different.'

I yelled with laughter. 'Oh, call a spade a bloody shovel, Jan! I may not have been your actual Gainsborough portrait before, but now I reckon I've been done by Lucien Freud!'

Todd looked up. 'There's a lot more to you than you let on, isn't there, Caffy?'

Why not tell them now? Like I'd just promised myself? Because I couldn't, any more than I could phone Taz. 'When this is over, I'll tell you everything, I promise. Meanwhile, I'll go and put my gear on and finish off that doorframe, if it's all the same to you.'

'It would be to us. But there's been a call from the police.

I'm so sorry, Caffy,' Todd added, putting a kind hand on mine, 'but that old postie didn't make it through the night. And now they want to interview you again.'

I was on my feet and ready to run.

'It's OK, it's OK. Jan'll be with you all the time – she's your legal representative, remember. And she's already spoken to some of her colleagues who are still practising.'

'You've been well-briefed?' I risked, winning a pair of answering grimaces.

'And the other thing is we've told them you're no longer in the Ashford area. They'll have to arrange to interview you in London,' Jan said.

'So I'll run you both up as far as the suburbs, where you can catch a local train. My feeling is that it wouldn't be friend Marsh who'll be talking to you.'

'So it could be someone quite straight?'

'Could be. But it could equally well be one of his chums. It's anyone's guess.'

I mustn't cry. As if it mattered, I asked. 'Which station?'

'Streatham.'

I felt very sick. Jan had fixed the interview for late afternoon, giving us enough time to get a wig almost the same as my original crop. Why hadn't I thought of simply buying a brunette wig? Because inside it was hot and itchy, not the sort of thing you want to wear when you're at the top of a fully-extended ladder, that was why. With a long-sleeved shirt and lightweight jeans, I didn't have to show too much of the new me. Jan had clearly enjoyed using her card – not gold, as I'd expected, but platinum, which I should have – and had come to a halt outside an optician's.

She pointed. 'That's what you need.'

'Varifocals?' I teased.

'No – Todd'll need them soon, though. No. Over there. Those coloured lenses. See – you can turn your blue eyes green or brown or whatever.'

'Ugh – putting things right in your eyes!'

'Doesn't hurt, honest. I do it myself every day. I wonder if my optician – '

'Your forking out for nail varnish remover's one thing,' I said, a bit more sharply than was necessary. 'And even for this wig.' Despite myself I had a little scratch. 'But the idea of your wasting hundreds of quid for something that'd turn my insides out – no thanks.'

'We'll see,' she said. 'And you don't need Harley Street, as you can see.' She peered more closely. 'Forty pounds for two months' supply. There must be somewhere in Ashford that sells them. All right, a bit close to home. Hastings or even Canterbury.'

I had a feeling than Jan didn't recognise the word 'no' when it applied to anything she wanted to do. She and Paula were sisters under the skin.

They kept us waiting at the cop shop, as I'd expected. They had the same posters as in Ashford.

'When did you and Todd get together?' I asked, not just to pass the time. To verify a theory I had.

'About thirty years ago when he did drugs. I managed to persuade the judge to send him to a rehab centre, not to jail. Since he wanted to dry out to please me, by this time, it all worked out rather well.'

So he'd been through it too. 'And then he dried out and asked you out? A famous pop star?'

'And I told him to dry out and then I'd ask him out. A famous lawyer. Then,' she conceded with a smile. 'At least he had something to look forward to, when the nights got darkest.'

'It's just when it's getting light it's the worst,' I said. 'At least for me.'

'I was speaking meta – I was using –' She stopped, blushing.

'Metaphorically. Well, I was speaking literally. It's the time people die, too. Several of my mates.'

She gave me a quick hug, but turned to look me in the eyes when she asked, 'You never gave up?'

'Oh, half a dozen times. But there was this social worker who really wouldn't let go. He broke all the rules and came to visit me.'

'Did he fancy you?'

I looked down the years, at his face. 'Oh, yes. He fancied me. And I fancied him,' I added, half to myself.

'But nothing ever came of it?'

Just that phone number twice a year. I shook my head firmly. 'A social worker. A client. Professional misconduct. No.' I had a very good idea she sensed that there was a lot more to tell. I'd told her all about the drugs and the rotten start I'd had. She knew I'd turned to education quite late in life. But she didn't know about my professional past. And now wasn't the time to tell her, not with a skinny black sergeant opening a door and beckoning me in.

Chapter Nine

'What I can't understand, Sergeant Taylor,' Jan said earnestly, 'is why your Ashford colleague – Sergeant Marsh? – treated my client as if she were the perpetrator of the crime, not the intended victim.'

You've seen the TV programmes where those facial reconstruction people take a skull and put the face back on, muscle by muscle? Sergeant Taylor's face was so thin it looked as if they'd only half-finished it. At least when he smiled, it crinkled into almost as many planes as Todd's. I preferred it that way – it was less a reminder of what Joyce called 'our last end'; you see, that set of short stories that Todd had recommended was coming in useful already. 'I'm sure your client was mistaken,' he said smoothly. There was no way of knowing whether he was practising a little *esprit de corps* or whether he was in cahoots with Marsh. 'I'm sure Sergeant Marsh was merely trying to establish if Ms Tyler knew who might have sent her the bomb.'

I itched to interrupt and yell, but I remained silent, even to the extent of sitting on my hands.

'That has been established, has it? You have forensic evidence that the bomb was addressed to her? The address label survived the blast?' Her voice expressed extreme doubt.

'We have been able to piece together fragments,' Taylor said.

And in double-quick time, too – Marsh had been sure it was mine within half an hour. Jan pressed my foot. She knew what I wanted to point out.

'What a pity he didn't ask me directly.' Damn. It had popped out of its own accord.

'You know who might have done it, then? One of your punters?'

I removed a fist from under my bum and pressed Jan's hand. I should have told her, shouldn't I?

'May I have a word with Ms Dawes in private please?' I asked humbly.

Taylor's eyes widened – back to the skull again – but he nodded courteously enough and left the room. He hadn't issued the routine warning about the interview being taped, there was no other officer with him – which may or may not have been a good sign – and he closed the door without displaying the irritation many other officers would have shown at such an interruption so early in the proceedings. So far I rated him a potential goodie.

'Caffy! Why didn't you tell us? A prostitute!' Or would she have been *Guardian* politically correct and called me a working girl or a sex worker, a term which always conjured up for me visions of women in white coats, like the Clinique girls in nice department stores. Whatever she'd called me, she'd have ended, 'Oh, you poor child!' That would have been the scenario I'd chosen. With one of her kind motherly embraces. What I got was a furious pair of hands on my shoulders shaking me so hard I was afraid my teeth would rattle. Can a shake that hard be loving? 'You little fool. You know it wouldn't have made any difference about how Todd and I feel about you, not an iota, and now you've made me look a complete amateur.'

'That's why I asked to speak to you,' I mumbled. I managed to look her in the eye. 'It's not something I'm proud of, Jan, my past. Being on the game – it wasn't a nice job. Even though I was never a street girl reduced to doing blow-jobs for a tenner. I used to meet my clients in a hotel. Oh, not the very posh end of the market. Not those women with degrees and such that call themselves escorts. Just a prostitute. Nice women don't do it. I mean, being involved with drugs was bad enough, but – '

'Was that why Granville cut his initials into your stomach? Because you weren't just his customer, you were his whore?' She didn't know what to do with her face; just as you thought it was trying not to cry, you realised it was brimming with anger – and then all the way back again.

'I told you I was his mistress,' I said, trying not to wince at the word she'd used, not to whine an excuse. But she might as well have a bit more of the truth. 'He'd bought me from my pimp. Yes, he owned me. When I escaped the first time he got me out of the unit and filled me full of heroin. And made his mark. The next centre I managed to get into was miles away, and he seemed to lose track – or lose interest. He's got another girl now, as I told you.'

'How many years –?'

'On the game, four. Nearly three years, on and off, as "his".'

She put her thinking expression on. 'So that's why he said "punters"?'

'Marsh hinted I was a tom the first day we met. I'm on file. Soliciting. When I was with Granville one of his turn-ons was to watch me with other men.'

'Jesus! Oh, Caffy! Why didn't you tell us? You poor child!' This time she did gather me in that kind and loving hug. 'Shall I ask that sergeant if you can have a cup of tea before we continue?'

'I'm fine. Glad to have it off my chest. You don't … mind? You're sure?'

'Even the most po-faced Christians love the sinner however much they hate the sin. And I've always said that if it weren't for men, women wouldn't have to do the job anyway.' She wasn't as relaxed as she liked to think – her voice was clipped, the way I imagined she must have sounded in court. She turned away – did she really dab at her eyes? – but turned back trying to smile. 'Come on, Caffy: you must know how much you mean to us.' Her voice broke. 'We – we never had a daughter, but if we had we'd have loved her to be like you.'

At least, that was what I hoped she said.

'But all I've done is put you to endless trouble and expense!'

She didn't know whether to nod or shake her head. One of us had to turn down the emotion. 'One day I'll pay you back. Well,' I conceded more honestly, 'I'll try.'

At that point there was a knock on the door – a knock! – and Sergeant Taylor popped his head round the door. He coughed meaningfully and glanced equally meaningfully at his watch. Of course, he had a shift to finish and a home to go to. He might even have the weekend free and be hoping to dash down to the coast. Jan and I smiled and sat down.

I felt so much better I didn't even try to sit on my hands. 'You were speaking about my clients, Sergeant.' I emphasised the word slightly. 'Most were very ordinary men out for a bit on the side, for whatever reason. Certain public figures have made it almost fashionable, haven't they?' I pointed out brightly. 'There's only one I'd imagine capable of such psychotic behaviour. The man who did this.' I lifted my shirt. To my horror the tan was as uneven as if I'd done it myself, but at least the scars glowed brightly. 'CG. Clive Granville. He's a big drugs baron in the Midlands. He caught sight of me in Tenterden on Tuesday. The bomb arrived on Thursday.'

Taylor sucked in his cheeks, more like the model for the Jolly Roger than ever. He raised very bright, shrewd eyes. 'Why didn't you tell Sergeant Marsh this?'

'My client's discussion with Sergeant Marsh was interrupted,' Jan put in smoothly. 'In any case, she was very shocked – almost to the point of needing medical treatment. He'd tried to prevent her taking so much as a shower to wash off the deceased's blood.'

'You were…' he gestured. 'The blood sprayed on to you? I thought you were in a van.'

'I was first on the scene. I tried to staunch the flow with my clean washing. I'd just returned from the launderette, you see.'

'That was very –' He seemed at a loss for words.

Jan wasn't. 'My client is a brave young woman. After Granville mutilated her, she still managed to put herself through college and get a steady job.' A nice bit of phrasing, there: no further mention of my drugs habit. Once a junkie always a junkie, you see. And junkies aren't the most reliable folk, as any neighbourhood cop trying to reduce the burglary rate will tell you.

'You tried to save – '

'Arthur. Arthur Mann. He always said he'd be a whole Mann when he'd got his new dentures.'

'You tried to save Mr Mann. And Sergeant Marsh didn't want you to clean up?'

'One of his colleagues. A young man with ginger hair and white eyelashes. I'm sorry – I didn't write down his number.'

With a wonderful dry smile, Sergeant Taylor said, 'I shouldn't imagine that that was uppermost in your mind at the time. I shouldn't imagine you'd have been the most coherent of witnesses at the time, so perhaps that's why these points weren't made at the initial interview.'

Not a coherent witness? How dared he!

But he was attempting another smile, which rather undercut what he'd said. 'I'll point our Ashford colleagues in the direction of Clive Granville. I should imagine we won't have to trouble you any more. But in case we do, can I have a contact address for you?'

Jan's foot sprang into action. 'You won't have been surprised to learn that Caffy has left the Ashford area. You can contact her via me. You obviously have my phone number.'

'And your address, Ms Dawes?'

'Care of my Chambers.' She produced a card, which he took.

'I think we should have an address – we may need to put Ms Tyler under immediate protection,' he insisted

'I'm moving this evening to another friend's,' I said. 'I don't know their house number. But I'll phone you to let you know as soon as I get there, shall I?'

'Very well. Don't leave it too late, though, will you? As

soon as I get off duty I shall be going up to the Midlands. My son's graduating from the University of Wolverhampton. Law,' he added, glowing.

I promised most earnestly, not intending to for one second, and we went on our way.

'Where now?' I asked, blinking in the vivid haze that passes in London for bright sunlight.

'Home,' she said warmly. 'Once we've fought our way onto the train – have you ever been on one in the rush hour?'

It must have been nearly nine o'clock by the time we got back to Fullers, but the Transit still lurked under a tree. The Pots rarely worked this late: were they expecting rain next week? Amazing how a couple of days without Rob McElwee could harm your professionalism.

Paula flapped a hand as I walked over to apologise for a very poor working week and to offer to work over the weekend to make up. After all, I hadn't anything else to do, and I needed my wages – but not so much that I could expect her to pay me if I hadn't done the hours. After her brother's mate's activities this morning, I also wanted to ask her not to tell anyone else about my background – if I said nothing, the niggle would grow into a big rankle, and I liked her too much for that.

Before I could say anything, she asked, 'Got a moment? Or a spare hour or so?'

'Plenty of spare hours. But Todd and Jan were expecting to feed me.' I looked at her more closely – she was bubbling with something. 'I'll tell them not.'

Jan went straight into mother-hen mode. 'You sure you'll be all right? I could leave something on a plate?'

'We're mates, Jan – we often go out for a drink. I'll get something in the pub.'

'Well, don't be too late back. And bang on the door if you're afraid of going in there on your own.'

'I'll be all right – don't wait up for me!'

My schoolmates had always moaned about their mums being like this, but I'd always thought they were secretly pleased as well as vastly irritated. Now I understood both emotions.

'He did what?' Paula exploded. 'The bastard! The absolute bastard! And Derek's a bastard, too, for not doing as he promised and ferrying you himself. But he didn't get the idea from me, Caffy. I promise you that. Him or Derek or Mum. No one knows.'

I've never known Paula so much as bend the truth, so I believed her. 'It must have been the way I looked,' I said sadly. 'Just like a tart, Paula – funny, really, considering.'

She didn't laugh.

'At least I don't look so bad now my nails are back to normal,' I suggested.

Silence.

'Where are we going, by the way? This isn't the road to the Hop Vine.'

'It's the road to Crabton Manor. I've got the keys. The dogs are locked up. We're going to have another look round.'

'How?' I meant the question to apply to everything; she took it that way.

'Tomorrow we're painting lower level windows – I need to be able to open them and close them afterwards.'

'What about the agent?'

'William Harvey Hospital – peritonitis.'

'Who's feeding the dogs and letting them out and getting them back in?'

'I am.'

'You what?'

'No need to screech – it puts me off my driving. They are, I have to say, being given doggy Prozac.'

'So long as it's not doggy Viagra. And since when did Paula's Pots work weekends?'

'Since they were offered double-time for Saturday and triple for Sunday. Van der Poele's hosting a big party soon and he wants the place looking good. He's having one of those garden make-over jobs – my cousin Tina's husband's got the contract. Lots of tidy bay trees – you know the sort of thing. Apart from the money, it'll give us the chance to look round – that's what really clinched it for me.'

I shook my head. 'A professional villain wouldn't leave stuff lying around.'

'You're sure he's a professional villain?'

'Aren't you? No one less than a pro would have a police sergeant in his pocket – unless they were particularly dedicated Freemasons. In any case, it feels too pat. Too easy. I've got these vibes.'

She pulled into a lay-by and cut the engine. Switching on the interior light she turned to face me. 'Your vibes? You've only ever had them once before and that was when you said those joists were rotten and I took no notice and landed in the bathroom below.'

I nodded. She'd come mighty close to breaking a lot of bones – though the sight of her descending slowly and inexorably had brought the rest of us to hysterical tears. 'Same vibes,' I said. 'You see, the doggy Prozac could be a two-edged sword. The dogs won't bark and snarl at us, but they wouldn't bark at anyone else, either. So van der Poele could get into the house without the Herald Angels singing.'

'But why should he suspect anything?'

'I've no idea.' And then I had. 'Has he missed me?'

'As a matter of fact he did ask about you. "That blonde tart."'

'Those were his actual words?'

'A manner of speaking, Caffy. I didn't tell him about your past, either.'

'I'm sure you didn't. But he might have heard the exact words from someone else, mightn't he?' I let that sink in, then asked, 'What did you tell him?'

'Family bereavement. It's what we all agreed. That you'd dashed off to see your nan in Manchester.'

'Not Brum? Brilliant. Well done, all of you. Did he believe you?'

'Don't see why he shouldn't. I was saying how short-handed I was and how we had two big jobs on and he moaned about painters and builders never sticking to just the one job and that's when he offered the double overtime. Actually, I said I was interviewing your replacement – I wondered if you'd want to come and help tomorrow.'

'I'm ever so tempted,' I said. All that lovely overtime. 'But I think I may have another vibe coming on. You couldn't get someone else to come along, could you? Just to double-bluff him?'

Now she sounded exasperated. 'Such as who? At this sort of notice?'

'Have you got any really basic, nasty work to be done? How about young Dean, then? I reckon he owes you one.'

One job I've never envied coppers – well, there are quite a lot I've never envied them, actually, including arresting junkies with active needles – is staking out premises. Sitting slumped out of sight in cold cars with nothing for company except a cup of take-out coffee and a full bladder. Well, the Transit wasn't cold, and we didn't have any coffee, just a couple of hefty bars of chocolate. And since we didn't have any coffee, our bladders weren't full. Or shouldn't have been. Except being nervous always makes me want to pee. In fact, I'd just slipped out and had a wee behind the van when I heard a car. Knickers still at half mast, I was back in before you could say 'obbo.'

Lights out and hidden well under trees nearly two hundred yards from the house, the van was surely undetectable. All the same, I had one hand on the ignition key, the other on the gear stick: that was what we'd agreed. Anyone approaching the house and we'd beat it, fast. And that meant me driving – the Transit usually started first pull for me, remember, and rarely for the others, even Paula.

Yes, the car was slowing. And coming to a halt. No, the dogs didn't bark, dreaming their sweet Prozac dreams. There was the light crunch of gravel – I thought I made out two pairs of feet. I might have made out the glint of a gun – but I was dead fanciful by then.

I looked at Paula; eyes so wide I could see the whites, she

nodded. The van rose to the occasion and away we slipped. Perfectly safely. There. We breathed again.

And then I had another vibe.

Chapter Ten

Believe me, it has to be a pretty strong vibe to get me to disturb someone at well past midnight, at least when their blinds were tight down, with no sign of any light. But that was what I had to do. I meant, of course, to knock firmly, but not obtrusively, and to greet Jan or Todd with a rational and well-expressed set of reasons why they shouldn't open any packages sent to them. And why they should take the mobile phone back to London and drive round using it all over the place before ditching it.

That was the plan. I even rehearsed under my breath what I should say.

What happened was that I was so panicky I started banging and hollering. In fact, I banged so hard you could see the bruises on my hands a week later, and my hollering turned to hysterical tears.

At long last, Todd, in Jan's black dressing-gown, flung upon the door and stared at me. 'Caffy! What on earth's the matter? Is someone after you?'

'No, not me.' I fell into the caravan, shaking so much he literally had to pull me to my feet. 'They're after you. You and Jan. Todd, I'm so sorry!'

By now Jan was with us, also in a black dressing-down. Ah. His and hers. Another time I'd have thought it sweet. 'For God's sake, Caffy!'

Todd almost dragged me to the sofa and pressed me down. I stared at my hand – a glass of something had materialised there. 'Get that down you and then talk,' Jan said, quite roughly. She was flushed. I dropped my eyes. I'd interrupted them when they least wanted an intruder.

I said baldly, 'Your phone, Jan. You gave them your number.'

'Yes.'

'And you've been using it all the time from here.'

'Yes.'

'And the police can put a trace on any phone and find where it's being used.'

'Yes.' This 'yes' was far less irritated – concerned, in fact.

'So by trying to protect me you've laid yourself – you and Todd – wide open. If Marsh can tell Granville where I am, he can look you up and do the same. If Granville can arrange a bomb for me, he can arrange one for my legal adviser. And will. And I'll bet my boots it'll be a much more stable one that only explodes when it's opened.'

Jan's flush drained completely. She looked ten years older. She sank down beside me.

'The police,' Todd said efficiently, reaching for the same bloody phone.

'I don't think so,' she said quietly.

And neither did I.

By now I was calm enough to explain my plans for the phone. Todd picked up the idea very quickly. 'But we can't be incommunicado,' he said. 'Even if I buy a new one, the police'll be able to check the registration and trace it back. The bent police, I mean.'

Before I could ask about pay as you go phones, Jan downed her whisky in one gulp – I'd seen people on TV doing that but even one tiny sip had set my mouth and throat on fire. 'I think we're being premature,' she said firmly. 'If a parcel should arrive, we'd dial 999. We wouldn't get Sergeant Marsh then. We'd get specialised police and maybe the bomb squad. That'd lead us to some senior and straight officers, surely.'

'What if they don't go for the parcel bomb option?' Todd said. 'What if they simply decide to fire bomb the caravan while we're asleep or maybe organise a car bomb?'

'The letter bomb's Granville's trademark,' I mused. 'But I think you're right. Which is why I think you and Jan should abandon ship for a bit.' I heard the words coming out of their own accord. I hated them – but I was sure they were the right ones.

'What about you?'

'If you can lend me forty quid for some of those coloured lenses, I shall be fine.' I gave what was meant to be a grin. 'I've got my vibes to look after me, you see.' I explained about the aborted burglary.

'You mean this van der Poele set a trap?' Jan went paler still.

'I think so. Which is why I'm going to try those lenses. If I'm working on Crabton Manor full-time, then I shall be able to nip in and out all the time.'

'But what about Fullers?' she wailed.

'If we can't pull things together, there may not be a Fullers,' I pointed out.

'You can't deal with this on your own!' Todd snapped, as if he were angry with me for even thinking of it.

'I don't intend to. But at least if you two aren't here, if you're back at Eastwell Manor or better still some big

London hotel, then you're safer and can work out a proper plan – talk to your legal friends, maybe, Jan. They must know some straight officers. They'll know what to do. So long as none of us try to play by our rules. We have to play by theirs.' Now I'd started to think things through I felt as if I were an inch taller, my shoulders an inch broader. 'I'm sorry I was so het up before. But I wanted to make sure neither of you ended up like Arthur.' I got to my feet. 'Now, I'll leave you to get some sleep. I think you should be away first thing.'

'What about you?' Todd asked.

'Back to my little eyrie in Fullers,' I said.

'Surely you'd rather stay here,' Jan said.

I shook my head firmly. However early they'd be up and around, I'd be up even earlier. 'I don't suppose, Todd,' I said casually, catching Jan's eye, 'that you bought another camera today.'

He flushed like a first-time punter. And then grinned, a naughty schoolboy grin.

'Could I borrow it? And could you spare five minutes to show me how it works?'

In the few moments it took to show me the camera – it was virtually foolproof – I also convinced him that I didn't need his assistance. It was far more important for him and Jan to get away.

'But wouldn't an extra witness – I take it you are going people-trafficker hunting? – be useful?'

I patted the camera, a neat compact job, though still equipped with a little zoom lens. 'This'll be my extra witness. If it's needed. They may not bring consignments in every day.'

'Consignments! You make the poor devils sound like a commodity – so many packets of fags, so many cases of booze.'

'Don't you think that's what they are to people-traffickers? They don't care about spiriting victims away from hostile regimes; they don't care that families back home have beggared themselves to get one relative clear. They're just interested in screwing the last penny out of them for the "voyage" and then taking as much of their earnings as they can.'

'Yours isn't the conventional view of illegal immigrants,' he laughed.

'I have another view, too,' I said seriously. 'If you bring folk in like that, they escape screening. Who knows what little charmer may come in and meet up with his al Qaeda cellmaster?'

Todd passed over his new toy without a word.

As we stood by their door, Jan rejoined us. She'd been crying. She passed me a set of spare keys, 'So we'll know you can have a shower and boil a kettle,' she said. We had a long hug. Then Todd and me. 'Promise me if I'm not around in the morning you'll just go,' I said, before I could join her in a little weep. 'Promise. We'll find some way of getting in touch. I know! Call Paula as soon as you've got a new phone. But please be somewhere like Kew Gardens when you do!'

I didn't get much sleep, but I got enough to clear my head, and was down in the fields near the verge with its little cairn by about five-thirty. I'd waved goodbye to the Daweses' caravan, blowing them a kiss, as I'd set out. There, that sounds easy. It wasn't. But never mind. Here I was, at the bottom of the steep slope, cold and damp with the heavy dew, lurking under fronds of cow-parsley poking the little zoom lens through a gap in the hedge. If – big if – the removal van parked where it had parked before, the number plate should be nicely in focus.

A glance at my watch told me that if they kept to the previous day's schedule I wouldn't have long to wait. Insects were starting to buzz. Birds were singing – but they seemed much quieter than they'd done yesterday. A fieldmouse scuttled a couple of feet from me: if it hadn't meant refocusing, I could have taken its photo.

A couple of cars passed. One of them might have been Jan and Todd's. I hoped so. I wanted them well clear of any action, much as I'd miss them. It was like finding my parents after all these years and then having them whisked away. And no, I didn't think for one moment that they might have been my true parents, handing me over to the Tylers for whatever reason. But I wouldn't have minded adopting them.

It was a good job the rumble of a lorry interrupted my thoughts before I could get sentimental and weepy. I flattened myself even more closely into my hide and waited, hardly daring to breathe. Was it the removal van?

I could have cried with frustration when it proved to be an ordinary bread van, one of those big jobs that deliver Mother's Pride or whatever all over the country. All the same, it stopped on the same patch of verge, and the driver cut his engine and got out. Perhaps he just wanted a slash. My luck was in. The jet of urine was directed six or seven feet away. He threw his fag end in after it. There was a little hiss.

Then I felt another vibration. Through my stomach.

God, I must be turning into some little shortsighted animal, dependent on other senses to escape predators. But there it was. Footsteps. I could hear them now. Not marching. Just ragged walking, the effort to stay upright on the steep canal banks obviously too much for some of them after the long walk from wherever they'd been put ashore. I squeezed the shutter release. No reaction from the driver, because he was just opening the back doors. I took picture after picture, one of each backside, refugee, migrant, illegal immigrant, call the men what you will. At last, long last it seemed to me, although I could see everyone was moving with the speed of desperation so strong I could almost smell it, the last set of feet disappeared, the doors were slammed and locked and the driver's feet moved back to his cab. A twig snapped somewhere close to me. For a moment he hesitated. Then he got in and drove off. I stayed where I was. One elephant, two elephants, three elephants, four elephants – all the way up to a hundred elephants before I eased myself free of the vegetation and pushed myself upright. Then I bolted.

Ladders apart, I've never been much of a one for exercise, and people like Paula Radcliffe simply amaze me; it's not just that she can run so far so fast, but that she does it regularly, day in, day out, just so she can do it on the big occasions. All I managed was a bit of a run, a bit of a walk, then a bit more of a run. I fell over a couple of times, once into a mixture of thistles and nettles. By the time I reached the top of the hill and Fullers I was hot, sore and breathless, and aching in silly places like my ribs. No question – I'd have to take advantage of the caravan shower. They'd left everything in their fridge and cupboards, with a little note telling me they didn't expect to find any of it when they got back, which they hoped would be very soon. There was also a wad of twenty-pound notes – For lenses! said the note. It would buy more than lenses.

I'd cleaned myself up, though my hair was still wet – and very frizzy – and I was just draining a mug of coffee. There was a knock at the door. My God – Paula (ours!) already? We'd agreed she'd pick me up at eight-thirty, and it was barely eight.

But it wasn't Paula. It was a handsome young postie, berry brown in summer shorts. His blue eyes twinkled as he smiled, revealing even white teeth. He had long elegant fingers.

'Morning, Miss. Ms Dawes, is it? Would you mind just signing for this parcel for Ms Tyler? Whoops!'

Chapter Eleven

Now, when there really was good reason for a wholehearted panic, and after all my fuss the previous night, I was remarkably calm: the cliché about seeing everything in slow motion seemed true, after all. I caught the package, signed, exchanged a quip about the lovely weather and closed the door, the package still in my hand. As soon as the young man had gone, I opened the caravan door, still clutching the package, which I took to the very far corner of the Fullers' plot. I laid it very carefully where we usually parked the Transit. If it exploded there, it should hurt no more than a wall. So that no one could inadvertently run it over, I pulled across the big plastic rubbish bins we use for stripped wallpaper and grotty plaster to form a crude barricade. There. Now I would wait for Paula, and, more important, Paula's mobile phone. Because now, in the warm morning sun, it was clear I had only one course of action. All this cops and robbers stuff wasn't funny any more – even if it ever had been. It was involving innocent people. I couldn't blame myself for what had happened to Arthur, but if the young man this morning or any of his colleagues in the sorting office had been injured, yes, I would have considered myself to some extent responsible.

Only then did it dawn on me that the young man probably hadn't been a postman at all. I'd seen neither bike nor van, and though I knew the delivery workers had summer uniforms, he'd just looked summery. And he hadn't been carrying any other mail, either. No, of course Granville wouldn't use conventional means again. He'd have known that the Royal Mail would be keeping a close eye open for packages, intercepting and checking anything suspicious.

What we needed desperately was that straight policeman we'd joked about, one we could trust with our lives. I'd already trusted Taz enough to do two lots of cold turkey, the second one, of course, courtesy of Clive Granville. What I couldn't trust were my emotions. Taz, or Tadeuzs Moscicki, the only man I've ever really, truly loved – the head over heels sort of love, as opposed to the deepening daughterly affection I felt for Todd. And Taz hadn't loved me quite enough. Enough to drag me out of my drug-ridden way of life, not once but twice: yes. Enough to set me on the course of study that got me – literally – where I was today: yes. Enough to send me his phone numbers ever year, of course: yes. But enough to make what I was terribly afraid he'd still think of as 'an honest woman' of me: alas, no. Nor even to get to that promising halfway point, sharing my bed. Don't think I hadn't tried. But I wouldn't use the skills I'd needed to make a living, and nothing seemed to happen without them. So there we'd been stuck, as seething with sexual tension as non-lovers in a D. H. Lawrence novel.

I'd known all along that if he turned up here in rural Kent I'd make another play for him. I'd also known, at a place very deep down that I didn't care to prod, that he'd reject me again. Because that was how it felt to me. A slap in the face. A turning away. A closing of doors. But never a final turning of a key in the lock.

I pulled myself straighter. What was I bellyaching about? No one had ever said that love should always be requited. In fact, we'd be a lot worse off in terms of books, music and plays if it were. What was a bit of heartache, compared with Arthur's death and the total disruption of the lives of two quite innocent people?

A nasty little voice informed me it was quite a lot.

Tough.

Action was always better than a mope. I'd cried enough with Jan to keep me dry for weeks; I'd played a sentimental card, to my shame. Even if there was no one to see me, I owed it to myself to straighten my back, start thinking about Taz purely as a policeman and get a life. And life would have to start with putting together lunch if I was to spend the day at Crabton Manor.

The Daweses' fridge provided some rich pickings for my lunchbox. I was determined not to feel guilty about taking stuff, because I was sure they'd have been really hurt if I hadn't polished off things that would have gone off by the time they could return. Less easily I pocketed the cash. The moment she arrived I greeted a surprisingly bleary-eyed Paula with a demand for her phone. She handed it over with no more than a raised eyebrow, and retired to explore the mobile home, the whole of it, squeaking with pleasure at each new space-saving item as she did so.

I'd clenched my stomach against hearing Taz's voice. So it was a bit of an anti-climax when I got this electronic message telling me he wasn't available. Well, I suppose a lot of folk are still decently in bed at eight-thirty on a Saturday morning, even in weather as gorgeous as this. I simply asked him to phone as soon as he possibly could. And then I added another sentence, not playing the sentiment card, believe me, just being dead accurate: 'I'm in very grave danger and so are some other people.'

'I'd hoped for a full day's work out of you!' Paula protested when I asked her to drive me into Ashford.

'I know. And I'm sorry. But if I change the whole of my appearance, then we should all be a lot safer. And could you leave your phone with me? You know there's no signal out at Crabton Manor.'

Paula wasn't normally one to tighten her lips, but believe me they were almost invisible by the time she dropped me. 'And how do you propose to contact me when you wish to be collected? I presume you do wish to be collected?'

Best to ignore the sarcasm. 'You could park up and hang around?' I said hopefully. 'These chains of opticians are supposed to provide instant service.'

'Or I could go and get on with a decent day's work – bloody Dean says he's too busy, by the way, bugger him – and let you bloody fry,' she said. 'OK, I'll send Helen to meet you at eleven-thirty. Parking will be impossible by then, of course. Meet her by the Stour Centre. I'll tell her to wait ten minutes and if you're not there then to come back without you.'

I couldn't really argue. But I wondered just how much of her bad temper was a result of last night's failed burglary. Paula liked to be proved right, not wrong.

To my amazement, the new lenses didn't hurt at all. They did all sorts of tests, and then found they hadn't got a pair in my first choice of colour. They could order them, of course. But

I had a van to meet, so I opted for the nearest shade – a rather tigerish hazel. Armed with detailed instructions about hygiene and handling, I was ready – and just about waiting – for Helen when she appeared. To my delight, she didn't recognise me.

There'd been no phone call, of course. I'd had to switch the mobile off while I was at the optician's, and had no idea how to get messages off it, assuming there were any. Helen tried to instruct me, but her idea of safe driving didn't coincide with mine, which involved the old-fashioned concept of at least one hand on the wheel and both eyes on the road. So we gave up.

Not knowing quite how much Paula had told her about the situation – nothing, I hoped, to affect her appetite – I talked mostly about the lenses and their fitting. But it seemed she was even more squeamish about eyes than I'd been, so the conversation faltered and lapsed. We'd just turned off the M20 on to Stone Street, the B2068, that is, where if you look back over your shoulder, as I always do, you get a view that makes you want to take up landscape art, when the phone rang. Pressing the obvious button, I heard just enough to recognise Taz's voice when we lost the signal. Bloody countryside!

'Stop! Pull over into that lay-by!'

Well, not so much a lay-by as a dumping ground for old cars and a trysting place for lovers, though there were much less public ones further up the road in various sections of woodland. However, this was good enough for some, as I proved as I tangled with used condoms. Now wasn't the time to get litter-conscious, so I sprinted backwards and forwards until his voice came back.

'I'll be down as soon as I can. Tonight at the latest.'

I made myself say as calmly as possible, 'Bring some really scruffy clothes. You may end up painting and decorating. This is where you'll find me.' If we met at Crabton Manor that would at least solve the problem of getting me home. I gave succinct directions, hoping he wouldn't hear the sound of my heart pounding as I talked.

'You want him to paint!' Paula exploded. 'You know this is a skilled job – how long did it take you to qualify? – and you tell me to put a complete amateur on my payroll.'

'Amateur painter and professional cop,' I reminded her. 'With lots of professional back-up.' I hope, I added under my breath. 'You can tell van der Poele that you're giving him a trial.'

'But he knows we're an all women organisation.'

'Tell him Taz is gay,' I replied. And wished I hadn't. I like the truth, remember, and wanted above all things for Taz to demonstrate to me once and for all he was straight. 'And I wouldn't worry about paying him – I'm sure a policeman's salary is quite enough to live on.'

She pulled a face.

'Anyway,' I asked, pulling off my sunglasses, 'how do I look?'

She literally took a step backwards. 'Do you want me to be honest? Really? Well, like a poor relation of Lucretia Borgia. Your colouring's sort of Italianish – it seems to have darkened a lot overnight. But you've got these weird eyes. You could be some sort of Traveller.'

Seemed all right to me.

Then, pulling her chin, she added, 'Trouble is, you still sound like you. I suppose you can't do any other accents, can you?'

'I could up the Brummie one – how's this, our kid?'

'You'll need an interpreter if you want a conversation down here,' she said. 'What about a new name? Caffy's a bit distinctive, in its own quiet way.'

'Trouble is, I feel like a Caffy. Ok, if I look like Lucretia Borgia, how about Lucy?'

'Provided you remember to answer when you're spoken to. And you'll need a surname, too.'

I recalled the apparently friendly sergeant back in Streatham. 'Taylor? Lucy Taylor?'

'Right, Lucy Taylor. Work. I've saved the bargeboards for you.'

Saved? Left the nasty boring things for me as penance, more like.

'And the soffits. OK?'

Great! I didn't think. 'OK.' I slipped into my overalls, grabbed my gear and shinned up as fast as I could. Not least because I could hear barking. No doubt the Prozac had worn off.

I was really glad to have some painting. As usual, it absorbed me. It didn't require anything really classy, but I would no more have offered slipshod work than Paula would have let me. Plus I was a long way from the ground, and although scaffolding is a great deal safer than a ladder, standing back to gaze admiringly at your work is not an option. So I was quite surprised to hear Paula yelling, 'Lucy! Get yourself down here. Lunch break.'

Hell, she meant me, didn't she?

'Sorry, I was miles away,' I yelled back, coming down as soon as I'd finished the section I was working on, and joining the others already lounging in their battered deck chairs.

'We always listen to the radio while we eat,' Meg said carefully, as if I really were a new girl. 'So we keep in touch with the world.'

'Sounds like we're nuns,' Lucy Taylor, the Brummie said, adding, 'Oh, Meg – not *Any Questions*! The news is one thing, but all these pompous and pretentious people sounding off about things they know nothing about really gets up my nose.'

'It's what we always do,' Paula said clearly. 'I told you that you'd have to fit in. Like it or lump it.' Addressing someone behind my left shoulder, she said, 'Afternoon, Mr van der Poele. We've managed to recruit someone to replace Caffy. Lucy. Lucy Taylor.'

I turned and raised a hand. 'Hi!' I said, Brummie as I could make it. I didn't gild the lily by removing my sun specs.

Van der Poele merely stared. 'I hope she's more reliable than the other one.'

Bloody hell! All the extra time I'd put in for him and he said I wasn't reliable!

'She's got good references,' Paula assured him. 'And although I only took her on this morning, you can see she's got stuck in.'

'I noticed you were late,' van der Poele observed.

'I've marked my time sheet.' Her voice was very clipped. 'And we shall work correspondingly longer.'

Time sheet? She was keeping time sheets for him, as if she were a kid earning pocket money? What a bastard.

'We didn't expect to see you, Mr Poele,' said Meg, not very helpfully. 'The boss said you were off for the weekend or something.'

'The kennels said I'd given them too little notice. You don't know any other places round here?' Was he acting, too? Or was his story true, and the hapless kennel-owner about to lose his custom as a result?

'I'm strictly cats,' Meg assured him.

He nodded, as if marking that against her, and strolled back to the house. Turning, he yelled, 'I shall be letting them out for a run soon. If you don't like dogs, you'd better be up that scaffolding or in the van. But I shall want to check the time sheets.'

To a woman, we finished our mouthfuls and packed up. With double time on offer, we preferred the scaffolding.

We got plenty of notice of Taz's arrival, the dogs being still on the loose although it was a couple of hours since they'd been released. Van der Poele emerged briefly to snarl them to heel, looking hard at Paula, who was halfway down the ladder.

'This could be another new recruit,' she said. 'Come for a trial.'

'And if she's no good?'

'It's a bloke, and I'll redo anything in my own time that isn't satisfactory,' she said.

Van der Poele nodded and retired with the dogs.

It was times like this I remember why I liked Paula so much.

As soon as it was safe, she climbed down to ground level, and approached Taz with the friendly but businesslike smile of an employer welcoming a potential employee. Her smile increased in warmth when she saw him properly. He was romantically dark and brooding, cultivating the image of a man wandering the earth in his search for a home. There's a portrait of the Polish composer Chopin by some French artist making him look both haggard and heroic: I think that was what Taz aspired to. In fact, his parents lived in Surbiton and the grandfather to whom he owed his name and his looks was running rings round the staff of the ex-servicemen's home he had been forced by failing sight to retire to. I'd met and liked them all, especially the grandfather, who'd got me to slip him a couple of audio-books the library at the home didn't think were suitable for men his age. They'd all made me very welcome. Pity I'd probably never get to see them again. Still, I don't suppose they were pining for me. Taz would have said brusquely that things hadn't worked out between us, and no decent parents would have argued about that. They'd always said to drop in whenever I was around, that the break-up wouldn't make any difference, but it was a promise I preferred to remember than to test.

I wish I could have blamed the dogs for the way my heart was pounding so hard I could hear whooshing in my ears.

Paula drew him over to the van, gesturing occasionally at the house and nodding as if he was making the right responses. It looked like a genuine job-interview, if on the hoof. How much was she telling him about his real job? After a few minutes, he disappeared from view, returning with a bundle of clothes. Paula pointed him in the direction of the out-house, still mercifully dog-free. When he emerged, she called us all down, and one by one we shook hands with him. Meg might have drooled over Todd. She positively slavered over Taz. Helen giggled rather a lot. I found it hard to look at any-one, especially Taz: no, nothing to do with the lenses. He spoke to each of us with rather less enthusiasm than the occa-sion deserved. He positively froze my smile.

'How are you on heights?' Paula demanded. 'Because I'd really like to finish the very highest level work today. However late we have to work,' she added firmly.

'I'm not fussed,' he said.

Second lot of Brownie points to him. I'd awarded the first lot for his prompt response – he'd taken only about three hours to get here – and for twigging so quickly what was needed. But I knew he didn't have a head for heights, and although I knew Paula had only suggested that he worked high up so he could talk to me, I countered, 'I've almost fin-ished. Couldn't he start preparing the window-frames on the level below me?'

Paula looked hard at me, and at him, but nodded. 'Those aren't too bad – should be just a matter of rubbing down and spot priming. But if you think anything else needs doing, tell me or Ca – Lucy. OK? We'll work on till six-thirty or so. The light may get awkward after that and I don't want anyone squinting into the sun and going splat.'

He laughed. I'd forgotten how he laughed. I turned away so he wouldn't see my face.

Although we could have talked, we didn't. I could look

down and see between the boards the top of his head and the quick movement of his hands. So why didn't I? Because something was definitely wrong with the electricity that should have been snapping between us. What had happened to Caffy and Heathcliff? I ought to be lusting for him: the only strong emotion I felt was a desperate hope that he wouldn't betray us by being incompetent.

Tea break, and great waves of blushes flooded both Meg and Helen. Paula smiled more than usual. I got back to work as fast as I could. No. I wasn't jealous because he was flirting with them. I was wondering why I wasn't jealous.

It was nearly seven before I got Taz to myself. Helen had giggled and blushed her farewells, after Paula had squashed Meg's suggestion that we all adjourn to the pub.

As casually as I could, I asked, 'Where are you based?' mouthing 'Ashford' so he knew.

'Ashford,' he said clearly.

'Well, would you mind giving Lucy a lift?' Paula asked. 'That way I get to keep the van and I can round everyone up tomorrow.'

'You want me tomorrow too?'

Paula nodded sagely. 'You've made a good start on the grottiest job. Maybe we'll see what you can do with a paint-brush.'

'Thanks. Shall I bring Lucy with me?'

'That'd be very helpful. Right, boy and girls – back here at nine tomorrow. OK?'

'What now?' Taz asked as we walked to his car. Whatever his normal vehicle, this was an Escort that had seen better days.

I waited till we were safely inside what felt like a Turkish bath. We wound down the windows as fast as we could but it seemed safer than outside. All the same, I managed no more than a mutter: 'We set out as if for Ashford, then you do some fancy nipping through the lanes making sure we're not being followed to where I'm living at the moment. A quick shower and then you can treat me to a pub supper.'

'Me treat you? Thought I was doing you a favour.'

'I bet you earn more than I earn per hour.'

'I doubt it.'

I told him my weekly pay.

He whistled. 'How can you live on that?'

'Truth is, it's hard. But it's better than my life in Brum, so I'm not complaining. If you prefer, there's some stuff in the Daweses' fridge.'

'Who are the Daweses?'

'I think,' I said as I fastened my seatbelt, 'that I'd better begin at the beginning, don't you?'

Chapter Twelve

Taz didn't reply.

There I was, ready to give chapter and verse of why and how we needed him and he was totally bound up in starting and driving his car.

I could have howled. But bloody well wouldn't. I didn't do howling, remember, not for men, and I wasn't going to start now. Hell, in an ideal world, Taz would have pulled over as soon as he could into some convenient lay-by – preferably one unsullied by reminders of my former life – and said something like, 'Let me look at you, Caffy. After all these years… Why, you're beautiful!'

In fact, when at last he looked at me it was out of the corner of his eye. He was far more interested in the bends ahead than in my appearance – which I suppose was only right. At last he said, 'I take it this is some sort of disguise. And they called you Lucy Taylor. May one ask why?' He sounded weirdly like his mother, a lovely woman as I said, one I'd have liked as a mother-in-law, but perhaps a bit twinsetty.

'It is best if I begin at the beginning,' I said. 'You may even want to take notes. Would you rather wait till we get back home? Left here, please.'

'That's taking us away from Ashford,' he objected.

'I don't live in Ashford. I live south of Tenterden, overlooking Romney Marsh. At least, I do at the moment. Not my own place, I hasten to add. I had to leave there in a hurry.'

'Rent problems?' he asked idly, dropping to second for a tight corner.

What had happened to the committed, concerned young man I'd known and ... loved?

'Bomb problems,' I said. 'A letter bomb, to be precise, and what may be another, probably sent by my old friend Clive Granville.'

At last I had his attention good and proper. 'Granville! What have you done to upset him?'

'Stayed alive. Not died in a drug-induced stupor. Not contracted HIV – not that he's to know that, of course, but –' But it seemed important that Taz should know. 'Anyway, one day I nearly run into him in Tenterden. Forty-eight hours later my favourite postie gets blown in to the middle of next week.'

'So this lot –' he pointed at me with his thumb '– is part of some witness protection deal. I'd have thought you'd be better off in some safe house.'

'That wasn't an option. The policeman who interviewed me wanted to blame me, not protect me. But I think he's bent, so he would, wouldn't he?'

'Look here, you've got to have pretty strong evidence if you're going to make allegations like that!' His mother's voice again.

'I told you I should have begun at the beginning,' I said sadly.

After a shower, courtesy of Jan and Todd, and a cold beer he'd dug out of the fridge, Taz seemed much more his old self. He was as intrigued as Paula by the fittings of the mobile home, wandering round as if he were a prospective buyer.

'Not a bad place to doss, this,' he said. 'Done well for yourself here, Caffy.'

'I told you. This isn't mine. It's the Daweses'. I've got what I call my eyrie in Fullers itself.'

'Surely they – '

'I'd have been in the way,' I said firmly. I wouldn't point out I hadn't been invited; I didn't want him getting the idea that the Daweses had been anything other than wonderful. 'And in any case, Fullers is safer.'

Something made him look at me sharply, the way he used to look when he was trying to rescue me. 'Why don't we have another beer and you can tell me everything? And then we'll go and get that meal and I'll tell you what I propose to do.'

We had a bite in the Crown, the local pub. It was still warm enough for us to sit outside, in the furthest corner of the garden, just like lovers avoiding interruption. In fact bats were the only things to venture into our air space. I was entranced.

'You're not scared of them?'

What a conventional question: he should have known me better.

'Not after that Scottish bloke dying of rabies?' he prompted.

'I'm not proposing to try and catch one. Anyway, these are a different type, I think. Weren't his confined to north of the Border?'

'And you're not scared in Fullers? All on your own?' Didn't he remember I'd never been girly?

'So long as no one knows I'm there, why should I be? More escape routes than in the caravan, for one thing. And anyway, if they're tracking activities via Jan's mobile, then they'll find them in London somewhere, so I shouldn't be bothered.'

'What about mice and other beasties?'

I turned to look him straight in the eye. 'After Clive Granville, how can a mouse scare me? Anyway, you told me that you were going to get back our lives for us. The Daweses have a house to renovate. Paula has a business to run. I have a job to do. And the only way we can do these things is if we're not afraid of death by parcel. Which reminds me, shouldn't dealing with said parcel be your priority?'

'Where did you say it was?'

'In a far corner of the garden.' I grabbed his wrist. 'My God! What if some little animal nibbles it? It'd activate it and blow us all up!'

'So might heavy dew, unless the bag's waterproof. Oh, well,' he said, sinking the last of his half in one gulp, 'I always did say it was better to think on your feet.'

Fortunately, the Isle of Oxney wasn't a mobile dead spot. The advice Taz received was simply to move the package into one of the bins, and make sure it stayed covered. The person at the other end of the line was clearly unwilling to ruin his or his colleagues' Saturday evening. He insisted that things were best done by daylight, though I'd seen on TV impressive lights illuminating enough scenes of crime to make me doubt this. But Taz assured me that the aim was to behave in a very low-key manner, not alerting any more people than necessary to what was going on. The army, complete with armoured cars and goodness knows what else, would become an immediate news item. Special Branch might not.

'Special Branch?' I squeaked. 'But I thought they chased overseas baddies.'

'There are far more links with organised crime and baddies, as you so charmingly call them, over here than you realise. And the death at Crabton Manor and those immigrants suggest big fish.' He patted the pocket with the film cassette in it. To his credit Taz hadn't doubted anything I'd said. Occasionally he'd stopped to ask for clarification of various details, but each time he'd nodded in what looked like agreement and continued with his notes. 'Tomorrow you'll have lunch, ever so casually, with a very senior policeman – '

It was I who shook my head. 'Can you really see that as a scenario? Me in my dungarees meeting some smart gent?'

I'd forgotten how he could wrinkle his nose in distaste. 'Are the dungarees really necessary?'

'If we're both to be safe undercover as decorators,' I said. 'In any case, Paula's got a contract to keep to. We're her employees, remember.'

'You really mean to carry on?'

'Don't you? OK, you don't have to. She can tell van der Poele that you didn't suit, and we're back to three women again.' So Taz would go back to the city where he belonged and leave us to it. 'But I can't let her down, Taz. She's been a good boss to me, never throwing my past at me even when I'd really pissed her off about something. Never. Ever. She needs the money from this job so that she can pay Meg and Helen. And me,' I added, almost as an afterthought.

'Well, you're going to have to talk to someone pretty soon, aren't you? For your own sake,' he observed coolly. 'Not to mention nailing Marsh, if he does turn out to be bent. No, I'm not doubting you, not for one minute,' he insisted, as my hackles rose. 'I'm more interested in sorting out the hows and whys and whens than expressing myself properly. Now, I'll make sure you're safe for the night and be with you early – by eight at the very latest.'

'Aren't you going to stay?' I asked stupidly. 'No, I mean here, in the caravan. I didn't mean – ' I ground to a halt while I was losing.

'I've arranged to stay with a friend,' he said, with both embarrassment and an obvious desire to end the discussion, 'in Maidstone.' And a flush worthy of Meg, starting somewhere near his navel, I should hope, spread slowly and inexorably up his throat, across his face and into his ears.

'OK,' I said, taking the hint. 'Let me finish here – the loo's cleaner – and I'll lock up behind us.' I waved him a breezy good night. And retired to my eyrie to cry my eyes out.

Except I didn't. Cry, that is. Giving up for the time being on the rather tricky language of *Evelina*, by the light of my friends' torch I got deeply involved in first one, then another of those *Dubliners* stories, ending with the two morally bankrupt young men in *Two Gallants*. That's the nice thing about books. They remind you that some things never change.

True to his word, Taz was knocking on the mobile home's door soon after seven. His friend must be very tolerant about his comings and goings. He couldn't have got there much before midnight and must have been up by six.

I'd found bacon and eggs and was ready to do an old-fashioned fry-up. There were even a couple of wrinkled mushrooms and a tired tomato.

'Cholesterol,' he said.

'Well, the milk's off and the bread's as hard as the devil's head. We'll have to stop off at a garage or newsagent's to get replacements. But until then, all I can offer you is a rather manky orange, a sad grapefruit and a French apple. Or dry toast, of course.' Jan had lashed out on one of those tiny packs of very expensive French butter. I'd forgotten to get any spread to replace it when I'd used the last for yesterday's lunch. Let Taz hair-shirt if he wanted to. I got busy with the grill-pan. (Even I don't fry bacon!) Very soon Taz was sniffing hopefully. I took the hint.

So the fluffy young woman who knocked on the door was greeted by the smell I've always dreamed of waking up to. And she had no qualms about accepting my generous offer of Jan's hospitality.

'Cressida. I'm from the Special Branch,' she said flashing an ID. In all probability she had degrees from the best universities and black belts in any number of martial arts. But she spoke in a kittenish voice that made me want to scream. 'Toby – that's one of my colleagues – is looking at your explosive device now. He'd probably welcome breakfast, too.'

I peered round the door. Not an armoured car in sight, just a couple of trailer vans, the sort people used to move house. They were taking 'low key' seriously, weren't they? 'That's tough, I'm afraid. That's the last of the bacon on your plate. Unless you want to share it with him?' I might have given him some of mine if he'd been a Troilus, not a Toby.

It was soon agreed that it was kindest if we tucked in and left no visible traces of the meal to distress Toby. He couldn't fail to notice the smell, however, and looked duly hangdog when Taz tossed the manky orange in his direction. The trouble was, his complexion rather resembled that of the fruit, as if he'd tried to cure acne by over-exposure to a sun lamp.

'I'm going to need specialist equipment,' he announced, peeling the orange reluctantly to reveal something nasty. 'So my aim will be to get it removed from here.'

'You're going to risk that? After what happened to Arthur?'

'Ronnie, our little robot, will risk it. He'll pop it into a blast-proof container. In any case, if it's made by the expert Taz tells me you suspect it is, then it'll be pretty stable.'

'Unless there's a timing device,' I pointed out. I wasn't sure he was patronising me by giving the robot a silly name or was following the custom of putting together a long and sophisticated set of initials to make one.

'I'll warn Ronnie to bear that in mind,' Toby said, a half sneer on his face – though that might have been in response to Cressida's offer of chewing-gum.

I left Taz to make whatever phone calls he had to make and retired to my eyrie to fit the lenses. They'd made me practise inserting and removing them, of course, and I'd had no difficulty slipping them out last night. This morning was a different matter altogether. The little things had lives of their own, and showed an affection for the index fingers supposed to be popping them in that was almost touching. Just when I thought I'd have to give up, they went in, one by one. There, I was Lucy again, not Caffy.

I'd taken so long I wasn't surprised to hear Taz yelling for me. I called him up, and showed him the rest of the place. To my horror he obviously saw it as a heap of old bricks that was going to cause far more trouble than it was worth. Even though all the major repairs had been done, and Fullers was simply awaiting our cosmetic efforts, he could hardly wait to get out of the place. But he steered me back to my eyrie.

'We'll meet my contact after we knock off work,' he said. 'So take your glad-rags with you.'

'Taz,' I said, with as much patience as I could muster, 'you'll find we're both filthy by six and need a shower.'

'He wants to see us at seven so we'll have to knock off early,' he said.

'The other thing,' I said carefully, 'is that I don't have any glad-rags. I've got slightly smarter jeans and this top.' I held them up for his inspection.

He looked aghast. 'Surely you can do better than that.'

'How? And indeed why?'

'Well, for this evening, for instance, we shall be meeting in a decent hotel.'

'The first decent hotel I've been in since I came off the game,' I observed deliberately.

He flushed again. 'You had good gear then – '

'And sold it all.' Time to see what being brutal would do. 'To support my habit. Remember, that's what drug addicts do. They sell everything, and steal some more and sell that.' Not that I'd ever stolen. A bit to do with moral probity, more to do with Taz's support. But I could certainly understand the temptation. 'If I asked Jan and Todd they'd fit me out from top to toe, but they've given me so much I couldn't ask for anything I didn't really, really need.'

'Sorry. Of course. You've done very well,' he said in a tone I couldn't place. Was he trying to get back into social worker mode? Or was he trying to remember what we'd once meant to each other. Straightening, he tried again. 'But think – haven't you really got an outfit you keep for what Mother would call "best"?'

'How long have you been in the police?' I asked.

Thrown, he asked, 'Why? Well, I must have joined soon after you started your second lot of rehab.'

'So you don't remember how hard up you always were when you were a social worker? Well, Taz, dreadfully paid though social workers are, they get lots more than the minimum wage; they get contracts involving sick pay and paid holidays. I'm on what the government in its infinite wisdom says is enough to live on. I've got a bit stashed away in case I get sick, because I couldn't even afford a prescription on my average week's take-home pay, let alone a couple of days in bed with flu. But I live so close to the wire I simply can't afford posh clothes.'

'Charity shops?'

I looked at him steadily, then reached to finger his shirt. 'How many people wore that before you did?'

He wrinkled a fastidious nose.

'Quite,' I said. 'So I'll put in these jeans and this top for this evening, shall I?'

It was such a wonderful day it was impossible to stay in sociologist mode. If only Taz had driven a soft-top – it would have been grand to drive through the sun-blessed lanes, the wind blowing through what was actually not very nice hair now. Perhaps it was something to do with the way I lay: how else could I explain the patch at the back which seemed permanently tangled and matted? It needed a good dose of the serum I used to use. Well, it would have to manage with some of Jan's olive oil and a polythene bag to cover it for half an hour before I shampooed it.

'Have you decided whether to stay or throw in the towel?' How's that for association of ideas?

'I'll stay for today. If you think there's a chance of getting in the house. We'd need proper evidence before I could get a search warrant, you see.'

'That's why Paula and I took photos. Yes, inside and out. And why Paula picked up a fragment of blue rope and slipped it into a poly bag for safe-keeping.'

'She did what?'

'I told you. I took some photos from the outside, and when she let me into the place we took more of the room where I'd seen the corpse. And she spotted some fibres of the rope the stiff had been strangled with on the floor and kept them. Just in case.'

'So why the hell haven't you told the police before now?'

'Because when I tried I got Marsh accusing me of wasting police time. Hell, Taz, don't you ever listen? I don't suppose you were listening when I told you I'd got photos of the immigrants – '

'Yes, I was. You gave me the film for processing. It's at the lab even now, I hope.'

'You hope!'

'My friend was taking it to Maidstone – that's where Kent's police HQ is, remember – this morning.'

'I hope he or she remembers,' I grumbled, unashamedly fishing for info. Of course I was nosy. Your ex-nearly lover's sitting beside you – you're entitled to know what he's up to and with whom. Well, to wonder, if not to know.

'I'm sure they will.'

Oh, ho. A no fishing sign. And his jaw was clamped in the way that made him think he looked like that dishy man who plays Hornblower on the TV. His nostrils were even giving a little flair.

'There's a garage over there,' I said. 'Bread and milk and sandwiches and stuff.'

As I walked to the shop, he rolled down his window. 'Get some butter, will you? Proper stuff, not marge. And a paper. The *Observer*.'

I walked back, and leant towards him. 'Haven't you taken anything in? I can just about afford essentials, but nothing more.'

'But a paper is an essential.'

'I've just crippled myself financially to change my appearance because one of your lot dubbed me in with some very nasty people. If you'd had to do that you'd have been able to claim on expenses, wouldn't you? You can probably claim your living expenses down here, if the case comes to anything. So why don't you pick up the tab – then you can get anything you damned well want.' I was supposed to be able to do anger without any other emotion, wasn't I? How come I had to turn away before he could see the tears welling up round my damned lenses?

I told myself it was the cleaning solution: I must have used too little. Or too much.

Chapter Thirteen

Paula popped our supplies into the big cool-box that also housed extra water and squash on days like this, raising an eyebrow at the obviously cool relations between me and Taz. She also gave us a post-it to stick on the Escort's dash to remind us to collect them. 'It's going to be a real scorcher,' she said, rather unnecessarily. 'So I want us to work as far as possible in the shade. I'm afraid the dogs are back in their outhouse, which means we're going to have to go behind Trev – that's the Transit – here.' That was Paula for you – self-possessed and forthright. Until she had to say, 'So make sure you let us know if you're going to – er – ' She blushed. 'And we'll warn you, too.'

'Not very hygienic,' he said, nose a-wrinkle.

'Well. With a bit of luck we'll all sweat so much our bladders won't get very full.' Now she sounded like matron in one of those old hospital comedy films.

'More to the point,' I said, 'does this mean van der Poele's out of the way?'

'Not yet. He said he'd be going out but didn't give a time. I'm feeding and watering the dogs. And yes, they are doped. So if you really need the loo – '

'Paula, stop wittering about our bodily functions!' I interrupted her. 'Sorry.' She was the boss, after all. 'The important thing is that we shall be able to check out the house. Uninterrupted.'

'Until he unexpectedly returns.' Paula's smile was ironic, though at whose expense I wasn't sure.

Just in case it was mine, I gave a cheerful grin. 'But we

shall have the excuse of needing to open and close windows. And you have the key.'

'After Friday night,' she said seriously, 'I want you to have paint all over you and a brush in your hand before you venture in there. And that applies to you, too, Taz. If he finds out you're not who you're supposed to be, what does that make me? And the rest of us?'

'Just taken in by a smooth-talking con,' he said, switching on a charming smile, as if putting himself down, just a little.

'I don't do taken in,' she snapped. 'And I don't think van der Poele does credulity, either. He knows Caffy was on to something. A copper turns up – '

'Oh, I wouldn't have to tell him I was a cop.'

Paula raised a warning hand. In the distance a dog yowled. 'It's hard to work out just how much tranquilliser to give them,' she said, calm again. Apparently. 'And it'd be a brave man who could keep his trap shut with them tearing off his balls. No, Taz, you do it my way or not at all. Do I make myself clear?'

He drew himself up to his full six foot, pushing out his chest as if on parade. 'Yes, ma'am.'

'And stop taking the micky. While you're here, you're polite to the boss. Otherwise,' she added, spoiling the effect, 'I shan't show you those photos we took.' She turned back to dig in the Transit's glove box. I noticed she produced just half the set; did that mean she only half-trusted Taz?

Despite taking plenty of drinks breaks, it was a hot and sticky crew that gathered for lunch. Taz was last down, and made straight for the far side of the van.

'I bet van der Poele only wanted us to work this weekend because he'd heard the weather forecast,' Meg sighed, slumping into a deck-chair and undoing more top buttons than strictly necessary. 'It must be well into the thirties.'

'No one would be mean enough to do anything like that,' Helen protested. 'By the way, has he gone yet?'

'He has and he would,' Paula declared. 'Which is why I've changed my mind and you three are going to take the sides of the house overlooking the road and paint with one eye open for van der Poele and I am going to show Taz round.' She stared at me as if daring me to contradict her. I hadn't even thought of such a thing. First, the person showing anyone the ropes would naturally be the boss. Second, I'd no particular desire to be with Taz. Third, if I was nippy on my feet at the end of the break I'd be able to get to the only part of the house still in full shade that had a view of the road.

Meanwhile Taz returned, via his car. 'Listening to *The World this Weekend*! What sort of outfit are you?' he demanded, no doubt taking in the fact that there were only four chairs, all occupied. He flipped over to me one of the three packs of sandwiches from the petrol station shop, and reclined at our feet with his two. He'd stripped off to reveal an already tanned six-pack and set of pecs to die for. Reclining showed everything off far better than sitting would have done.

'I don't know why you're laughing,' Meg rebuked him quietly. 'It helps my kids with their homework.'

Helen said, 'And I thought I might start college in the autumn. Get qualifications like the others.'

'You don't need a knowledge of current affairs to learn how to slap on emulsion,' he chortled.

'There's no reason why women shouldn't know what's going on in the world, for all we don't have any fancy degrees, is there?' Meg demanded. 'And I think you'll find NVQs involve a bit more than slapping on emulsion.' Quite a mouthful from someone he must have realised fancied the socks off him.

He dropped his eyes. So he should.

Thinking of my spot out of the sun, I hauled myself to my feet. It wasn't emulsion I was about to slap on, but gloss paint where the frame met the window. You need to get an eighth of an inch, no more, on the glass. That requires a bit of skill and a very steady hand. If I heard any more of his lip I might not be able to manage the steady hand part, I was getting so angry. How had I ever been in love with this patronising young man? Or was I just angry because he was taking more notice of the others than of me?

Come on, Caffy – whoops! Come on, Lucy. Paint that window-frame. I looked at my hand. Some folk used masking tape to get a straight line. I'd prided myself on never needing to. Today, just in case, I sneaked a roll from the back of the van.

It was I who, an hour or so later, spotted van der Poele's car and knocked the window hard. I wasn't surprised to see Taz and Paula emerging on to the scaffolding above me, though it wasn't the wisest move. They were a bit obvious, and van der Poele knew we'd done that particular section. Paula was soon beside me, however, using the ladder as easily as if it were an escalator in a shopping mall. To my dour amusement, Taz was clearly uneasy, making sure he steadied himself before moving a foot or releasing a hand. There was a lot of ladder to go before he reached solid ground, though. Ground as solid as his feet. Feet of clay, eh? I had a nasty suspicion I was falling briskly out of love with our Taz. I didn't need so much as an inch of the masking tape.

Because the heat was still intense at five, Paula told us we could knock off if we wanted.

'What about you?' I asked. 'And what about your contract?'

'You've done more than I expected already. Taz isn't bad at rubbing down. But someone'll have to repaint his windowframe tomorrow.' She paused, presumably for him to hang his head and apologise, eventually resuming, 'I'm going to stick it out a bit longer, but you could run the others back, Lucy, and then bring Trev – the van – back here for me.

'It'd make more sense if Taz did that,' I objected. 'I could carry on painting.'

'True. Will you start it for him?'

Taz bustled forward, holding out his hand for the keys. So his deafness had been temporary and selective. 'I can do that – no problem.'

Winking at me with the eye Taz couldn't see, Paula handed them over.

'So long as he doesn't flatten the battery,' I cautioned, hearing the starter motor whine and cough over and over again.

'I don't think he's that stupid. There you are. He's given up. Go and show him, girl!'

A triumphant moment later, and Paula and I were on our

own. We worked on open windows, so we couldn't say much. At last, both finished, we were putting away our brushes and making sure the lids were firmly on the paint tins when she said, 'When Taz comes back, don't forget that butter and milk.' In exactly the same tone, she continued, 'I had an idea you were sweet on him.'

'You had the right idea,' I admitted. 'Once. I think absence must have made a fond heart wander, though. In his case, at least.'

'His? What about yours? I mean, he's very good-looking and he's looked after his body very well. Very well indeed.'

'I don't know what I ever saw in him,' I said honestly.

For all that, we were to spend the evening together, weren't we? And in any case, he had to drive me back, which he did in silence. The only time he uttered was when I let us into the caravan again and I handed him one of my towels.

'You can't manage a decent dress but you buy expensive things like this!'

'Try drying yourself on a posh frock.'

'I don't remember your having a chip on your shoulder like this.'

I curled up inside. Was that what it was? A spot of invert-ed snobbery? Resenting other people's good fortune and sneering at them for better clothes and cars? Jesus. Not a good thing. There was only one thing worse in my social book than inverted snobbery and that was snobbery itself, people with money or birth judging people like me who had neither. Funny, I'd never suspected Taz of snobbery before. Surely he didn't think that being a cokehead in designer jeans was better than being a decorator in jeans from the market. But the funny thing was, I really did resent his having money and being mean with it, and might be playing up my uncouth side a little more than usual. If I was, I certainly never felt tempted to do it to the Daweses, apart from that awful Little Nell moment, which made my toes curl just to think about it even now. They could have bought and sold Taz and not bothered with the small change, but I didn't covet their money. Heavens, they were so generous with it I had to stop them overspending on me.

Maybe I ought to have quipped with black humour that my old ones had come to a sticky end and turned the conversation that way. As it was, I said quietly, 'I wrapped my last towels round Arthur, remember, the postie who died. I had to buy replacements. If that comes across as an inferiority complex, so be it. The shower's there, remember. And make sure you shut the door properly.'

By the time I emerged, he'd ponced himself up in neatly-cut cotton trousers that flattered an already tight bum and an open-necked shirt. No jeans and T-shirt for him, then. To be honest, even without him pointing it out, I felt very dowdy beside him. Dowdy and a mess. My hair was drier and more brittle than ever. I grabbed a handful. When this was all over, I'd go to a barber – cheaper than any salon I knew, except Stell's! – and have a short back and sides.

Meanwhile, there was a short drive west to our rendezvous. I suppose I'd hoped for one of those converted country houses that this part of the world is rich in – pun intended. What I got was a rather anonymous modern place, one that wouldn't have been out of place in the centre of

Brum, for instance. The Mondiale Hotel and Golf Club. Hmm.

Coughing awkwardly, Taz led me into the foyer and introduced me to our host. In tones more suited to a church, he said, 'This is Assistant Chief Constable Moffatt, in charge of Crime for the Kent County Constabulary.'

One of those things that could have been better expressed, I thought, refusing to giggle, even though I recalled a car park slot at a nick in Birmingham announcing it belonged to the 'Crime Manager'. The police weren't at their best when it came to titles, were they? At least, I hoped they weren't.

Moffatt at least didn't seem to think there was any ambiguity. He bent over my hand (I noticed too late some paint under my cuticles) like an elderly courtier. 'Miss Tyler.'

'Ms Taylor. Lucy Taylor. I'd rather everyone used my new name until I get used to it,' I said. 'Like my new appearance.'

He gave another half-bow. I had a nasty idea that he was the type to judge by appearances. Immaculate himself in a middle-aged version of Taz's outfit, he might have shaken my hand with something like old-fashioned courtesy, but he swiftly ushered us to the far corner of the hotel bar where my appearance wouldn't be so obvious. No, I was being paranoid. He wanted no one to overhear us. That was the reason. The main reason, anyway.

He leant towards me, his grey eyes cold under salt and pepper eyebrows. 'You realise, Ms Ty – Ms Taylor – what a serious allegation you've made against one of our officers?'

'Dead serious, isn't it?' I agreed pertly. 'Almost as dead as Arthur.'

Taz would have preferred a little serious humility. Well, he was mixing with a very senior officer, and was presumably pretty well the lowest of the low himself. Not that he'd want anyone to think that. He'd insisted to me that he was on an accelerated promotion scheme. 'I'm sure Ms Taylor realises that a man's career is at stake here.'

The trouble was, the more serious he wanted me to be, the more mouthy I wanted to be. 'What's a career compared with a life?' I asked.

To my surprise, the older bloke had to look down to hide a smile. Doing so revealed his growing bald spot, almost round like those tonsure things monks used to have. It was freckled with age spots.

'By the way,' I pursued, 'have the robot and his hungry little human friends, Troilus and Cressida, drawn any conclusions about that package they took away?'

He smiled, but with the air of someone fending off a tricky question – which was what I realised too late was what he was doing. 'The main conclusion,' he said, 'is that you are a brave young woman.'

Any compliments I'd had in the past tended to be about my anatomy. A couple of college tutors had said nice things about what lurked between my ears, but no one, fellow addicts in rehab. apart, had ever used the word brave. Not knowing how to respond, I just asked, the words coming out in a husky whisper, 'It was a bomb, then?'

'It was a bomb all right. More stable than the one that killed your poor postman. But just as powerful.' He smiled again. Another digression coming, no doubt. 'I hear you've been brave and resourceful throughout.'

For the first time Taz smiled at me with the sort of

warmth I'd been hoping for. But not a single frisson did it give me. I'd still have liked a frisson. It would have told me my years on the game hadn't destroyed normal sexual desire.

'What I'd like to ask is if you'll carry on being brave and resourceful. You see, we've come to believe, as you do, that Marsh has illicit contacts with two major criminals.'

'Just the two?' I asked tartly – if you'll forgive the pun. 'Still, I suppose when they're the calibre of Granville and van der Poele that's probably enough.'

He was about to reply, but a barman with a swarthy complexion the texture of grapefruit skin brought over a dish of nuts, which he placed without speaking between the two men. Those sandwiches seemed a very long time ago. Didn't I see a TV programme once, where they experimented on some rats, keeping them hungry and placing food just out of range? The idea was that the rats would use will power to bring the food nearer. Perhaps this was a rerun of the same experiment. Should I participate or not? Not. I reached for them. The will power I'd thus saved could be used to stop me from snaffling the lot.

The waiter returned with leather-bound menus and a tentative smile. No wonder he tried not to open his lips: his teeth needed urgent attention. He asked, with a thick accent, 'You like drink before meal?'

Meal! That was just what I wanted to hear. I must go easy on the nuts, then, to save some space for what I hoped would be a real treat.

'Oh, yes, a drink – but I don't think we shall be eating – ' Moffatt began.

I must have had some will power in reserve.

'Or would you, er, Lucy –?'

Yes! 'I would, please,' I said, quietly but firmly.

'In that case, could you find us a table out on the terrace, perhaps? It's such a lovely evening, isn't it?' he added, smiling at me. He seemed to be treating me as a niece he enjoyed indulging. Or was he softening me up for something? Just how long would he expect me to be brave and resourceful? Not to mention just how much Bravery and Resourcefulness might he require?

The waiter distributed the menus, and hovered hopefully with his order pad.

A little bit of B and R might be called for right now, come to think of it. I was used to a half, or at most a pint, of Bishop's Finger at a session. If I started swigging alcohol now, on an almost empty stomach, I might be too tight to follow as closely as I ought what was going on. One of my old mates, in similar situations where she needed to keep one step ahead of a punter she didn't quite trust, used to have a Bloody Mary – without the vodka. She'd bought me one a couple of times. I can't say they'd have got the ducks off the water, but they were a damned sight safer than innocent-seeming alcopops.

Moffatt went for sherry – I didn't realise people still drank that – and Taz for a predictable half of lager. Moffatt seemed amused by my choice, but didn't argue. Once we had drinks before us, the waiter seemed happy to wait till kingdom come for our order. Neither man opened his menu. God, I was so hungry. Instead of taking the edge off my hunger, the nuts seemed have sharpened it up. Perhaps if I went to the loo it'd stop me staring at the empty dish.

It was so long since I'd used ladies' rooms like this! The hotels I'd worked from weren't this class. One or two nicer punters – or simply ones hoping to impress me with the size of their wallets, if not of what Paula would call their wedding-tackle – had booked into better places, ones like this where there were tissues free for the taking and good quality soap and towels, not stuff that dripped from a dispenser and hard paper. If I hadn't had the run of the Dawses' place I don't know how I could have resisted nicking a bar – not until I saw the beady lens of a little CCTV camera. I smiled at it, and retired to a cubicle.

Soap, no: that would be greedy and tempt that camera. But paper hankies, yes. I grabbed a fistful and shoved them in my bag. Why not? The hotel's profit margin on the meal would no doubt be enough to pay for them twice over.

Thank God the menus were open when I got back and the men were talking about starters. Again, I ought to go easy. I'd not eaten a three-course meal for several years now – what if I filled up too early? I certainly wouldn't risk, as Taz was suggesting, a pint of mussels. Or homemade soup with a crusty roll. Especially in this weather. Would choosing smoked salmon be pushing my luck?

Not if I didn't have the expensive steak the men were ordering. But I had too much pride to ask for a smaller, cheaper one. I almost wished I hadn't asked to eat. And then, relaxing my shoulders, I had a sudden rash of sanity. These men were only here because of me and my B and R. I deserved the best just as much as they did. Smoked salmon and steak it would be.

And Moffatt turned not a single silvering hair. He didn't even ask for house wine. He chose a bottle of white and red from the main selection. This was going to be an evening to remember. All I had to do was to stay sober enough to remember it. And remember what I was committing myself to.

I was happy to let the men talk about cricket and the forthcoming football season: I quite like both, but top class sport had long since priced itself out of my range, so all I knew was what I gleaned from the newspapers or Meg's radio programmes. The conversation turned to a leading footballer who was in the media spotlight after being caught betting.

To my surprise, Moffatt turned to me. 'Are you a betting woman, Lucy?'

'Can't afford to be. I used to do Lotto if we got a bonus, but then Meg told us the odds against actually winning anything. By the way, what do I call you? I make a point of never accepting a meal from a man whose name I don't know.'

Taz coughed.

'John,' Moffatt said, apparently unfazed. 'I have an idea, though, that even if you could afford an account at a bookie's, you'd still prefer money you earned to that you got in a windfall.'

I reflected. There was plenty of time. The waiter wanted to show us to our table. It was hard not to gasp with pleasure. The terrace overlooked what was obviously a golf course, but in the evening light looked just like a park with a beautiful lake. Magic. The waiter pulled back my chair for me and then for the men. When he'd flapped open starched linen serviettes – or were they napkins in these surroundings? – and laid them on our laps, he left us to it.

'All circumstances being equal,' I said, 'I think you're right, John. Much as I'd like a fairy-godmother, I like earning my money with the toil of my hands.' I spread them out. There was still paint under some of the nails, too. 'But I've an idea that you're not introducing this simply as a theory.'

'You're right. Basically I'm asking you to make a choice – not now, but in the course of the evening – whether you want us to spirit you away to a safe house or whether you're content to continue as you are. You know you're at great risk if Marsh discovers you and tells his friends. But you might be very useful to us if you stayed out in the open.'

Before I could say anything a waitress had appeared, offering bread rolls. We all chose wholemeal. They were rounder than the white and she had a terrible job picking them up with a pair of tongs. It was all I could do not simply to grab one to put her out of her misery.

But there were more urgent things to think about than rookie waitresses. My life, for a start.

'I saw a TV programme once,' I said at last. 'One of these nature documentaries. About great big lizards on some idyllic island. Tourists pay a lot of money to see these lizards, and get stroppy if they don't. So to make sure the main act turns up, the locals tether a live goat where the lizards will hear it bleating. A sort of living dinner gong. Except the goat then becomes the dinner. Is this what you want me to be?'

'Exactly. Except we shall do our utmost to see you don't get eaten.'

I nodded slowly. Not quite irrelevantly, I asked, 'When the first parcel bomb arrived, I'm sure that there was a lot of publicity and Granville – '

'We don't know for sure it was Granville,' Taz interrupted.

'Granville or whoever would have known he'd missed his target. What about publicity for today's? He'd know it had arrived: I'd bet my boots that it was one of his men that delivered it.' I was about to spout my theory when Moffatt interrupted.

'None – yet. That's another thing we need to discuss. We've given a lot of thought to this.'

'"We" being?'

'Quite a lot of people. The police have their own team to investigate internal corruption. A couple of them. Then,' he continued, counting on his fingers, 'the National Crime Squad, since Granville's attracted the notice of a lot of forces all over the country, Kent County Constabulary – that's me and some colleagues, and, since you've invited Taz to help, the Met. Is that enough? Oh, I'd forgotten the Immigration people and the Human Smuggling Unit given what's in your photos.'

'Plus MI5 for the bomb.'

'Quite a party,' Taz said dryly.

'If it's mine, does that mean I can cry off if I want to?'

'Exactly,' Moffatt smiled. 'But I rather hope you won't.'

Chapter Fourteen

To do John Moffatt justice, he stuck to his promise that I need make no decisions till the end of the meal and didn't press me at any point. The conversation turned to the food, which was so good I almost wished I hadn't nicked those paper hankies. The wine made me forget I had. But there were some things I hadn't forgotten.

'Did you find anything at Crabton Manor?' I asked Taz.

He shook his head. He seemed to have rather more mussels left – in a stylish bucket – than he'd started with.

'I told him not to expose anyone to any sort of danger,' Moffatt said firmly. 'Your boss – Ms Farmer?'

'Paula Farmer,' I agreed. 'Except of course she's not a farmer, any more than I'm a tiler. Or indeed a tailor.' Hmm. I'd better go easy on the booze. If the white was anything to go by, the red would be heady, powerful stuff.

So ought Taz. He jumped in. 'Paula's tour meant I know my way around now. I should be able to put together a rough ground plan – '

'You don't need to,' I said. 'Paula's got one already. Precise and detailed. For doing estimates,' I explained, realising I'd been a bit unkind. 'At one time van der Poele said he might want us to decorate the inside as well, but he seems to have gone off the idea. Pity. Nice big indoors job for winter. At least we've still got the Fullers contract, though.' I reached quickly for the water.

'Why the hell didn't you tell me?'

'You needed to case the joint anyway,' I said reasonably,

sitting on an urge to point out that he hadn't asked me. I'd thought, after all, that he was going to do a superficial search. 'And some people can't read plans – like some can't read maps or music. Or read full stop.' At least two glasses of water before a drop more alcohol. For good measure I covered my glass when the waiter flashed the bottle again. When he'd gone, I downed the first glass of water. I wouldn't have expected the effect to be so immediate. 'That business about money, John. Were you implying that if I just swanned off and let you people look after me you'd actually pay me?'

'We'd make up what wages you missed. The problem is that once you go into the scheme you literally give up your old life. Your whole identity. You'd probably get retrained in a new skill.'

'No more Paula's Pots, no more working for the Daweses at Fullers?'

'No. If we get a conviction, of course, you might well get a reward from Crime Stoppers.' He smiled.

'And if I stay where I am, working for my living with people I like, do we – do they – get any protection? And does someone keep an eye on Fullers so that the Daweses can be safe? For a long time? Clive Granville has a long memory and a lot of money – he can pull more strings even when he's inside than most men can when they're completely free.'

He didn't give a straight answer, of course. 'The courts have powers to confiscate ill-gotten gains these days. Especially where drugs are concerned.'

'You know about his drug-dealing activities, then? I thought it was just the bombs and immigration scam that –'

'I told you, Caffy – there are a lot of people in the team. Ah, our main course.'

Little lights were coming on all over the golf course. Some were reflected in the lake. The waiter lit candles on the table. I could get to enjoy living like this. Perhaps I could retrain in hotel management. Now that was an idea – a real plus for the protection scheme.

At the next table, some old bat was snarling at the waitress, who had to smile and take it. No, I was better with Paula. At least I could swear back at her and she wouldn't blink. At least, not very hard.

We all tucked into the main course without saying very much. Taz was probably glad of the excuse: it must be very hard to be closeted with such a senior officer in circumstances like this. Moffatt appeared to be thinking, looking up at me almost speculatively from time to time. I was happy simply to eat and be grateful. I'd probably said all that I needed to say – we all knew I'd carry on as I was. It was OK even to drink. The red was so smooth I could have sunk the bottle without noticing – until, that is, I'd come to stand up again. As it was, I paced myself. I couldn't see Moffatt as a dessert man, but I could imagine him suggesting liqueurs with the coffee. And I could definitely see myself accepting one: I'm an absolute sucker for Tia Maria. Or that stuff they put coffee beans on and set alight. That'd look really pretty in the dusk. But, as I relaxed, something clicked in my head. I'd have been sick with horror, only that would have wasted time. 'That bomb. So they know it was signed for and received. So do they assume the bomb didn't go off or that it did go off and for some reason there's been a media black-out or that someone twigged and disabled the thing?'

'What difference does it make?' Taz really shouldn't have had that last glass.

'All the world to me and Fullers. Granville isn't a man to be left in doubt. He'll want to make sure I've been wiped out. If he suspects I haven't, I'm – '

'Very much at risk. Excuse me while I make a quick call.' Moffatt fished out his mobile. The old bat coughed ostentatiously. Raising an irate eyebrow, he got to his feet. 'We'll get an immediate press release out. Explain the delay by saying that the family had to be informed.'

He headed for lights at the edge of the lake. Without speaking, Taz headed in the other direction, presumably for the gents'.

Moffatt was back first. 'I'm still not happy about your returning to Fullers or the caravan till we've checked them over. How would you feel about staying here?'

I managed a dry laugh. 'I don't think so. Hotels like this aren't entirely happy about accommodating young women looking like me and having no luggage.' Especially after they've dined in the company of two men. But I wasn't going to say that to him. I wondered with a sudden shiver if all those speculative glances hadn't been… No, surely not. I hadn't had a bad vibe all evening. But I was sure as hell getting one now. 'No, I'd rather go home, please. I was hoping Taz might give me a lift but he's in no state to drive, is he?'

'I had an idea,' he said, dropping his voice, 'that you and Taz were an item. If you two wanted…' Maybe I'd got the wrong vibe.

'No. We're not an item,' I said flatly.

'In that case I'll get my driver to drop him off.'

'Driver! Wow!' Hell, I'd got diverted. How much had I sunk?

'Doubling as an extra bit of security for us. If you swim with sharks, Caffy, you want to make sure your cage is as strong as possible. Which brings me back to your safety this evening. I've sent a few colleagues to check that Fullers is safe – and that mobile home that so fascinated Taz. So it's Todd Dawes who's taken you up, is it? He was a bad lad in his younger days, Caffy. Very bad. He's supposed to have dabbled in every drug going.' He sounded almost tetchy. Or was it speculative?

No, I'd better miss out on a liqueur. 'So he must have gone through every cold turkey going, poor bugger,' I observed. Then it dawned on me what he was implying. Taken me up, indeed! 'He and his wife have become my friends, John. Dear, dear friends – both of them. Like second parents to me.'

'Well, I hope they're kinder to you than your first.'

Golly, the police had been doing their homework, hadn't they? But they seemed to have forgotten one thing, as I should have pointed out to Moffatt when he'd talked about dropping Taz off. They'd worked out how to get Moffatt home – and he'd sorted out Taz's arrangements. But what about me? A cab? Out here at this time on a Sunday evening would cost an arm and a leg. I certainly didn't have enough cash on me.

Taz was just returning to the table when Moffatt's phone rang. As one person, all the other diners turned to him in shocked reproach. He scurried back on to the grass.

'Taz – can you do me a favour? And charge it to your expenses?'

'What?' He sat down.

'Moffatt's sorted out your transport to Maidstone. But what about me? He's checking it's safe for me to go to Fullers but I've no idea how to get there except have a cab.'

'And you've made the state of your finances pretty clear.'

'Sorry.'

'No, it's me that's sorry. I'd no idea. You always seemed so well set up when – '

'Quite,' I said dryly.

'Look,' he began, taking my hand. 'I've been – pretty off-hand – all weekend. Some of it was the shock of seeing you like this. And there's other stuff too. Would you feel safer if I came back to Fullers with you? I could phone my friend.'

He was being suspiciously cagey about this Maidstone friend, but all the same I couldn't stop myself blabbing out, 'Would you? That'd be great. I'd feel a lot safer.' But very uncertain. I'd no idea where he'd want to sleep – on his own or with me. And all the all hopes and uncertainties were thinking of bubbling up. Taz and me. What if it could be Taz and me? What if all his stroppiness and awkwardness had been because he'd really started to have feelings for me?

Or what if he'd been stroppy and awkward because that was the real Taz, and I'd put my own version of him on a pedestal?

But Moffatt was back, looking very serious. The waiter hurried forward tactlessly, flourishing the sweet menu. Without consulting either of us, Moffatt waved it away. 'Coffee. And the bill, please.'

Bye-bye, Tia Maria.

Moffatt looked me full in the face. 'It seems we were too late with the press announcement. Someone's booby-trapped the caravan door – '

'They haven't hurt Fullers!' I wailed.

'Let's just say, we'll have the fire service standing by in case there's a similar device attached to any of the doors. But we want to leave everything till daylight – for the same reasons as today's low-key activities. But I rather think we're going to have to generate a very loud bang, loud enough to convince our friends that this time they've been successful. Otherwise, Lucy, we have no choice – it's witness protection for you, my girl.'

I knew what the Daweses would want. Or at least I thought so, until I heard the words come out with such finality. 'You'd better blow up the caravan. At least it'll mean they should lay off the house.' Swallowing, I continued. 'Todd and Jan haven't been in touch with me since yesterday morning. They promised to leave their number with Paula. But we've been in a mobile dead spot all day.'

'What's her number?' He passed over his phone.

The old bat coughed.

'Hell and buggeration!' He glowered at her and at the other diners. 'Take her down to the lake, Taz. I'll settle up and book her a room.'

'Lucy Taylor,' I hissed, just to be sure, and set out with Taz.

Romantic or what? A stroll in the lamplight, with a sickle moon just appearing. Me and the most handsome man I'd ever seen. Oh, I might mock, but he really was stunning.

Still, I'd better make that call, and he'd better have something handy to jot down the number I hoped Jan had left Paula.

A voice from behind us grated out, 'Well?'

Moffatt. Maybe just as well. Better forget everything but praying Paula would answer, and have good news. 'They left a message? Oh, thank God! Taz – write this down!' I dictated the new number.

'And do you expect to be at Crabton Manor tomorrow?' Paula continued. 'One or both of you?'

'Me certainly,' I said crossing my fingers. 'Not sure about Taz.'

'Someone else?'

'Don't know.'

'Let's hope if there is a replacement, whoever it is hasn't got such a bob on himself. And knows what to do with a paintbrush. Oh – hang on! You want us to pick you up?'

I knew they'd enjoy the experience as much as I would. 'I'll be waiting in the foyer,' I said, adding in my poshest voice, 'or you could always have my room paged.'

Jan and I made contact. They'd changed phones and were safe in an hotel favoured, said Jan, without apparent irony, by the rich and famous who demanded a high degree of security. Before I could say much, Moffatt retrieved his phone. He explained the situation gravely.

There was a moment while we waited for their response. Then he burst out laughing, and cut the call. 'You know what they said? Exactly what you said. "You'd better blow up the caravan. At least it'll mean they should lay off the house."'

I did what I'd done the other day, and the shock of it was just as toe-curling. I burst into tears. I'd never before shared exactly the same thought with someone: I'd heard lovers say they did it. Todd and Jan were better than lovers. They were my closest friends. My family. And I was responsible for the destruction of their home, albeit a temporary one, and was putting their dearest possession at risk. OK, if it hadn't been for a circumspect phone call, I might have been in Fullers and at risk myself. But I'll swear it was for the synchronicity I was weeping.

It's amazing what coffee and strong drink will do for hysterics. Moffatt was quite adamant that a decent single malt would be better for me than Tia Maria, though on what grounds he wasn't clear. Perhaps it was because he felt he ought to have one too, just to make sure it was all right. Taz sat awkwardly, occasionally pithering with the sugar. I'd have loved to know what was going on in his head – or more particularly in his loins. Did I owe that to being afraid? I'd read that people who'd lost loved ones suddenly wanted to bonk like bunnies – often quite inappropriately. So it was all biological. The urge disappeared as fast as it had come.

Moffatt's Visa card and the receipt for the meal lay on a little silver plate. It was time for polite goodbyes. Someone had to initiate the process. It had better be me. I said, 'I'm sorry. All this emotion's knackered me.' I was just getting to my feet when Moffatt's phone rang. Would we troop back to the lawn? Or head for the foyer, where calls were allowed. I headed for the foyer. It was nearer the lifts. The others had to follow.

'It's for you,' Moffatt said. 'Todd Dawes.'

I pressed the mobile to my ear. 'Jan says if you can't get into Fullers, you'll need clothes and things. We're paying. OK?'

'But – '

'And then,' he said, as if he knew the information would mean I wouldn't argue, 'we shall claim on our insurance policy. Just go somewhere decent, open an account, and make sure you keep all the receipts.' He rang off before I could even start thanking him.

I started to howl again. Through my tears, I managed to croak to Moffatt, 'You're right: they're much kinder parents than my first ones.'

Whether it was my damned waterworks or the firm hand Moffatt placed under his elbow, Taz seemed to lose interest in renewing his moonlight emotion. We all said polite farewells, and I was given my key. I was just heading for the lift when Moffatt called me.

'Just remember, young lady, you don't open your door for anyone. Is that clear? Anyone.'

Chapter Fifteen

The hotel produced, at my embarrassed request, complimentary toothpaste and toothbrush on top of what appeared to be their usual range of toiletries and goodies like a shower cap. But it seemed terribly sad that the price of my stay in all this luxury was the sacrifice of that lovely mobile home. Or was the sacrifice of the mobile home really to protect Fullers itself, and this simply a by-product? Whichever it was, it was all my fault.

I twanged an imaginary rubber band on my wrist. No, of course it wasn't all my fault. Some of it was. My first career had set it all off, no denying that. But it hadn't been my fault that my pimp, Oscar, in many ways a decent man and certainly one who loathed violence, had passed me on to Granville to pay off some debt he'd foolishly incurred. Oscar was so mild-mannered he wouldn't have dreamed of selling me, if he'd known about Granville. Or would he? I suppose it depends on the size of the debt and the other measures Granville was threatening to use if it wasn't settled. Not just threats, of course. Granville had ways of fulfilling them. If I thought about those, however, it would be very hard to keep cheerful.

OK, it might have been my fault in the first place – though there had been extreme circumstances that drove me into prostitution – but recently I'd been pretty blameless. All I'd done was to pass on information to a bent cop about a crime possibly committed by a very unpleasant man. And the cop and a thoroughly evil man had conspired to kill me.

If anyone was the victim here, I suppose it was me. No. Caffy didn't do victim, remember!

I lay back: it was time to let the bath foam do its work and relax me. I could forget all about the criminals and their crimes, just as they'd taught me. Start with the feet, then the ankles, then … off I was going…

Except one thing niggled me. In my ruminations I'd used the word information. It had seemed the right word at the time, but there was something about it… In fact it was still buzzing round by the time I'd finished my bath, cleaned my teeth and stowed the contact lenses in the little bowls I'd kept with me in case they'd become uncomfortable during the day. The optician had dinned into me that I mustn't ever wear them without cleaning them properly, so I'd have to get some more fluid. I'd have to get a lot of things: I'd be able to retrieve most of my possessions from Fullers when I could eventually get back in, but until then I hadn't even a pair of clean pants to my name. Swathing myself in the bathrobe made of thicker towelling than the laundrette tumble dryer would have coped with in a morning, I started on a list.

Pristine pad. Pristine pencil. It was like being a child again. Such little things giving such huge pleasure. What surprised me, as I picked up the pencil intending to write

Knickers

Contact lens solution

T-shirt

Trainers

Socks

Bra

I wrote the word,

INFORMATION???

and just to make sure drew a big, swooping oval round it. Only then did I write the list.

What next?

Should I raid the mini-bar? On the whole I thought I'd had enough alcohol. And I was much too hot. That bathrobe would be fine when it wasn't still about twenty degrees Celsius outside. Then damn me if I didn't spot that what I thought was just a heater doubled as an air-conditioning unit. Trouble was, it sounded like an aircraft taking off.

I might as well go to bed and try to sleep. And then I realised one huge, gaping gulf in all the arrangements. There was no paperback to fall asleep over. It seemed a bit disrespect-ful to take a Gideon Bible to bed. But disrespect or not, in it had to come. There'd been one or two Bible-bashers in Rehab. I'd always found them tediously lacking in humour. But tonight I must confess I found the story of the woman taken in adultery spot on. I must have done. It was still open at the page when my alarm-call came through the next morning.

It promised to be another scorcher. I was just about to have a shower when I noticed that there was a swimming pool avail-able. I was halfway down the corridor before I realised I did-n't have any swimmies. But I'd dimly registered you could buy all sorts of trashy jewellery in the hotel lobby; maybe they sold swim things at the pool? I could charge it to my room! No, I couldn't ask the tax-payer to subsidise me to that extent. Could I? It wasn't as if I was a very good swimmer. And then that therapy bit about the inner child popped up in my brain.

Those lengths I swam in my new suit – people with personalised abdomens like mine don't go in for bikinis – might not have been very elegant lengths, but at least there were a dozen of them.

Yes!

A luxurious shower sluiced off the chlorine. I found a hairdryer, which blew my witch's locks into some semblance of order. And then I strode off for breakfast. Given the amount of food I'd put away the previous evening, I surprised myself by tackling it so enthusiastically. Well, juice, as much fruit as I could afford in a week, the full mixed grill (except someone ought to tell the chef to source his bacon from local free-range pigs), and then toast and conserves. Tea or coffee ad lib. Well, not too much coffee, not remembering Crabton's loo provision. .

I have to confess I shoved into my bag all the half-bottles of shampoo and bath oil on the grounds that they'd only be thrown away anyway if I didn't take them. The list and that note too. Looking round the room – I'd nothing to leave, so it must have been simply to fix it in my mind – I flapped a hand in farewell. Much as I liked my eyrie, I had to admit that this had a few more home comforts. Home comforts? A bit of a misnomer there, Caffy.

Bugger it: Lucy.

'And you will be in for dinner this evening, Madam?' the immaculate young Frenchman at Reception asked. At least, he was pretending to be a Frenchman, but his accent creaked and I didn't believe him. It was certainly nothing like the genuine French accent purveyed by one of my clients – and I knew he was genuine because he was in senior management in Renault and used to pop across to see how his cars were selling in the outlet in Brum. He'd offered me a Clio once, lots of Va-va-voom: I didn't accept because I knew who'd get his filthy mitts on it, and to my mind Granville had enough wheels anyway.

I shook my head. 'I'm just checking out.' I slapped the key card on the desk as evidence.

'But is there something wrong? We have a reservation for you for five nights. Last night, that was what was booked.' No, definitely not French. Somewhere much further east, surely.

'In that case,' I said, with what I hoped was aplomb, though I'd never been entirely sure what that was, 'I'll be in for dinner.'

Which meant a couple of additions to that list. It was going to be hard enough eating on my own in a place like this – how on earth did Cinderella feel going into that ball-room alone? – I wasn't going to make it any worse by turning up in the jeans and top that, for want of anything else, I'd had to wear for work. If it had been the Daweses' money paying for everything, I might have had second thoughts about all this spending. As it was – and though somewhere deep down I realised that everyone who took out a policy would be paying for my treat – Todd's insurance company seemed so distant and anonymous I should really enjoy spending it.

The question was, as I realised when Paula strode into the foyer, when.

'I suppose you could take Trev into Folkestone at lunchtime,' she said, getting into the passenger seat. 'It took me five whole minutes to start the bugger this morning,' she explained. 'He must be missing you.'

'Needing a service, more like.'

Paula didn't like helpful suggestions. 'I suppose Canterbury's got a better range of shops, but at least you can park in Folkestone if you don't mind paying through the nose, and there's a Debenhams right in the middle. Plus a Marks and Sparks for undies and things. Your mate Moffatt called me this morning. He said to make sure you bought enough to last several days. The police would fork out for what Todd's insurance wouldn't.' She was quiet for a bit, then said, 'We've got ourselves into something big here, Caffy. Do you think we can cope with it?'

'It's either that or go under.' It wasn't quite the answer to her question but it was the best I could manage. I tried again. 'Maybe Moffatt'll come up with an undercover cop to look after us.'

'He didn't say anything?'

'I think he's worried about the money involved – remember all that stuff on Meg's radio about police budgets?' I refused to think about that swimsuit. 'Unless he didn't think he could find someone who could paint.'

'Not Taz again?' She dropped her voice a little as if she were speaking to an invalid.

I breezed back, 'Well, he's really with the Met. And he's very junior – he wasn't really here in any official capacity.'

'He seems to have known who to speak to, though. I didn't know quite what to make of him,' she continued. 'I mean, he's a real dream to look at – he ought to be on TV, in one of those costume dramas. Imagine him in knee-breeches.

Heathcliff! Caffy!' she called out, clasping her hands on her chest, as if the joke were new. Believe me it wasn't. Then she looked at me. 'Do you know what I think? I think he's like one of those gorgeous chocs you get given at Christmas, no other time, not just inside a lovely box but specially wrapped, too. Lindt, I think.'

I didn't comment.

'Imagine a choc like that, only when you bite into it it's hollow.'

I nodded. I got the gist, at least. 'But he's not, not really,' I protested. 'He got me out of ten kinds of mess – before.'

'You know something,' she said. 'I reckon you may have been in ten kinds of mess but the person who got you out wasn't him, but you.'

'I couldn't have done it without him,' I insisted.

'Or what you thought was him.' Paula always liked to have the last word, so I thought it was best to let her.

There was a beat-up old utility truck parked outside the manor gates. The driver waved Paula over as she got out to open them. After a few moments' conversation, she pointed. He followed me in and parked alongside me.

Paula's smile was as dry as they come. 'This is Sid,' she said. 'Come for a day's trial, he says.'

We shook hands solemnly.

Whereas Taz looked a likely subject for a painter, Sid looked ready to slap the old pigment anywhere it was needed. He was built, to use the elegant Midlands expression of my childhood that fear of offending Paula had once made me stifle, like a brick shithouse, giving the impression he could carry not just a hod of bricks but Paula and me to balance the other shoulder, so to speak. 'You give the orders, Guv,' he told Paula, 'so far as this job's concerned.'

To my ears, everyone south of Watford talks like Eliza Dolittle before the Professor got at her, but this was the thickest Southern accent I'd ever heard.

Paula took him over to meet the others, simply introducing him as Sid.

'Morning, girls – a nuvver nice day. Jus' wo' ve doctor ordered. Wo' we go' to do today, ven?'

Girls. We always referred to ourselves and each other as women. And no professional painter would welcome broiling heat like this. Our smiles were polite, no more.

Paula sent him to rub down the window Taz had botched. She turned to us all: 'Well?'

'It's the way he talks that does my head in,' I said.

'Glottal stops,' Meg said.

'What's a glottal?' Helen asked.

'A glottal stop is where instead of moving your tongue forward to say "t" or whatever, you just stop it. "Wha'ever", not "whatever": get it?'

'So what's a glottal?' she repeated.

'Maybe it's something to do with an epiglottis,' Meg pondered, and off they went, still talking.

Van der Poele was in the house all morning, so there was no opportunity for heroics, with or without glottals. Sid rubbed down and dusted off and even applied a turpsy rag to his window frame before applying primer. His movements were surprisingly delicate, quite finicky, for such a big man, his great bananas of fingers curling round the brush-head almost protectively.

God, it was so hot. We'd all been known to paint in shorts and bikini tops, but for various reasons none of us seemed inclined to strip today. Either we felt it would be wrong with a male in our midst, or we couldn't face the thought of Sid's naked beerbelly flopping round overhead. At lunchtime, the van was like a sauna, despite being parked in the shade with the windows and doors wide open. It started first time and I got into reverse.

''Ere, young lady! Wha' d'you fink you're up to, ven?'

'Going into Folkestone for a spot of shopping, Sid. Want a lift?'

In answer he zipped round to the passenger door and popped inside. 'At least I should be able to use this,' he said, flourishing his mobile.

'Not until about a mile down the road. Pain, isn't it?' We set off.

'You know what it means, though: it means His Nibs in there has to use a landline – should be able to get a tap on that.' In private, his accent, though pretty strong, was at least no longer impenetrable.

'Emails?'

He tapped his nose, settling back to enjoy a really scenic ride in what seemed like contented silence.

As we picked up the motorway, he dabbed away with those enormous digits, and was soon muttering into the handset. As the one most intimately involved, I'd have liked a decent chance to eavesdrop, but he hunched away from me, and the van's engine noise – it really did need a service, by the sound of it – and the nasty concrete road surface combined to drown him out.

The traffic in Folkestone was holiday-season bad, and parking, when I got to the town centre car park I wanted, was dodgy. I might have squeezed into some of those tiny spaces in a Fiesta, but I was after something a tad more spacious. At last a little old lady pulled her Nissan Micra out of a slot big enough for a Sherman tank and I dived in, much to the chagrin of a family in a people carrier. Tough. I'd only twenty minutes to shop and they had all day to drift round.

'See you back here at ten past?' I asked Sid.

'See me every time you turn round, more like,' he said. 'I'm sticking with you, kid.'

'I've got to buy undies,' I said firmly.

'I shall be an embarrassed hubby. OK, embarrassed dad,' he corrected himself.

And I would be an embarrassed young woman, unless I could shake him off. I set a cracking pace.

The bugger kep' up with me, step for swea'y step.

'This a'ernoon,' he informed me, 'I dun 'alf fancy having a quick shuftie round the building. Any ideas?'

'Provided van der Poele's out of the way, ask Paula to do what she did for Taz – give a conducted tour. Your boss should have told you: she's got a detailed ground plan you might find useful.'

He nodded. 'And if he doesn't go out?'

'She probably wouldn't want to risk it. The only thing she might do is go inside herself to open a window for you to paint the frame. But if you went in for no reason and he caught you out, she'd sack you in front of him. Assuming the dogs left her anything to sack.'

'Ah,' he said. And fell silent.

I felt quite sorry for him as the women descended on my bags of shopping, Paula quite forgetting to point out that I'd extended my lunch-hour. I'd have extended it even more had Sid not driven while I chomped a Marks and Sparks sarnie. And sorry for the women too – much as I'd wanted to splurge, I'd had no time to do more than grab the essentials on my list, and there's not much to squeal about when it comes to multipacks of knickers, socks, clean jeans and a couple of T-shirts. Even my bra was bog-standard. But they did have a little squeak over what I'd bought for evenings in the hotel, a slinky wrap-around skirt and skinny tops – two for the price of one. The trouble was, if I often ate the sort of meal put before me last night, I'd soon need a bigger size: there's nothing like being poor to control calorie intake. Except, of course, for the temptation to buy filling, comforting junk food. Thank goodness I've never had a sweet tooth, and an early tendency to spots kept me off the greasy end of the market. But there was a clear stone less of me than when I was on the game, and I'd not been fat then.

Paula coughed and looked at her watch. The stuff went back into the bags and into Trev, and we started work. Paula's only concession to the heat was individual water bottles for each of us and a reminder to wear our floppy sunhats.

It was a good job Sid was handy with a paintbrush: there was no chance for him to do anything else. Van der Poele lurked inside all day, only appearing – just as we were about to descend for our tea-break – with the damned dogs, one of which took instant exception to Sid, snarling furiously at the bottom of his ladder. Sid appeared to take no notice – but he stopped working on those tricky window edges and addressed himself to the sills instead.

Paula, descending from her ladder to snapping distance, called coolly, 'Bring them to heel, Mr van der Poele. They're putting my workers at risk, rushing at the ladders like that.' When he took no notice, she added, 'An investigation into a fatal accident by the Health and Safety inspectors would set us back days. If not weeks.'

Not to mention bringing all sorts of unwelcome visitors to the site. Van der Poele scowled and whistled. These days he seemed to be able to manage them without that whip. The dogs slunk back to him, but not without a couple of farewell growls.

'You've brought in another man,' he said, as if blaming Paula for the canine fuss.

'You asked for speed: that means more workers.'

'What happened to that pretty boy?'

'I had to let him go. You didn't see the mess he made of the only window he tried.'

'Hmph. OK. So what time are you finishing tonight?'

'We'll take our tea break as soon as the dogs are inside,' she said pointedly, 'and work on till five-thirty.'

'But there are still a couple of hours of daylight after that.'

'That's the standard day, as I explained when you accepted our estimate. We have to abide by the European directives on working hours. Unless,' she added, with a limpid smile, 'you pay cash overtime like you did this weekend.'

There'd be no overtime tonight, that was clear as he stomped off inside. And I don't think, as we eased our sweaty bodies inside soaked clothes, that we particularly cared.

I transferred my purchases to the utility truck, Sid having informed me that he'd be running me back. I assumed he meant to the hotel, and was basking in anticipation of a luxurious bath, followed by dinner in my new gear.

But he pulled into a lay-by only half a mile from Crabton Manor and poked his mobile. 'Zilch. No effin' phones, no effin' roads. What a bloody place. Bet you wish you were back in Brum sometimes, don't you?' he added, as if to encourage a bit of a natter – if without any 'T's'.

'Not very often. Except I do miss a good balti.'

He put his phone away. 'Funny bugger that van der Poele of yours,' he said, without remarking my choice of food.

'His dogs didn't think much of you, did they? Perhaps it's true what they say – you can smell a copper a mile off. Though you're dead nifty with a paintbrush,' I added, not wanting to offend him.

'My dad was in the trade. He'd have skinned me alive for a single paint drool.'

'Quite right. Tell me, are you here to protect us or to get access to the building? Or a bit of both?'

'Whatever, I was wasting my time today, wasn't I? Strikes me that Paula could have taken on Hitler and won. Pity she doesn't play cricket – we could do with her in the England team, couldn't we?'

I explained about sport in the paper and the radio being dedicated to Meg's news programmes.

'That's what's so different about your lot,' he said, snapping his thumb and finger. 'No nasty little trannies, all tuned to different stations.'

'If we want music, we wear Walkmans.'

'A bit hot for anything extra, even that light,' he sighed, mopping the back of his neck. 'Can you navigate from here, like?'

I looked at my watch. 'My betting is that now he thinks we've gone, van der Poele will have gone out. I had to leave a couple of windows ajar. If you fancy a shuftie I'll keep watch.'

Despite his apparent eagerness earlier, he asked cautiously, 'What about them bleeding dogs?'

'He usually locks them in an outhouse.'

'Bit rough on the poor buggers in this weather. I wonder if we could call in the RSPCA.'

'You're welcome – when we've finished. We need the money, remember.'

'You really expect him to pay?' he half-sneered.

'Paula shares your view of him, so he's paid in advance for the materials. And he paid cash for the weekend overtime, which is why he was miffed with us for finishing on time today.'

'I wondered about that. Bit of a risk, isn't it?'

'You mean you'd expect us to work all hours God sends and be surprised when we end up with damaged joints from climbing all the ladders or repetitive strain injury from too much waggling the wrist back and forward?'

'Well, I –'

'Would you expect a team of men to work extra for no more pay? Well, then. We're just the same as men – only we're women.'

He threw his head back and laughed. I had to join in. At last, he wiped his streaming eyes and asked, 'You're sure about these dogs, then?'

'No. But we can case the joint.'

'And not take any risks.'

'Sid, if you'd rather, we can wait until you've got a search warrant, I's dotted and T's crossed. I just sense you found today a bit of a waste of time.'

He looked guilty. 'Thing is, Lucy, I ought to wait for a warrant. I'm supposed to be a cross between undercover and doing obbo, not to mention a spot of protection. So I really shouldn't be in there. Not unless I have a really good excuse.'

'In that case,' I said, 'do you want to keep an eye on things while I have a hunt? – so long as you tell me what I'm supposed to be hunting for.'

Chapter Sixteen

Sid was tempted, there was no doubt about that.

'That's one reason why I changed my appearance,' I pointed out. 'Van der Poele had already caught me taking an interest in the house and I thought if I turned up as someone else I could carry on working here and have a sniff round if necessary. I don't usually look like the raddled oldest inhabitant of some inner-city whorehouse,' I added brutally.

'I never said you did. But it's risky, see, now we're not working – and I'm supposed to be keeping an eye on you, not you keeping an eye open for me.' Why was he backtracking as fast as he could? 'I'm supposed to get you back to that posh hotel of yours, too, all in one piece. Plus your shopping, of course,' he added. 'You've done well today, haven't you?'

'How do you mean?' I kept my voice flat as the Marsh.

'Buying all this stuff. Pay-rolled by this posh geyser.'

Ah. A none-too-subtle allusion to my past. But I'd keep cool. 'And his wife. My legal adviser.'

He looked taken aback. Good.

'Who have made me a loan.' I stressed the last word slightly. 'I need essentials, since the police haven't got round to getting my own gear back. In fact,' I said, suddenly tiring of the game, 'why don't we go and see what's happening in my Des. Res. right now? Turn left at the end of the road here. No, hang on.' I grabbed a couple of bags and opened the passenger door. 'I'm going behind that hedge and no peeping.'

So when we turned up at Fullers, in my clean jeans and T-shirt and lurking under sunhat and sunglasses, I wasn't recognisable as anyone in particular. Moffatt and his men had done a good job publicising the poor caravan's demise: there were still a couple of TV vans and several bored looking reporters currently flaking out in the shade of handy trees. I had half a mind to join the reporters and ask a few questions, and was even tempted to duck under the police tape, but rejected both ideas as silly – I wanted to see, not be seen. I nudged Sid, now also stripped down to jeans and T-shirt, into action. 'Go on, just sidle over to that bunch there and ask what's been going on. Go on – just think of it as a bit of detective work, but stay in role.'

'In wha'?'

It took me a second to realise he was sending me up. He winked and set off, rolling his bulk in an exaggerated waddle.

Of course, as we both knew, we could have simply phoned whoever was really working on this case. The question was, who. Last night Moffatt might have been a kind old geyser enjoying playing Santa Claus to a poor vulnerable girl, but by day he'd be sitting at a desk delegating like mad. As for Taz, he was now back in London doing whatever young constables do. I blushed. I'd never even asked him about his real work, as opposed to the Saturday job I'd wished upon him. A few years ago and I'd have hung upon his every word, as he described to me the horrendous pressures of his job – oh, he'd always changed the names in his case-load, in the interests of confidentiality. Come to think of it, I wonder how many fellow-clients he'd told about his whore with a heart of whatever. Funny, such a thought wouldn't even have entered my head a week ago.

Broiling in the utility cab, I wondered how much Sid

really knew about the set-up. I was sure he'd have a contact number for emergencies, but he hadn't been awash with information, had he?

He came toddling back. He really was a small-framed man – yes, lanky, but light with it – who'd put on a huge amount of weight. When I knew him better, I'd talk to him about a diet. I reckon I'd saved several punters' lives in my day, pointing out the only exercise they ever seemed to get was with me and that I preferred them not to smell of beer and chips. Blood pressure, too – I succeeded in getting one chap off salt when he'd simply ignored the doctor's threats. Well, it brings it home to a man, the thought of an undertaker collecting him from a bed other than his wife's. They never pointed out that they'd not be alive to feel embarrassed – perhaps they'd hoped I'd break my rule about mouth contact and give the kiss of life. And maybe I'd massage their hearts, having experience with other apparently lifeless organs.

'Well, well,' he said. 'It seems the poor young lady staying at the caravan is currently fighting for her life in the William Harvey Hospital. Under police guard, of course.'

'Is she expected to live?'

He shook his head sadly. 'Terrible facial injuries. If she lives, there'll be years of plastic surgery ahead of her.'

'Poor girl. Any idea how it happened?' The well-placed police vans meant you couldn't see either the front of Fullers or the caravan itself.

'There's talk of a Calor-gas explosion. But no one seems to believe that.'

'You couldn't use a bit of your influence and go and look at the house?'

'You're off your head, girl. How can a painter get beyond the lines? Hey, you're really upset, aren't you? Tell you what, in that outfit you could always claim to be the deceased's sister, casting her beadies over the scene of death. Nothing odd in that, these days – they even fly relatives to where aircraft have crashed, though I must say it seems dead ghoulish to me.'

Although I'd be unrecognisable, I didn't think the press'd buy the idea of a grieving relative emerging from a decorator's ute., so I said, 'Perhaps we'd better wait till she's properly dead. OK, time for an early bath, I'd say.'

Sid was backing the van to turn into a gateway when he was tooted loudly, indeed offensively.

'Effin' Volvos,' Sid muttered, offering a small selection of fingers for the driver to count.

'Just get the hell out of here,' I muttered. 'I know you'd like to dot him, but I'd rather you didn't.'

Obligingly, Sid simply pulled on to the road and drove back towards the hotel. To any onlooker, I was too engrossed in the crime scene to turn my head.

'Find a lane and pull into it,' I said, 'and phone Moffatt or whoever. The bloke who tooted was Clive Granville.'

'Not a big-time player like him in an effin' Volvo!'

'It isn't just you and me who can go down to the woods in disguise,' I said. 'Pull over there and dial while I can still remember the registration number.'

He obliged. I'd have loved to hear the reaction of the person on the other end.

I don't know what I expected at the hotel. Some sort of

welcome committee from the police updating me? I checked
with the receptionist when I picked up my key that there
were no messages. Nor was there anything on my room's
answerphone. Hmm. Nothing to do except have that early
bath, then. As I stripped I slapped my head in anger. I never
take a bath without the company of a good book, and I had-
n't had the nous to buy one in Folkestone. Paula wouldn't
really have begrudged me the extra five minutes it would
have taken. True, she and the others wouldn't have demanded to see the contents of a book bag, but a good paperback
would have been a better investment than any of the clothes.
Well, as good. Slinging that fluffy robe on, I watched a bit of
early evening TV, flicking between channels till I found an
item on 'my' explosion. The footage was pretty poor – just a
few hot, sweaty policemen and a load of tape. Would that
have been enough to convince Granville that he'd got me?
That he could lay off and return to his usual occupations of
kinky sex and money-making? Certainly the newsreader did
his bit, eyes downcast and voice as sombre as if he were com-
mentating on the Queen Ma's funeral. It was all I could do
not to dab away a sympathetic tear.

After the news, it dawned on me that I ought to eat.
Maybe a swim first? That was a good idea. A swim, then the
early bath. And bother the poor old hair.

But what about a book?

I managed a further dozen or so lengths, then hopped
into the Jacuzzi for a few minutes. The subterranean gur-
glings weren't all plumbing induced, however. My tum was
joining in. I'd have to eat. On my own. In the posh dining
room.

I put the process off as long as possible by showering and washing and drying my hair, now the texture of a politically incorrect golly I dimly remembered from my childhood. I even toyed with a meal from room service, but I dismissed that as cowardice. In any case, there was nothing on TV and no book to read as I ate.

Hair apart, I was chic enough as I presented myself in the bar where Moffatt had entertained us last night. When no waiters leapt to my side, I simply bought a drink at the bar. I'd done that time enough in the past, goodness knows. This time I didn't scan the bar for the potential client, and I asked for it to be charged to my room. Kent Constabulary could surely afford a chilled white wine. Keeping my eyes demurely lowered, I retired to a table by the open window and sat studying the menu as if I was to be tested on it at the end of the evening. At longish last, a waitress sauntered over to take my order. Her body language told me where a woman on her own with no executive briefcase to fiddle with would find herself sitting – in a corner by the service table. My mouth demanded a table on the terrace. She opened hers to tell me that they were all booked, but perhaps she caught something of the steel in my eyes.

So I ate overlooking the golf course, my back to my fellow diners. Logic told me I should be facing the room with my back to a wall, as one or two of my police clients told me they preferred. But I couldn't face an hour of avoiding eye-contact with people. And the view over that neat grass in the evening light was pleasant enough.

For company I'd brought the notepad and pencil I'd used earlier. A list for the following day was headed by the simple word book. In fact, that was the list. Bored, I turned to what I'd written the previous night. Information. Why had that word stuck? What information had I given? And to whom? The smoked trout and avocado didn't give me any clues, nor did the herbed chicken. But as I debated the merits of a sweet or coffee, something seemed to fall into place. I must have said something to Sergeant Marsh that had triggered his interest. When had he got up? What was the precise moment he'd said he'd talk to his colleagues?

When I'd said we did jobs of all sizes, one day a pensioner's bungalow, the next – yes, I'd said we hoped to get the contract to restore the interior of Fullers. Fullers on the Isle of Oxney. It was at that point he'd bolted.

It was back to Fullers I had to go, then.

But how?

Now I came to think about it, it was something I'd rather do without any police assistance. Telling myself I was simply going for a walk in the evening sun, I mooched round to the part of the hotel guests don't normally see. The bins. The bottle bank. The staff going to and fro. To, in this case, involved a kid on a pushbike, hot and bothered and obviously late for his shift.

'Hi. My name's Lucy. Could I borrow your cycle? Just for an hour or two? It'll be back here when you need it.'

He snorted. 'Gives you a bit of time then – I'm on till two. Twenty quid. Mal.' He shoved out a hand. I couldn't blame him: he was probably earning even less than I was.

'I'm borrowing it, not bloody buying it! Fiver.'

We settled for one of the Daweses' tenners.

* * *

Fortunately for me the hotel lay to the west of the Isle, so I had a long gentle upwards slope to deal with, not the steep one I'd run up the other day. All the same, for someone not used to a bike – it was true, thank God, you didn't forget how to ride one – it was bloody hard work, and at last I had to get off and push. It wasn't as if I was in any hurry.

There were still a couple of cops there, trying to look as if they were doing something meaningful, not just having a smoke and basking in the sun's last rays. I flipped a mental coin: to talk to them or keep mum? In the event it was no contest. They couldn't have been as dozy as they looked, because one clocked me, despite my quiet arrival. He beckoned me over, unsmiling.

Good job I'd got a story ready. 'I'm a friend of Caffy's,' I said. 'They won't let me see her yet, and I just wanted to see – you know, where she'd been …' My voice quivered.

'I'm not sure the SOCO team have finished yet.'

I might have known he'd be a jobsworth, though he was a bit young for that sort of attitude – twenty-five or -six, maybe, and scrawny with it. His hair was thinning already.

'I wouldn't touch or anything. The name's Lucy Taylor.' I gave my old address.

The older guy shrugged. 'Why not, so long as you wear these?' He ferreted in his back pocket and produced a pair of overshoes. 'You'll have to take her, mate.' So he could return to the fag half-concealed behind his back, no doubt.

'Have you known this Caffy woman long?' the young cop asked. Marks for knowing the background, at least.

'Years. On and off. I was telling one of your mates. Sid, I think his name is. Big bloke, drinks a lot of beer I should think.'

The young man shrugged.

'If I'm Lucy, what's your name?' I did a bit of hip-swinging, just to encourage him. It was awful how familiar the routine remained, though I hadn't practised for years. Perhaps I should have used it on Taz, after all.

He responded with a swagger of his bony shoulders and narrow hips. Bingo. 'Simon. Simon Wallace. You won't touch anything, will you?' The way he was standing he might have meant the direct opposite.

'Cross my heart,' I promised, doing just that.

He registered breasts even I had always thought quite good.

We turned the corner and suddenly I didn't feel so perky. The side of the caravan had been blown off, breaking some of Fullers' windows. They'd been boarded over. Despite myself, I gasped and covered my mouth, turning away instinctively. Wrong. I turned towards the caravan, not away from it, as I'm sure I'd have done if I really was imagining a friend's suffering. But Simon didn't seem to notice.

'Must have been a nice place before. We have to make sure it isn't looted, of course,' he said proudly, nodding at the caravan.

'Anything left in one piece?'

'Not a lot. Still, they're stinking rich and there's always the insurance.'

'What about the house?' I wasn't much good at this, was I?

Simon shrugged. 'Needed a lot doing before – just needs a bit more now. Fancy taking on a dump like that.'

'Caffy said it was nice inside,' I said wistfully. 'I suppose I couldn't …' But the team who'd boarded up were used to people like me, and there wasn't a single crack I could press an eye to. I shook my head regretfully and turned to go. I knew the lie of the land, now, and there wasn't much point in hanging round. After all, if the house were being used for people smuggling or whatever, then all the fuss on the TV would make sure it wasn't used again, at least while there was a police presence. Unless Marsh put his cronies on guard, cutting them in on the deal. Now that was worth thinking about. Meanwhile, if I went quietly this first evening, maybe I'd get friendly with young Simon and wheedle him into letting me into the house. Something else had occurred to me: if my sleeping quarters were almost undetectable, then I'd bet my teeth that there were other hidden places. Priest holes, cellars for smugglers and their booty. There'd be something, wouldn't there? And if anyone could find it it'd be people like Paula and me. The only question was whether we should come back illicitly, as in my original plan, or be open about it to Sid. I'd give it thought as I headed back to the hotel. At least it was almost all downhill.

I hitched myself on to the bike.

'Oi, Lucy Whateveryournameis, where d'you think you're off to?' Simon's mate yelled.

I nearly fell off. 'Back home,' I said inaccurately.

'Not on that bike, you're not. No lights. And it'll be pitch dark before you get back to Ashford.'

'Cycle lanes,' I said with more hope than confidence.

'Still need lights. Don't she, Simon?'

'Absolutely.'

'I shall have to push the bloody thing,' I said.

'I'm sure young Simon'd be happy to give you a lift, soon as we finish here. Tennish, that'll be.' He jerked a thumb at the police car.

'I suppose you can't leave till someone else takes over,' I said, all winsome.

'That's right.'

'Well, bollocks to that.' But I only said it in my head. And I did what I'd seen kids do, dab a foot on a pedal, shove off, and swing the spare leg across the crossbar while on the move. I couldn't quite manage the leg bit, not without risking intimate acquaintance with a healthy bank of nettles, but I managed a damned fine scoot. It wasn't until the men were beyond earshot that I stopped, pulled under a tree and got on properly. Good job I did, actually. A police car swished past me, right down the road I'd been heading for. I found what claimed to be a bridlepath going roughly the same way. Roughly indeed. It was so rutted my teeth were nearly shaken out of my head. But I stuck it out. And, at last having picked up a proper tarmaced road, I had time to wonder exactly why they'd been so keen to bring an errant cyclist to book that they'd abandoned an important crime scene. Pity I was simply too knackered to cycle all the way back up again and take advantage of their absence to let myself into Fullers. No, not to hunt for priest holes. To rescue a book.

Chapter Seventeen

It was lucky I'd worked out how to set the phone wake-up call because, book or no book, once I collapsed into bed, I slept like the dead. All that exercise, I suppose.

True, I hadn't gone all the way back up to Fullers. Once off my track and on the main road I'd realised the wisdom of the two officers' objection to my cycling without lights. I was simply invisible to passing motorists. Perhaps I'd been paranoid: the cops really had wanted to protect me, not to hunt me down. I quickly abandoned any hope of arriving in one piece if I cycled back the hotel, so I swallowed my pride, dismounted and pushed the damned bike all the way back on the right side of the road, facing oncoming traffic. At least that way I'd see them even if they didn't see me. If I did manage to get into Fullers the following night, then I'd rescue that powerful lantern torch too.

I was dog-tired and hot and sticky when I made it back to the area behind the kitchen. So when I saw the cycle's owner propping up the back door, lighting up, I lost my rag. How could he manage to smoke, on his wage? And if he could afford cigarettes, he could afford lights for his bike! I slapped a fiver in his hand. 'No bloody lights!' I snarled. And realised, rather late, that I was dependent on the bike for transport later in the week. I fished out a reluctant tenner. 'But you can have this if you make sure you've got some for next time.'

'Next time?' He pocketed it.

'Like tomorrow.'

He shook his head, innocent as a cherub. 'Evening off.' And he disappeared inside.

The sad thing was, my legs were too weary to give chase. A shower and bed called.

'The ground-plan of Fullers?' Paula queried as soon as I could get her on her own at Crabton Manor. 'Why?'

Sid had been rather more in policeman-mode when he picked me up this morning, I thought. He'd checked to see if I'd heard any more from Moffatt and asked how I'd spent the previous evening, pressing quite hard when I was evasive. Surely he couldn't be in cahoots with the men up at Fullers? All my life I'd lived in a world where I could trust no one. Now I'd met Paula, the rest of the Pots and now the Daweses, of course, I'd learnt there were people you could believe in. It was disappointing to say the least to be reminded of the other world. Now, narrow-eyed, Sid turned to see why I wasn't following him up on to the scaffolding.

I touched the side of my nose. 'Have you got one?' I pressed her, very quietly. He'd have had to come all the way back down again if he wanted to eavesdrop.

'Not here, but – '

'Are you here all day or out and about?'

Unless they knew her very well, no one would know from Paula's face that she was trying not to laugh. 'If I have to go and estimate for a job down in Hythe, you'd like me to pop into the office and bring it back here?'

Office! Her front room, more like.

'I'd like it even more if we could go to the pub after work

and you give me a lift back to the hotel. I'm sure Sid would appreciate being let off.'

'I'm sure he wouldn't. Watches you like a hawk, doesn't he? He seems OK, but you never know with men that size,' she added obscurely. 'I'll have to check the diary, of course – but it seems like a good idea to me.'

Cheered immensely, I was up the ladders like a monkey and painted with a will all day. Sid was mutinous when Paula announced she was leaving us on our own. She was quick to explain to him that she was responsible for drumming up new business and she trusted us to be as professional as she was. Both jaws set. To prevent an anticlimax, I nipped round and started the van for her. She hopped in and was away, leaving the rest of us debating which was worse, another day in the hot but increasingly milky sun, or a day zapping round in a van the cooling system of which was happier in winter. The answer was probably neither. The scaffolding platform was like a high-level sauna, as the day got progressively more humid.

'What's the forecast?' I asked Meg over a mid-afternoon bottle of water.

'Storms in France may drift north. May not.'

'Wouldn't bet on them staying put,' I said.

'What'll you girls do if it does rain tomorrow?' Sid asked.

Meg stared. 'What all decorators do – work on an indoor project!' She didn't ask on which planet he'd spent his working life, but might just as well.

'Is that where Paula's gone? To find something for you to do tomorrow?'

Even Helen sighed. 'She's doing forward planning, isn't

she? You don't just turn up at this house and say, right, lady, we'll do your hall now. You have to give estimates and negotiate dates and then when you're ready and they're ready you have to check they still want the same colours they originally chose. And then we start.'

None of us seemed to want to tell him that on a wet day we'd be busy at Fullers. Meg looked at her watch. Without another word, we resumed our stations and worked with a will. At least the women did. Sid pithered round down below – the sort of time-wasting that gets our profession a bad name.

Paula was back about five, up beside us checking on our progress, nodding as we outlined any problems that had made us take longer than expected. By the time she gathered us together as we cleared away the paint and brushes we could see that all was not well.

'Helen – what you've done is meticulous. But when the sky's this colour, and you're doing bits you can only see from the ground if you lie flat on your back and use binoculars, you don't have to do the Sistine Chapel act, you know.'

Helen produced a sly smile. 'More like Angelica Kauffmann since I'm female.'

Paula snorted. 'Been talking to Caffy, have you?' She stopped short, flushing crimson.

'Not,' Helen replied, attacking her hands with white spirit, 'since she went away. Oh, Paula – have you heard from her? Do you think she's OK?'

I've no idea how many women from Kent have won Oscars, but Helen certainly deserved one. Her voice was near to breaking, her little mouth quivering. So why hadn't Paula told them who Sid was? They'd certainly known about me and Taz, and had, come to think of it, said suspiciously little – zilch, indeed – since his rapid departure. It was clear Paula and I needed a long talk, and not just about the internal dimensions of Fullers.

'Now, Sid,' Paula said, 'I need a word before we go.' She indicated that he was to step aside with her. He stepped.

Helen's eyes rounded. 'Looks like bollocking time,' she whispered.

'That's what you get if you don't pull your weight,' Meg observed.

Sid seemed to be suffering a slow puncture. Quite a fast one, actually. You could see him shrinking. Paula could be quite caustic if necessary. Then it dawned on me that we weren't alone. Van der Poele was exercising his dogs – on leads! Well, if Paula could put the fear of God into that hard-headed brute, no wonder Sid was stuttering an apology. Words like 'earn your keep' and 'passengers' echoed round.

At last Sid slunk to the cab to his utility truck. He stuck a humbled head out. 'Will you be wanting a lift, Lucy?'

'I think Paula wants to talk over a new job with me,' I said. 'But tomorrow morning – yes, please. Same time, same place.'

We prepared to pile into the Transit. One of us had to squat illegally in the back, of course. I'm sure van der Poele wouldn't have turned a hair, but given Sid's real job, he'd have to shove his oar in. I caught her eye. Almost imperceptibly, she nodded. But she made sure Sid gave both Meg and Helen a lift. They lived in the opposite direction from the one he'd offered to take me. Lots of smiles and waves,

including gracious ones to van der Poele, who responded
with a sneer, and we went our separate ways, me in the driving seat to make sure the van started.

'Daft bugger, to be idling when van der Poele's watching,'
Paula observed. 'Don't think much of these undercover cops,
and that's the truth. That Taz of yours…'

'Not mine. Why haven't you told the others Sid isn't
kosher?'

Though I kept my eyes on the road, I could feel her eyes
on me.

'Did I need to?'

'Suppose not. Just wondered.'

'I don't like him,' she continued. 'And I'm not sure how
far I trust him.'

'Or some of his colleagues,' I agreed. I told her about the
previous evening.

'So why do you want the plan if the place is guarded and
you can't get in? Plus no transport. And don't look at me like
you want to look because the answer's no. The van's far too
public to try and sneak in unnoticed.'

'That's the point,' I said with as much conviction as if
that had been part of my plan all along. To be honest, I was
thinking on my bum. 'We go all open and above board.
You've got the contract to decorate Fullers. What more likely
scenario than that you want to go and check out what we
need to start work on a nasty rainy day like tomorrow's going
to be? And that I'd be with you?'

'They'll recognise you.'

'Like this? With these shades?' For good measure I pulled

my baseball cap back to front, so all my golly-locks were covered. 'I looked quite chic last night,' I said. 'New top, new jeans. I go in with you in my painty T-shirt and dungarees and no one'll give me a second glance. Specially if you fix them with your Medusa eye.'

'It's one thing putting up with you talking posh if you're Caffy,' she objected. 'But not when you're Lucy, if you don't mind. OK. Pull over into that lay-by and put your overalls back on.'

'But it's miles yet. I shall melt!'

'So what?'

I was getting out of the cab when she relented. 'OK. Let's grab something in that pub over there first. You can cast your eyes over these plans while it's still light.' She pointed upwards. 'The way those clouds are building up it'll be dark well before it's officially dusk – or anything like it. And the murkier it is, to my mind, the better. I take it there's a torch there?'

'A whopper up in my eyrie.'

I parked up. Without hesitating, she pointed to a picnic table in the furthest corner of the garden and strode off to the bar, returning with two mineral waters topped with ice and lemon and dropping the bar menu on the plans beside me. 'My treat,' she said, offhand.

I knew better than to be effusive. 'Thanks. How's your maths, Paula?' We both knew it was good enough for her to do all her working out without a calculator. Once a hapless client had tried to prove that she'd quoted for more wallpaper than was necessary. She was both faster and more accurate than the calculator she later kindly showed him how to use.

My ambition was to be as quick and accurate as she was. And certainly better than the average client. I set to, as well.

'What have you found?' she asked.

'Nothing yet. But if you take that side and I take this, I reckon we should see how many feet we know we've got and how many we should have. I'm thinking some of these walls may be thick enough to hide – well, all sorts of things.'

'You add, I'll order. What do you fancy?'

After all the fancy fare at the hotel, courtesy the police, I was happy to read the menu from right to left. Paula was more than my boss, she was my friend, and I knew how little she took home, even though the firm was hers. She might be Business Woman of the Year in my book, but fat cat she certainly wasn't.

She narrowed her eyes shrewdly when I asked for salad, but headed for the bar, leaving me with her mobile phone. Which rang almost on cue.

A possible job? We can all be Paula's efficient secretary when called on, so I didn't hesitate to answer. To hear a familiar voice.

'That's Caffy, isn't it?'

'Jan! How wonderful! But should you be talking to me?'

'This hotel has a very big switchboard, love.' It was a long time since anyone had called me that and sounded as if they meant it. 'How are you getting on?'

I gave a brief account of my hotel holiday: my painting days wouldn't rate anyone's phone call, not at hotel rates to a mobile.

'How are you finding the police?'

What could I say? 'Someone seems to be taking me seriously,' I managed, 'given the cost of my accommodation. But Jan, your poor caravan – '

'Tin and cardboard,' she dismissed it. 'But what about Fullers?'

'Well boarded-up. But I shall know better tonight. Rain's forecast, so we may be working on it tomorrow.'

There was a pause while I heard her muffled voice repeat what I'd said.

'You don't take any risks, do you hear?' Todd's voice came, like an anxious father's.

'Of course not,' I said, grinning so he could hear the smile in my voice. 'Don't worry: Paula and the others will be there. And I'm afraid that if it doesn't rain we shall still be at Crabton Manor.'

'Have the police done anything about that yet?'

Or indeed about Granville's car. They weren't very informative, were they? 'You know, I've been too busy painting to think about it. But now you come to mention it, no. Not that we've heard. We know they've got photos and the bit of rope that Paula gave them, and I'd trust Taz to have seen they went to someone reliable. Moffatt seemed terribly keen on sorting everything out at Fullers. But no one's done a lot at Crabton. Mind you, van der Poele's been in residence, so Sid, our undercover guy, hasn't had time for a sneak round.'

'Sneak round! They've surely got enough for a search warrant. I wonder what the hell's going on.'

'So do I. Todd, Paula's just coming back, did Jan want to talk to her?' I waved the phone at Paula, mouthing, 'Jan Dawes for you,' and took myself off to the loo so they could talk business if they wanted. I had a good scrub and returned to hear Paula's laugh. They'd had a good long natter, then. No, I wouldn't get wistful. Especially not when I saw how

Paula had interpreted my request for a salad. Greenery yes, but with a burger and chips on the side, as it were. She tucked into hers, passing me the phone.

'No risks, remember,' Todd repeated. 'I've told Paula that we shall do a little stirring from this end. You know what worries me most? They tell you they've got all these agencies involved, but they don't keep you informed about what's going on. I thought the police prided themselves on their communication skills these days.'

'They were very chatty on Sunday. But since then,' I conceded, 'zero. And nothing from Taz, even. Of course, not having a phone I'm a bit elusive. And no, Todd, that's not a request for one. Coloured contacts are more than enough.'

He laughed. 'Jan's bouncing up and down to say something. So I'll say goodbye, Caffy – and remember, nothing, nothing at all, not even Fullers, is enough to make you take risks. Here she is now.'

Jan, in motherly mode, said much the same. We said an affectionate goodbye all round. We'd never let each other go, not even when the Fullers job was finally over. Even as I smiled with happiness, I shivered: these lovely people were still at risk. And so was I.

'Nice pair,' Paula said at last, dabbing the chips she always keeps till last in a tiny heap of salt. 'I'm glad you talked Todd into letting us do his house. Though between you, me and the gatepost, I don't really know where to start.'

I grinned. 'But I'm sure you'll have decided if those cops start asking awkward questions.'

'Eat up. We've got a plan to look at and I don't want any greasy fingerprints on it.'

Chapter Eighteen

'Eureka!'

Paula looked at me sideways. 'Even I know that's Greek meaning you're likely to leap up and run round in the nude,' she said, 'and I tell you flat, that's a sacking offence. But it is interesting,' she said, eyes agleam, 'that the internal dimensions don't match the external ones. Look, we've somehow lost six feet on this floor, a good eight on that.'

'I think that one's my sleeping quarters,' I said, pointing to the storey missing six feet. 'A good, deep cupboard. But the doors aren't exactly invisible. Where's the missing eight feet? Much harder to lose that.'

'We'll have a quick shuftie tonight,' Paula said. 'I don't know if we'll have enough light or time to do a real search. Tell you what, though – if we find anything interesting you can stand me a half of Bishop's Finger at that posh dosshouse of yours.'

'If we find anything interesting, I'll stand you a glass of fizz.'

'Your account or the police's?'

'Which do you think?'

'In that case, we'll make it half a bottle. Ok, let's get this show on the road. Dungarees on time, I'd say.'

There'd been a lot of activity out at Fullers. The caravan had been taken away for a start, the tyres of a low-loader or whatever doing no good at all to the lawn, despite the dry weather. But if Jan and Todd were as committed to the garden as to the house, then I was sure it would look as good as new this time next year. Correction: as good as old. I'd bet my teeth they'd want a knot-garden or something equally in keeping.

The same two as last night, looking just as bored, guarded the place. Apparently to wake them up, Paula drove to within a foot of their toes, leaning out of the cab to ask where she should park and giving the completely wrong impression that she didn't care a lot how she did it.

Where, not if. One thing Paula didn't lack was authority. Or the confidence that went with it.

They pointed.

She reversed swiftly, but as precisely as if her licence depended on it. We got out, Paula walking swiftly over to the cops, me slouching in the background oozing resentment from every pore. If anyone had considered the matter, they might have said I was a badly dressed ugly dyke who hated overtime. I found some gum and would have chewed, my mouth insolently open, but I thought that would be gilding the lily. In any case, I wasn't sure how old the gum might be.

Paula raised her voice. 'You really want me to call Mr and Mrs Dawes, do you? They're sitting having dinner in some posh restaurant like Quaglino's with their poncy friends and they have to take a phone call from some jumped up plod who won't take an honest worker's word? OK. Here's the phone. You'll find their number in the index. Or would you like me to find that too?'

While they debated she jangled the house keys ostentatiously.

Damn me if they weren't about to call her bluff. She dialled, had a few words with Jan or Todd and passed the phone across to Simon, the scrawny one, whose blush practically glowed in the poor light. I didn't need to hear his grovels: I could see from his body language he was ready to die of embarrassment.

Snapping the phone shut with an air of contempt, Paula flapped a hand over her shoulder to tell me to join her, and shoved the key into the lock. It turned sweetly. And we were in. While I started looking, she went back for clipboards, tape and a variety of other clutter, promising to scowl at the men as if it was their fault she'd forgotten them. I could hear her snarling at them when she dropped them, no doubt deliberately, just so she could give another scowl.

She dumped most of the things where anyone opening the door in a hurry would fall over them. We'd hear them and they'd be slowed down. Right: the plans and some light were all we needed.

'I thought this place had been re-wired,' Paula said crossly, flicking a light switch but getting nothing.

'It has. It's just that some stupid Sparks "forgot" to put in light bulbs except where he fancied. I'll nip and get the lantern torch Todd gave me,' I said, glad of an excuse to nip and get my reading matter before I got side-tracked.

Yes, there were *Evelina* and *Dubliners*. I hugged them to me like old friends. But I couldn't find my other ally, the torch, anywhere. Don't think I didn't check. There were plenty of places I might have put it, if I'd been in the habit of carrying it round. But surely I'd left it by my bedroll?

Shaking my head, I ran downstairs, dropping the books by the rest of the booby-trap and calling to Paula.

'In here. The kitchen. Or where it was and maybe where it will be.'

The Daweses' delight in the past hadn't extended to old lead pipes, that was clear from the array of shiny new copper ones. But they'd found a range more or less in period, at least to look at, which was currently sitting sadly in the middle of the floor, awaiting installation. For some reason my torch – Todd's torch – sat on the top of it.

'Someone's been in here,' I said flatly. 'That isn't where I left it.' I explained.

'What about the rest of your stuff? Your sleeping bag? Clothes? Hang on, I'm coming too.'

I didn't ask why. Paula would never have forgiven me if I'd made her confess she was scared. Together and armed with the torch, however, I'm sure we both felt a good deal braver.

Tidiness, as opposed to cleanliness, has never been my strong point. If only I'd left my bedding neatly rolled or spread out to air. If only I'd hung clothes in a graduated row. Those that I'd shown Taz were still in a jumble on the floor. I'd an idea they'd been neat when they were in my knapsack: shouldn't the stuff still inside be folded? Whoever's hand had been in there had stirred them up something shocking. Trouble was, whose hand? I shook my head at Paula, who tutted, more in sorrow than in anger, I thought.

'Are you going to bring it down?' she asked. 'We can't hang around much longer, you know.'

'I'm not sure if – well, if mine was the last hand to touch it,' I said. 'If it wasn't, maybe I should leave it here in case whoever it was comes back.'

'Not much chance of anyone coming back anyway if we're working here tomorrow.'

'All the same.' Truth to tell I didn't want my pathetic rags anyway. They hadn't owed the first owners anything when they'd arrived at the charity shops. Now they looked more like disgraceful dusters. No wondered Taz had been horrified when I'd worn them to meet his boss.

Maybe Paula picked some of this up. Not usually a great one for touching, she slung an arm round my shoulders and drew me from the room.

Not entirely to my surprise, she led us down to the kitchen again. 'Hang on here while I go and look at the window from the outside,' she said, checking she'd got her electronic measure in her pocket. I produced mine – only a cheap and cheerful tape, not her professional job, but good enough for what I was sure she had in mind.

Her face appeared briefly at the window, pointing at the nearer edge of the house. The she disappeared from view. I knew better than to look for her until I'd got a measurement from the middle of the window to the outside wall of the kitchen, then, for good measure, from the same place to the inner corner. Then I saw her head bobbing round.

'What kept you? The police?'

'Finding something to focus on. You need to point this thing at something for it to tell you how far away it is. In this light it needed a big stone. Very big. I had half a mind to ask PC Pea-brain there to move one for me.'

The readings were identical. All of them.

'But the kitchen's the logical place,' I wailed.

Without speaking she stomped off to the room at the far

side of the house. It might once have been a library, with deep embrasures allowing shelving for massive tomes. A big, elegant window dipped from near the ceiling almost to the floor.

'Not much light given the size of the room,' Paula murmured. 'I dimly remember having seen other windows bricked up – something to do with the tax on windows, whenever that was.'

I thought it better not to tell her. 'That'd make it easier to put in a false wall along here,' I said, tapping hopefully.

'Forget it! If they were building a priest hole they'd make sure no amount of tapping would betray it. Which room's above this?'

'Mine. Eventually. There's a passage sandwiched between, of course, on the middle floor. No window. Very solid walls.'

'Think enough to make a little run of steps? To your little cupboard. Which is almost wide enough to convince anyone that that's all it is. Come on, we're going back – what are you waiting for?'

We stared at the wall, frustrated. Barely detectable, there was a closely fitting panel running ceiling to floor.

'You'd need a jemmy to open it from this side,' Paula sighed. 'But I reckon it'll open sweet as a nut from the other. And that we'll find a little set of steps going down through that thick wall to the library.'

'And then where? You see, it's not just priests who had to hide. Later on it was Free Traders. And their booty, of course.'

'Not a good time to look now, though,' Paula said. A

sheet of lightning had just lit up the big window. She held up her finger: I could see her counting. 'About eight miles away, I should think. Whoops! And that one was even closer. My vote is, Caffy, that we abandon ship now. Before the rain.'

'Too late.'

'OK, then. Before the power goes.'

Even as she spoke, the pale glimmer of the mean electrician's forty-watt bulb quietly died.

She pressed the van keys into my hands, plus the plans. I grabbed the books.

'Oh, for goodness' sake! Don't blame me if you drop the lot.'

I didn't. Nor did she drop her load as she locked Fullers' front door. It was a good job the locksmith had been more efficient than the electrician.

We were both pretty soaked, of course, but to my surprise Paula signalled me to pull up by the police car. I did, nearside to nearside.

'I've had to give up, officer,' she said, grudging as if he'd turned on the storm. 'Yes, I've locked the front door. See you tomorrow.'

That was enough conversation. And it was raining in on to my lap. I slammed into gear and set off. We weren't far from the summit of the Isle. All around, celestial fireworks were exploding. I knew better than to leap out of the van yelling, 'Off, off, ye lendings!' Instead, I asked quietly, 'Half a bottle of champagne or just a glass?'

Paula sighed. 'If I'm going to drive home through this, it had better be water.'

* * *

In the event we had nothing: in the wet there was no knowing if the van wouldn't take it into its silly head to refuse point blank to start again. So I stopped and got out without cutting the engine. Paula slid across and, waving, put the van into motion.

'What now?' she demanded, braking as I danced in front of her.

'The books,' I said.

The expression on her face as she passed them across told her how crazy I was. I couldn't blame her. I shoved them down my dungarees. By the time I'd reached the hotel foyer I was as wet as if I'd lain fully clothed in a bath.

I stared down. Which would be worse manners, to paddle across their polished pretend-marble in my working trainers or to slide across in my socks? I was sure the chicest guest wouldn't care a damn for the poor cleaner who'd have to sort out the mess. I set out as I was. I'd almost reached the lift, my finger poised to press the button, when a voice rang out, 'Lucy? Ms Taylor? Can I have a word?'

It was Assistant Chief Constable Moffatt.

I turned, managing a self-deprecating smile. Well, it could hardly have been any other sort, the rain dripping off my nose and chin and joining the muddy puddle around the trainers.

His was less easy to read. I was sure it wasn't as comfortable as the ones he'd managed on Sunday evening, but I didn't feel any really sinister vibes.

'Working late,' I said.

'So I see. I've made a table-reservation for dinner,' he said, laughing as he added, 'I think I'd better get them to put it back. Half an hour?'

I was just about to tell him ten minutes when I thought of my lovely books. Two minutes to shower, two to dry my hair, and a last two to get dressed and slap on some make-up. Twenty-four minutes with what I knew were my friends.

Moffatt greeted my reappearance with a kiss on my cheek. All very friendly, the sort of kiss Todd might give. But there was something about the way he took my hand that set off the tiniest vibe.

Actually, I was dead worried about my own reactions, I should have told him I'd already eaten, and suggested he cancel the table altogether. I still could. But I'd had enough lean years to know that meals were things you didn't refuse, not without a very good reason – and a burger nearly three hours ago wasn't necessarily the best excuse. On the other hand I'd also learnt, also from experience, that there was no such thing as a free dinner. (I know, I know – but who eats lunch at nearly half-past nine?)

It would have been much better if I'd worked out with Paula how much to reveal of our evening's discoveries. On the whole, I thought, very little. The man hadn't done anything to get in touch till I'd been to Fullers twice in two evenings. Were the visits connected with his sudden interest in my affairs or was the meal entirely coincidental?

I'd have to stay on my toes. Hell, that meant I probably ought to stay on the wagon, too. And I'd have murdered for a Bishop's Finger – not that this classy bar would have been likely to sell such plebeian stuff as ale. Spritzer? In my opinion that merely ruined both wine and water. I settled for what one of my clients always called Tart's Tipple: dry Martini and lemonade with lots of ice. The menu arrived with the drinks. They were obviously desperate to close the restaurant on this vile night – there were only a couple of tables occupied in the far corner. It was lucky for my cycling friend that this was his free evening.

Moffatt seemed inclined to dwell on the torrential rain, but I knew about that from an experience he lacked, and decided it was time to push the conversation the way I wanted.

I ordered soup and salmon and looked him straight in the eye, cutting across an observation about an overflowing gutter. 'How did our photographs come out? The ones of the people being loaded into the van?' Whether I asked him about our other photos, the ones of the bed indentations, and the rope fibre Paula had picked up, would depend on how I felt about his honesty.

'Very well,' he said, effortlessly polite in the face of my rudeness. 'You must have used a good camera.'

Hmm. 'I borrowed someone's. What do you make of them? Your team, I mean – I'm sure you're too busy to take a day-to-day interest even in major crime.' He wasn't to know it but I was quoting one of my most messed-up clients, one with as much braid and stuff on his uniform as Moffatt – again, incidentally, in very smart casual.

'Not too busy to keep an eye on things. And, as you can see, to report back.'

Victim liaison was hardly the job of someone of his rank.

I wished desperately that Jan were sitting beside me – legal adviser or friend, it didn't matter.

'Unfortunately the bread van had been stolen – to order, no doubt. The shelves were found in an industrial estate in Canterbury. Someone reported having their removal van stolen in Southampton. Nothing's been found yet, of either van.'

'So someone's got a big place to hide them till they can be repainted – or enough open space to torch them without some helpful person calling the fire brigade.'

'Not every citizen is as helpful as you, Lucy. Anyway, our scene of crime officers have looked closely at the area you pinpointed and yes, they've got the impression of a shoe we believe comes from Eastern Europe. Nothing conclusive yet. The trouble is, in an operation like this, where we suspect one of our own may be involved, we want to do things as unobtrusively as possible. Which means what must seem intolerable delays to others involved.'

'That explosion couldn't have been unobtrusive,' I said, smiling at the waiter who'd brought the wine. He looked tired enough to drop.

Moffatt didn't reply until we were on our own again. 'We wanted to convince… people… that the intended victim was unlikely to survive.'

'And did she?'

He looked at me oddly. 'She's deeply unconscious.'

'How long can she be kept alive?'

'As long as it takes to find her killer. They've taken away the caravan for full forensic examination.'

I nodded, as if it were news to me. All those lovely books

destroyed! Before I could ask the next question, we were summoned to our table. I drained my glass and followed Moffatt.

He hadn't ordered any wine. Terribly apologetic, he told me he'd stick to water since he was driving home, but pressed me to have half a bottle. We compromised on another glass.

I felt as if I was in the ascendant. 'What about the photographs of the interior of Crabton Manor? We passed them and a fibre of blue rope to Taz. He said he'd deal with them.'

He reached in his jacket for and flipped open a little notepad. 'I've no idea. I'll get on to it first thing. How are you getting on with Sid?'

'How does he say he's getting on with us?'

Moffatt laughed. 'He finds Paula a bit tough.'

'He shouldn't try to mess her around. She's one of the best people I've ever come across. Honest. Decent.'

'But doesn't suffer fools gladly.'

'Do you?'

He looked completely nonplussed. 'No. But that's different.'

'Not in my book. Oh, the organisations you run are different in size and organisation, but you both take decisions that affect other people. Hers are more important, in some ways. If you make a mistake, you can cover it with press statements and internal enquiries. If Paula makes a mistake in her figure work, we don't eat breakfast. If she makes a mistake where she sites a ladder, one of us might die. People tug their forelocks at you because of your uniform. They see our work clothes and try to fiddle us out of meal breaks and deposits and make us wait sometimes for years for money for materials she's bought on their behalf. That's why Paula takes no prisoners. She also took me on without a single word of criticism about my past – something some of your colleagues have found hard to do.'

He flushed a deep crimson, avoiding my eyes. My vibes had been right. Deep, deep inside, so deep he probably didn't have to acknowledge it, he'd harboured designs on me. Once a tart always a tart, that was what some little voice inside was telling him. He might think he was being gentlemanly, avuncular, even. But his hormones urged him differently.

Tough.

The arrival of the soup allowed him to regain his cool.

'As for how we see Sid,' I continued, as if I hadn't noticed, 'we're not at all sure. Helen and Meg don't know he's not a genuine decorator. He's asked no questions, shown no signs of being – what's the word? – proactive, that's it – at all. He's not a good workman. Van der Poele knows he's not a good workman. That's why Paula had to give him a verbal warning this afternoon.'

'I didn't know that.'

'I shouldn't imagine it was the first thing he'd put in his report. Tell me, is he there to protect us or to spy on van der Poele? And if he's spying, what's he looking for?'

Cornered, he said, 'Well, things like the presence of your friend Clive Granville near Fullers.'

Yes, he side-tracked me. 'Does he live down here? Or is he just visiting? And is there any evidence he believes the story of my death? OK, my coma. He may be hanging out for one of my kidneys for a transplant!'

Moffatt threw his head back and laughed. 'A man for his pound of flesh, eh? Sorry, I didn't mean – '

'I know. You were quoting Shakespeare.' I didn't admit how difficult I found his plays, though I'd tried hard to read the famous ones. Perhaps you needed to see them on the stage. I'd seen a modern dress *Merchant of Venice* on TV and it had bored the socks off me. 'Anyway, what's the latest on him?'

'He's an elusive man. There's no doubt he's down here – he's used his credit card a couple of times in Tenterden – but we haven't run him to earth yet. And until we do, I'm very much afraid you have to stay as Lucy.'

There was something about the way his crow's feet crinkled that made me grasp my tufty mane and say, 'I can't wait to get this cut off.'

'Off! You mean – !'

'Shorn. The perm and the dye have made such a mess of it it'll have to go, most of it.' Mistake. Huge mistake.

Moffatt leaned across and stroked it. 'We must make sure we temper the wind to the shorn lamb.' And then his hand strayed to my cheek.

If there's one thing I should highlight in my CV it's skills in freezing off amorous males. By the time he'd finished his salmon (that old dodge of ordering the same as your dinner partner!) he was practically calling for his scarf and gloves. I wasn't rude or unpleasant, don't for a moment think that. After all, I should have known better than to get matey with a middle-aged man who'd given me even such a tiny vibe. But I picked at the food (not difficult when you've already had one supper), and allowed myself an occasional yawn.

Very soon these became quite genuine. It had been another long day and my books were calling me to bed.

If he'd offered me hard evidence about anything, of course, I'd have been bright and alert. But still a little more cool and remote than I had been.

One way to cool him down might be to talk about Taz, which I proceeded to as if I were a member of his fan club.

'But he never made it clear exactly what job he's doing in the Met,' I concluded earnestly.

'Rookie constables on probation do a lot of work but not much they can boast about.'

I had a nasty suspicion he used the verb boast deliberately – a touch of the old stag scoring points off an absent young one.

'But he had access to you.'

'He has – access – to a senior Met officer, who was sufficiently interested in what Taz passed on to him from you to contact me. Wheels are turning, Lucy, I promise you.'

'I shan't mind if they're like the mills of God and that grinding exceeding small compensates for their grinding so slowly.'

That's another way to put a self-assured man off you: out-quote him. Preferably from a hymn I'd last sung when I was about ten. It didn't take long to establish that we both had work to do the following morning and that neither could take coffee at this time of night.

So I had a solitary bed. Apart from the company of various Irish reprobates who reminded me vaguely of my dad.

Chapter Nineteen

As luck would have it, it was a brilliantly sunny morning, the sort that makes you leap out of bed and throw open the windows. It was only as I did my twentieth length (it really was quite a small pool, so I wasn't being entirely honest when I boasted of yesterday's twelve lengths) that I realised I should be cursing the sun and praying for the safe return of the rain. It'd be painting the exterior of Crabton Manor for us, not exploring the interior of Fuller's.

Sid was moaning how the storm had kept him awake last night. 'What about you?' he asked eventually.

'Slept the sleep of the just, Sid. Plus I was tired,' I conceded. I'd mention dinner with Moffatt if he asked, but by now I'd definitely decided to volunteer as little as possible about one policeman's activities to another. If anyone asked point-blank, that was another matter.

As if he'd been reading my mind, Sid slowed and asked, 'What did you and Paula get up to last night?'

'I told you – we needed to do a bit of forward planning. She's brilliant at working things out, but sometimes even she needs to have someone agree that she's right.'

'And she was right? Better than a calculator?'

My God, the bugger hadn't planted some sort of bug, had he? Some nasty listening device that transmitted everything we'd said? Paula had said she didn't trust him. I answered his question with one of my own. 'What are your plans for today? Are you going to try and case Crabton Manor?'

'Anything rather than spend the day like yesterday. Jesus, I bloody ache every sodding where. Why should my leg muscles ache? It's as bad as bloody toothache.'

'Ladders. Not just climbing but balancing on them. That's why we were happy to knock off when we did yesterday. And it's a good job we did. That rain wouldn't have done fresh paint any good at all.'

'Hmph.'

I added more kindly, 'Have a word with Paula. She'll find you a patch where you can keep both feet on the ground.'

'More likely to send me up to paint the sodding chimney, that one.'

'She has to maintain the front that you're a professional painter, Sid, and don't you forget it. If van der Poele thinks you're a poor workman, or simply skiving, he'll dock the money the rest of us should be getting. He'd just tear up the contract – you know he would. He's what my dad would have called a nasty piece of knitting.'

'Did your dad know about your being a whore?'

Just like that. Not an eyelid must I bat, even at the deliberately offensive term. He mustn't see my efforts to breathe normally. But I had to say something. 'You like to call a spade a spade, I see. As a matter of fact he didn't. He buggered off when I was about six or seven. But forget about my dad. I usually do. Can't think why I should have mentioned him then. Let's talk about van der Poele instead. Taz passed on what Paula and I thought was possibly evidence that someone was killed here. I can show you the room – from the outside. We'd love someone to take us seriously.' I didn't tell him that Paula had kept a duplicate set of photos in case the first got mysteriously lost. She'd have teased a few spare fibres from the rope too, knowing her.

'We are taking you seriously – you know that. Not everyone gets to eat dinner with an assistant chief constable, do they?'

'Not everyone needs to,' I said. 'Look! A heron, just taking off over there!' An ungainly grey shape organised itself into slow, efficient flight over the placid, gentle fields, dotted with sheep so round and white they looked like toys. As a city woman, the sight of lamb chops on the hoof still amazed me. Mind you, I ate far fewer of them, for one reason or another.

Sid wasn't impressed by any of it. He drove as far as Dymchurch in grumpy silence.

'You can't even see the sea along this road. This huge sea wall, whatever it is, fair gives me the creeps. Fancy living in one of them little houses and looking at that all day.'

'The upside is that all they have to do is cross the road and climb up those steps and there's the beach.' My mouth was working but my brain was trying to work out if that was how my poor immigrants had come into the country – simply been dropped the far side of a huge wall and being made to leg it before it got light. But surely there'd be coastguards to stop that sort of activity? Unless someone had squared the coastguards.

'And a force ten gale to blow you straight back home. And look over there – that ruddy great gun emplacement! Martello towers, they're historical. But that – ' He shuddered. Perhaps world wars weren't yet sanitised enough to be history. And yet one of my best ever days down here had been at Dover Castle, exploring the war rooms tunnelled deep into the famous white cliff. Sid pointed again. 'And the bleeding army practising killing folk all the way along here with their nice tidy firing ranges.' Anti-military? A policeman? That struck a very bum note. 'No, you don't kid me into taking a holiday down here. Spain, that's where I'm retiring, soon as I can.'

He sounded so disillusioned I glanced at him. 'It sounds as if it can't be soon enough for you.'

'Nor can it. The police isn't what it used to be. All paperwork and looking over your shoulder to make sure you're being PC. PCPC. PC Politically Correct. Geddit?'

On that positive note he fell silent. I was too preoccupied on my own account to disturb him. Or to laugh.

'Bugged? You mean, bugged?' Paula was so angry she almost squeaked. It wasn't because I'd broken our rule and followed her behind the van when she'd obviously been about to have a wee.

'I don't know.' I touched my finger to my lips. 'Maybe they trust us as little as we trust them. Tell you what, just check your bag when you come out. And I'll check mine.'

'Do you know what to look for?'

I shrugged. 'All I know was that Sid spent a long time faffing round here doing sweet F. A. all yesterday.'

'But I'd taken my bag with me. So it's more likely to be in yours.'

'I'll check. But do you know something? I think I'll do it in front of him. Look, we'll have to talk away from the van later – he'll be thinking we're having a lesbian moment and trying to sneak a look.'

I emerged first to find Sid, arms akimbo, staring at the ground floor. It was clear that that was where he wanted to paint. When Paula emerged from behind the Transit, he toddled over, heaving a stepladder out and planting it firmly in his new territory. Paula raised an eyebrow, but didn't argue, not until she came down from aloft a few minutes later to find him half kneeling on one of the ladder's steps.

'Sid, that's the way to damage joints.'

'I'm three-quarters crippled the way you got me shinning up and down ladders,' he whined.

'You must be very out of practice. I suppose,' she added, very clearly, 'that'll teach me to take someone his last boss let go. Very well, paint down here until your muscles feel a bit better. But for goodness' sake stand tall and keep those knees relaxed but straight.'

'Sounds like you're giving orders at some sodding antenatal class.'

By now white with anger, she snapped, 'I wouldn't know. But I do know that as your employer I'm responsible for the health and safety of all my workers. I'm warning you, Sid, fit in or drop out.'

We women exchanged scared rabbit looks. Paula had never had to speak to one of us like that, and certainly not in public, and we didn't know how to react. Should we rally round in support of the miscreant or be teacher's pets for the day? I knew that there was another, more serious problem. If Sid was one of Moffatt's men, how could Paula sack him? There must, apart from anything else, be a limit to the number of undercover officers capable of wielding a professional paintbrush.

Paula made a slight sideways movement of her head, drawing Sid to one side. I suppose she should probably have done that earlier so that his bollocking was in private. Funny, it was unlike Paula to make that sort of mistake. Along with the others, though, I decided that discretion was the greater part of valour, and applied today's paint as if I were wearing blinkers.

Perhaps that was the problem with Meg. She was so busy not looking that when she went back to the van to top up her paint can, she succeeded in spilling several litres of the stuff. The more she tried to stop it, the worse it flowed. God knows what she thought she was doing, standing there screaming and watching this stream of creamy-white flow everywhere. The rest of us were down there with her, ready to defend her against Paula if necessary. But Paula was coolest of all, simply grabbing the big tin and steadying it. Fortunately most of the paint had fallen in the deep tin tray she always insisted the paint tins stand on.

Taking Meg gently by the arm, she led her away. 'Why didn't you tell me you had a migraine?' she asked quietly.

Helen and I didn't need to be told what to do. We tidied up without speaking. Technically we shouldn't really use this paint again, in case it had got bits of dust and so forth in it. But the only place to tip it was the tin, so that was what we did.

'She's lost the vision in one eye,' Paula reported. 'She's done this before. She's taken two of her tablets, but I still think I should take her home. I'd better buy some more paint too. Can't have van der Poele complaining we're using mucky stuff. But I don't suppose Mr Green'll argue if I offer him a freebie tin.'

Mr Green was the old boy whose bungalow we'd be doing between big jobs. Cost price.

On impulse I gave Paula a hug, which clearly amazed her almost as much as it amazed me. 'We'll be OK here.'

We were. Helen was a bit scared, but once she'd heard from Meg's own lips that she'd be all right after a bit of a lie down, she buckled down as she always did. Sid might have been a Trappist monk for all we heard from him. But I couldn't help seeing that he still used the step-ladder as a kneeler, and wished I'd got the authority to repeat Paula's warning.

By the time Paula got back Sid had given up his stepladder and was kneeling on the ground so he could paint the underside of a windowsill. He might have been praying it glossy. She raised her eyes heavenwards, but simply said, 'There's a fresh can of paint in the van.'

'How's Meg?'

'She was well into what she called her Technicolor zigzags by the time I got her home. She says she'll be all right. Funny, you'd have expected a migraine before a storm, not after it.'

Towards the end of the afternoon, the wind changed direction; it became noticeably cooler, and Paula started looking to the west. 'The last thing we need now with the end almost in sight is an Atlantic front,' she said. 'I know they're talking about a hosepipe ban, but I could manage without washing the car if I could finish here in time.'

She hadn't mentioned penalty clauses, but it sounded as if the miserable bastard had insisted on one. With the English weather, for goodness' sake! And now we were one and a half down, one being Meg, and the half being Sid, now painting more slowly than ever. Paula couldn't fail to notice. Nor could anyone miss the pain he was obviously in. Perhaps he should have had Brownie points for carrying on. Paula didn't seem inclined to award any.

'Bursitis,' she said crisply. 'You've gone and given yourself bursitis. Better get off to your GP while you can still drive. Anti-inflammatories and hot and cold compresses.'

'What are you on about?'

'Your knees.'

'Bursitis,' he said, almost as if he was proud to have an 'itis'.

'Yes,' she said scathingly. 'Housemaid's knee.'

And it was precisely the diagnosis the A and E doctor gave, at the end of a four-hour wait at the William Harvey. There'd been a pile-up on the M20 and personally I'd have been ashamed to take up the time of people who'd been under so much pressure. But it seemed Sid had never got round to registering with a GP, so even if I'd driven him back to his base in what he vaguely called Sarf London he'd still have had a wait in an A and E there. Maybe, he said, almost proudly, an even longer one, what with the gun and knife crime in the neighbourhood.

Why was I involved? Sid claimed he was in too much pain to drive, and Paula wasn't going to put Helen at risk by not taking her home. So I'd got the short straw and the keys to Sid's utility truck. I didn't ask who owned it, so I never knew whether to blame its lack of maintenance on Sid or on the Met or even on Kent County Constabulary. OK, I was sulking. And why not? The William Harvey's a nice bright modern hospital, but sitting waiting for someone who wouldn't have needed so much as an aspirin if he'd carried out orders was niggling me. Not least because as time ticked inexorably by, it became clear that Paula and I would miss out on further explorations of Fullers that evening. I hadn't got a book and I was bored.

So bored I at last remembered to do what I'd been planning to do all day. I accidentally on purpose tipped over my bag. And – guess what – inside I found something apart from balled up tissues and old till receipts. A ballpoint I didn't recognise. I was just about to hold it up for Sid's inspection when a sodding nurse didn't take it into her head at that precise moment to call him in.

Frustrated, I had to vent my spleen. Especially when I unscrewed the ballpoint to find something inside – not, I was sure, a refill – small enough to sit on my fingertip. Who better to avenge myself on than the hidden listener? I retreated to the outside porch, where there was a congregation of mobile phone users, and, with my lips right close up to it, whistled as loudly as I could all the tunes I could remember before reassembling the ballpoint.

That'd teach someone. The question was, who.

Chapter Twenty

It would have served Sid right if I'd obeyed my next impulse, which was to follow him and shove his equipment where the nurse might have shoved a thermometer. The alternative was to return to the waiting room and confront him when he came out. Or I could have handed the ballpoint complete with its little cargo to the receptionist, telling her I'd found it on the floor somewhere, and then driven off in the ute., leaving Sid high and dry. That would have been very satisfying, but might have meant him taking up an emergency bed someone else might need. The thought I might be nicking official property had somehow escaped me, and when I remembered I found I didn't care all that much.

Meanwhile, of course, without the ute. I was as high and dry as Sid.

No. Think positive. The William Harvey wasn't all that far from my flat in Kennington. I could walk it. I still had the key, and could bunk down there. Without sheets and towels not to mention food and drink. There had been times, not so long ago, when I could have managed without any of those, and thought shelter a real luxury. But that was then. Then I perked up. There'd be tea-bags and dried milk and some of the books I hadn't been able to take with me. And a radio. Now all that was luxury indeed. Leaving the ute. keys but not the pen with the woman on reception, I strode off.

Ashford isn't, to be honest, your actual metropolis. It's a huge dormitory sprawl and very little else. Once it was a nice little country town. If you don't believe me, check out the

Chinese restaurant in the middle of the town, where they've got an eighteenth century engraving blown up to occupy a whole wall. Better than flock wallpaper and machine-embroidered silk pictures, anyway. I wonder if that was the Chinese restaurant where a triad kept someone kidnapped in the basement for a week. Like we said in that conversation a million years ago, Kent has its fair share of undesirable residents. Anyway, the once thriving market depicted in the old print is a now very pale imitation of its former self, and various stalls had disappeared even in the short time I'd been there. There's a big out-of-town entertainment area, so the centre, quiet during the day, is like a morgue in the evening. Were it not for some architect – with more sensitivity for looks than the comfort of women pedestrians in strappy sandals – putting down great swathes of granite setts, the place'd be silent as a graveyard at night. As it was, it sometimes sounded as if supernatural fingers were taking a typing lesson. I was padding almost silently in my paint-covered trainers, of course, grateful that if some man emerged who'd had a couple too many in the County Hotel or wherever I could easily outrun him. Not the young woman ahead of me, though. It was clear she'd registered the middle-aged bloke lurching sideways towards her like a giant crab but she didn't know quite what to do. The matter was partially solved when he collapsed at her feet, grabbing at her knees not because he was attacking her but because there was nothing else handy.

'I do apol…Terribly sorry!' He repeated himself a dozen times but seemed to have no idea how to let her go.

I circled so that she could see me and he couldn't. What I meant to do was grab him by the shoulders and prise him off. But at last, simply by backing away, she managed to free herself.

He tried to crawl after her. 'I did apolo – I did. I kept apologising. I did. I positively ejaculated my apology.'

I was fairly sure he'd hit on the word by accident but now he'd found it he was going to have a spot of harmless fun embarrassing a young woman.

'I ejaculated,' he repeated, adding in a confidential tone that rang round the square, 'I often ejaculate.' He lurched towards her again. I moved in swiftly behind him. 'I often ejaculate.'

'I'm sure you do,' I told him as I grabbed his arms above the elbows, wheeling him round. 'And prematurely, if I'm any judge.' A simple shove was enough to pitch him face down again. I didn't think he was hurt. Drunks seem to bounce, don't they?

Linking arms with the girl, I propelled her away from him more briskly than he'd ever manage, even assuming he'd get to his feet again. The pace was soon too much for her. Well, she was wearing those strappy sandals. I'd recognised her at once – she was the police station receptionist with the messy mascara. She clearly didn't recognise me, and I was happy not to introduce myself. What did surprise me was that she was so shocked – I'd have thought she had plenty of practice dealing with the drunk and the insane in her job. But upset she certainly was. She'd been heading for a swim down at the Stour Centre, she said, after a late shift at work.

'Next time, slam your bag full in the guy's face,' I suggested. Then I realised that I had a plan B for the damned eavesdropping pen. 'Look, you look awful. If I walked you back to wherever you work, wouldn't someone look after you? Give you a cuppa? Run you home?'

All this solicitousness must have convinced the poor kid she was at death's door. Alas, I'd conveniently brought her to a halt by a pizza place that also sold coffee. Plan C. 'Look, at least come and have a coffee. Sit down till you feel steadier.'

She nodded. 'My boyfriend – that's Dave, he's a trainee manager at the big Asda by the Outlet – is picking me up at half-nine,' she said. 'From the Centre. So I mustn't be late. But I do feel a bit wobbly – must be shock I suppose, though fancy being shocked by a little thing like that. Maybe a swim wouldn't be a good idea.'

Just about the best therapy, I'd have thought, but I was in selfish mode. I couldn't justify what I was going to do. I was using her, and I didn't approve of using people. Even for something good. If getting someone off my back were good, which I certainly thought it would be. And it wouldn't get anyone into trouble either. Yet. It might of course precipitate a little crisis, with me at the centre, but I seemed to have been dealing with crises reasonably well, weeping episodes apart. That's what I told myself, anyway.

My plan would mean I had to fork out money I could ill afford for her drink, though. 'You might do better with hot sweet tea,' I said thoughtfully, as she collapsed at a table, 'or hot chocolate.'

To my surprise it was waitress service. The girl who drooped over would clearly have preferred us to order double pizza with plenty on the side, but since we were the only ones in the place she could hardly protest that tables were for eaters only. Messy Mascara proved to have a name, Sherree, poor girl. Sherree Wagford. I clearly wasn't going to be Caffy, and rather hesitated to be Lucy, given my current state of paranoia. No, they definitely were out to get me, and I'd err on the side of caution. I told her I was Karen. When the drinking chocolates appeared, we both grabbed our purses. I let her out argue me: she could hardly be paid less than me, and there was a boyfriend in the frame. As I returned my money to my bag, it was easy enough to drop the Judas pen into hers.

We talked a bit about Ashford.

'It's really grand these days, with the Outlet and that. And all these nice little starter homes they're building. We're saving up for a starter home out Park Farm way, really convenient for Dave's work, though of course it'd be even better if he worked at Tesco, but maybe he'll get a promotion there when he's finished his training. The trouble is, we're both on shift work, so there are days we don't see each other. Though they do say that absence makes the heart grow stronger, don't they? Have you got a boyfriend?'

I shook my head. The less of my voice that disembodied listener heard the better.

'Pity – we could have got up a foursome, if you like bowls, that is. Dave's ever so good. I'm still learning and he's ever so patient. Mostly.'

At last she felt strong enough to walk the few yards to the Stour centre. Waving her across the pedestrian lights, I hoped that Sherree and her bloke didn't get vocal if they got amorous, and that the spy in the sky wasn't hovering in Ashford Police Station.

* * *

I told myself that my flat felt no worse than if I'd come back from holiday. The mustiness would soon disappear. I opened a couple of windows, not all of them, because by now the evening was quite chilly, at least compared with the previous balmy ones. I tipped everything in the fridge, not a lot, really, into a couple of carrier bags which I tied off. Then, gathering them and what change I could, I nipped down to the phone box. I'd need a lift in from Paula, wouldn't I? I popped the bags into a convenient litter basket.

'You left him there! Well, his bosses aren't going to be too pleased with you. But as his other boss, I tell you, I'm bloody furious with him. How many times did I warn him?'

'He should have taken notice after just one warning,' I agreed. 'Did you find anything to suggest a bug, by the way?'

'You know, I forgot to look.'

'It might be worth it. You see, I did – and I found some-one had planted a very clever pen on me.' I explained what had happened to it.

'You think Sid –?'

'I'd like to think it was Sid. Because the only other obvi-ous candidates for the job would be either Taz or John Moffatt. Would you do something for me, Paula? On your way over here – not at home and nowhere near your usual route – could you phone the hotel and see if you can find out who's really paying for my stay?' If anyone could sound as official as the police, Paula could.

'What?'

'Say that you haven't had an account from them yet, anything,' I said, deliberately misunderstanding her.

There was a short silence. 'You don't think an assistant chief constable could be bent! For God's sake, C – I really think you're paranoid!'

'The pen, Paula,' I said.

Another silence. 'OK. And where shall I meet you?' She sounded almost humble.

'Not my flat. The Stour Centre?'

'Half-eight. On the dot.' That was the Paula I knew and loved. But she added, in a voice I didn't know, 'You will take care of yourself? Promise?'

'Promise.' But my money had run out and she might not have heard.

One of my favourite escapist books was *Northanger Abbey*, where a naïve but decent heroine has an adventure but is rescued by a kind and pleasant young man. A bit of wish-fulfilment, I suppose, with me as Catherine Morland. Maybe it would work its magic again. I burrowed through the books. No, it must be one I'd thrust at Jan. In any case, I wasn't a naïve young woman, not any more. What was left? I burrowed again, rejecting book after book. Well, my closest friends would be with Catherine Morland. At last I found a rather battered *Jude the Obscure*. Would that work?

'You look rough,' Paula said as she let me into the Transit the next morning.

I didn't argue. I felt rough. Very rough. The rough you feel when you're cold and hungry and had a sleepless night.

Those children being hanged, of course. Or did I identify too closely with the self-educated Jude? Whatever it was, something had driven sleep away and the nightmares had come flooding back in the brief moments I had had. Funny: I'd been in real danger, I suspect, for some days, but hadn't woken so much as whimpering. This time – well, what a good job the neighbours were used to my yells.

'No electricity,' I said briefly. Who the hell had told them to cut me off?

She slammed into reverse.

'Where are you going?'

'Back to the Centre. You can get hot snacks there.'

I didn't argue. The Centre was already full of people all looking refreshingly normal. A sweaty middle-aged couple carrying badminton gear held the door for me. Kids seethed around the pay-desk while the teacher tried to count heads and pay. Wet-haired swimmers with the most enormous bags slung on their shoulders to the danger of everyone else, shouted their preference for the snacks machine. We slipped between the lot, past homely adverts for bowls and women's cricket and over-sixties aerobics into the deserted café. Deserted because it wasn't open, of course.

'Sit down anyway,' Paula said, heading for a payphone and counting out change. I didn't argue. A public phone might be safer than her own mobile.

Listening to her was a treat. Sounding just like a bored clerk, she asked for the accounts department. 'I'm just checking why you haven't invoiced us for Ms Taylor's room. Number 703. Kent County Constabulary. No?'

My stomach clenched.

'In whose name is it booked then? Who? What? Can you spell that?'

I didn't need to look at the clear block letters on the back of a gas bill envelope she laid before me. TADEUZS MOSCICKI.

The counter staff came in, laughing as if the world was still turning. Paula patted me on the shoulder and flourished her purse again. A big pot of tea appeared in seconds, toast a minute later.

'Well?'

'Well what? It's like it was before. I don't know what's happening or who to trust. And, Paula, I'm bloody scared.'

She didn't shake her head at the swear word. She gripped my hands tightly. 'So am I,' she said. And she burst into tears.

The sight of safe, solid Paula crying shocked me as much as anything I'd seen during the last couple of weeks. 'I don't know what to do,' she sobbed. 'I've got to hold the business together and everything seems to be against it. Taz can't wave a paintbrush to save his life; Sid ends up in Casualty; Meg gets her migraines and next you'll say you've got to disappear again. If I don't get the money off van der Poele, how am I going to pay everyone?'

Well, it was a different set of priorities from mine, but I could see that she was thinking of the greatest good of the greatest number.

'If I disappear,' I said firmly, if listening to myself with some surprise, 'it'll be to Fullers. I can work away there without anyone knowing and – once I've found that priest hole or whatever – be as safe as houses. And once work's underway, Jan and Todd'll be more than happy to pay as we go. Not that they wouldn't anyway. They don't expect the whole job to be completed before dipping into their pockets. Come on, Paula, they'd bankroll you interest free if they had the slightest inkling you'd got a cash-flow crisis.'

She nodded, but I could see Jan and Todd would have their work cut out to persuade her to accept their largesse. 'And it's bloody van der Poele, isn't it? Mean bugger. And knowing he'll be standing there with his watch like some dreadful Victorian father checking what time we arrive.'

'Which had better be soon, then,' I said, sinking the last of my tea and gathering my things. 'What about the others?'

'I gave Helen my car and told her to pick up Meg if she was fit.'

'You've been up and about for ages then?'

She nodded. 'And still nothing done.'

'If I know Helen and Meg, they'll have finished the south side already. Come on, we've broken the back of it.' I passed her her bag. 'You're absolutely sure there's no bug in this?'

'I used another one. Nothing but tissues and purse in this.'

'Good.' I suddenly felt I was in charge. 'Now, the way I see it is this: if I stay my last night at the hotel, no one's going to suspect anything's –'

'Yes, they will. They'll know your bug's not transmitting from where it should be. And they'll have a description of you from Cherie or whatever her name is.'

I nodded. 'Look, three of you should put on a convincing performance for van der Poele. We're on safe ground with him. We know he's evil and possibly a killer with a nasty taste in domestic pets. But all he seems to be worrying about now the "blonde tart's" gone is progress on his house. He knows members of the team come and go but tend to come back. If he asks about me, tell him – oh, I don't know… Yes, tell him Sid's off sick and I'm going to talk to an old friend to see if they're free.'

'And where will you be?'

'On the nine twenty-seven to Charing Cross.'

'What?' This seemed to be becoming one of her standard exclamations.

'I've got to talk to Taz, haven't I? And it'd be a lot better face to face.'

'But –'

'I'll get a cheap ticket. I'll be fine.' Of course I would. So long as I could find Taz, and, better still, Jan and Todd.

Chapter Twenty-One

'How on earth did you get here?' Jan demanded, almost in lawyer mode, now our welcoming hugs were over.

'The train.'

Her eyebrows asked about money.

'Look, Jan, being poor teaches you all sorts of tricks about travel. Just don't ask. You really don't want to know.'

Laughing, probably as much as the shock on his wife's face as at me, Todd intercepted room service and laid a tray on one of their several occasional tables. They might prefer playing camping at Fullers, but they weren't having a bad life here. Goodness knows how much a simple room cost at a place like this: they had a suite. No wonder the guy on the big front door had wanted to keep me out; no wonder the concierge had stood me in front of a security camera and beamed up my image for them to OK. I wasn't all that bad, either, hair apart. I'd stopped off at Debenhams so I could at least present myself in clean and decent clothes. I'd remembered all too clearly that it wasn't my money I was spending so I hadn't bought more than was absolutely necessary, just a clean top and skirt, both in the sale. But absolutely necessary wasn't good enough for a place like this. Come to think of it, even a damned good splurge on clothes like mine might not have been good enough. Look at Jan: her slopping-around-in-her-room outfit was a good deal more chic than what was now scheduled to be my Sunday best.

To my relief, Todd's gear wouldn't have been out of place on one of Paula's sites.

'Drink up, and then we'll sort this out,' he said, ruffling the top of my head as if I were a favourite puppy. 'Including, I have to say, your roots before you're much older.'

'Pray God it won't be necessary,' Jan said, squeezing my hand. 'I don't even know how you like your coffee – or would you prefer tea?'

The coffee smelt as if a princess could have bathed in it, with or without cream. And the biscuits … Well, I'd thought the hotel I'd been staying at was fine, but this was simply in a different league. Or was it simply that I'd never had coffee poured with such love before. No, I'd enjoy – I wouldn't cry. Paula's tears had been more than enough for one day. Which is where I started my account. I continued, with only occasional interruptions.

Todd plonked himself down beside me. 'Taz booked your room? You're sure of that? And is paying for it?'

'That's what the hotel told Paula. And it's hard to think they'd get a name like that wrong. The thing is, does he know he's paying? Or has Moffatt pulled a flanker?'

'You mean, discredited Taz and put himself in the clear?' Jan asked, sitting opposite us.

'I thought he was a good guy. Yes, Taz and Moffatt. I trusted them both. Almost –'.

'Almost?'

Almost as much as I trust you two. No, nowhere near as much as that. 'Almost is as far as I got with trusting Moffatt. Taz – well, with my life, at one point. Two points. I told you. I'd be pushing up the daisies without him.'

'That was then,' Todd said sombrely. 'Think now. Is he still the same Taz?'

I thought of the awkwardness between us, his embarrassment during the hotel meal. Was it because he'd changed? Or because I had? I shook my head, not to say no but to show I didn't know.

'You need to see him. Somewhere you can really talk,' Jan said. She and Todd exchanged a tiny unspoken conversation, I've no idea about what. It was almost as if he were reminding her about something. Hell – were they supposed to be meeting friends for lunch or something? I hadn't even considered that they might be busy.

All I could do was nod dumbly. In both senses.

'Why don't we leave you to it?' Todd was on his feet, reaching to haul Jan to her feet.

I shook my head. 'There's nothing between us. Nothing to make a phone call private.'

He passed over the hotel phone. I dialled. And got nothing but a long burr. He'd disconnected his number. Without telling me.

I held the phone so they could hear.

Todd tutted with irritation. 'What's the number again?' Taking the phone, he punched the numbers in as if daring them to defy him.

To my amazement, they didn't. The tone came over sweet as a nut. And then the familiar plastic voice of his answering service.

My mouth left a message without consulting the rest of me. 'Taz: last time it was me in danger. Now I think it's you.'

I was just about to give the name of the hotel when I saw that Jan was scribbling figures on a sheet of paper. 'Mobile phone number,' she mouthed.

I read it out to him.

'There,' said Jan, as if the whole thing had been her idea. 'Now, when did you last do the sights of London? Because it's a lovely day and a sin to be inside.'

We were at the Tower of London, appropriately enough, when Jan's phone rang. She handed it straight to me.

'Taz? Are you paying for that hotel room?'

No wonder he asked me to repeat the question.

'No, of course I'm not. Moffatt said he'd put it on to the Kent Constabulary account. Or get them to pick up the tab or whatever.'

'The hotel thinks different.' I realised I was in the way of a Japanese family armed with more camera equipment a jackdaw could shake a wing at. 'You're being set up.'

'We'd better talk. Not here. Where are you?'

'Just by Traitors' Gate.'

Todd and Jan sank into the shadows when Taz appeared.

'I phoned the hotel. You're right. Caffy, you've got yourself into something big here. Bigger than I thought, even,' he added after a moment.

'What are we going to do?' I thought that after you've got yourself I was being generous to say we.

'It's all right for you,' he grumbled. 'You can just disappear. Do a moonlight. You've done it before.'

Implying I was in practice, so no doubt it would come easy. I ought to put him right. But there wasn't time. 'How do I live? Like I did before?'

He flushed. 'There must be casual work...'

There was Todd and Jan's apparently bottomless pocket, but I wouldn't say so. 'What about you?'

'I'm being set up.'

'Quite.' I didn't point out that I'd used the same words only half an hour before.

'If you weren't around, perhaps that'd get me out of it.'

'Do you really think so?' I tried to suppress the scorn in my voice. 'You say nothing, Taz, and you're theirs forever.'

'But – '

'But me no buts!' Now where on earth had that sprung from? 'You have to take this to the very highest authority you can. You've got me as a witness. You've got Paula's photos and rope to back you – Taz! What did you do with them? You handed them over to Moffatt, didn't you?'

He looked at his feet. 'He seemed such a decent guy. Plus being a very senior officer.'

'"A man can smile and smile and be a villain."' Or something like that.

Taz blinked. 'You're right.'

And this was a man with the best public school education.

I didn't blame him for falling for Moffatt's charm. I had myself – nearly. And of course, young cops naturally fall into respect mode when with a man further up the promotional tree than he can even aspire to. Wrong there, Caffy. Taz aspired to head the Met. Well, if we could pull this one off, maybe it'd help.

'We're not quite on our own, Taz.'

He didn't need words to tell me that he didn't rate Paula's Pots high in the fight against crime.

'You remember the caravan. All that ducky equipment. Well, there are the owners. Todd and Jan Dawes. You remember,' I prompted, 'the pop star.'

'A pop star!' Another sneer.

I'd wipe it off his face as I ought to have wiped the first. I said mildly, 'And his lawyer wife. I think we should join them for lunch.' We'd spoken about a picnic here. I almost called them over. But I saw a little glint over Taz's shoulder. Security camera! Security cameras everywhere in a place like this.

'Meet us by the exit. Meanwhile, Taz, I don't know if you did any acting at school, but you're up for an Oscar now. You're going to tell me to get out of your life and never darken your phone again. And I'm going to burst into tears and run away. You'll stalk off in the opposite direction. And it'll all be videoed by CCTV.'

Jan and Todd joined me a few yards from the chaos of the exit. 'You poor child!' Jan enveloped me in a warm hug. 'Let him go, the shit. He isn't worth it.'

'I know he's not,' I whispered. 'But all that lot was a charade for the cameras. He's agreed to accept your advice. There he is, over there.'

We sneaked into a loud, nasty pub. We sneaked out again, Todd, tapping his ear.

'Loudspeakers,' he said. 'Lost a lot of hearing in both ears. I'm fine in small groups, but with background noise all I can do is try to lip-read. It'll be a hearing-aid soon, but somehow that's an admission of defeat.'

Jan squeezed his hand. I wished I could. It was a big confession to make for a man who needed the Megs of this world to believe he'd be young forever. After a moment, I reached for the other hand, and squeezed that.

We walked higgledy-piggledy back towards Charing Cross, eventually finding a café with outdoor tables. Goodness knows what traffic muck we'd eat with our food, but at least Todd would be able to hear the conversation. Taz was despatched inside to order.

'Are you sure he's up to this?' Jan asked, not mentioning what this was.

'He's got to be. If he gives in now he'll be under their thumb forever. Moffatt and the others will have bought him, just as Granville bought me. And their brand will be even deeper than mine.'

Taz was coming back. I started to talk about historic buildings.

'You're prepared to go back to Fullers?' Taz squeaked when I told him my plans.

'If you're prepared to go with Jan or one of her colleagues to the Police Internal Investigation people, yes. You see, I reckon Paula and I know what may have started out as a priest hole but which may not be a hiding place for something even more valuable than the hooch I suspect Free Traders used to keep there.'

Todd shook his head. 'They wouldn't risk keeping illegal immigrants there. People leave evidence.'

'Who says,' Jan reflected slowly, 'that people are the only things – oh, what a dreadful word to use! I'm sorry! – that need hiding? People smuggle all sorts of commodities.'

'We'll find out if I go back,' I said, trying to stop my jaw setting in a stubborn line. 'Paula and I were nearly on to it.

You see, Marsh only got interested in what I was saying about the corpse at Crabton Manor when I mentioned the Pots were hoping to work at Fullers. The moment I mentioned the name, he was out of the room. And when he got back in, he'd found out all about my past. Then he slung me out.'

'If only you had a witness,' Jan sighed.

'No, I don't. But I do have a friend at court. In the police station at least. Her name's Sherree. She was kind to me when I turned up. Funnily enough I returned the favour last night.' I explained. And then remembered. 'The terrible thing is I might have got her into trouble too.' I told them about the pen.

'Well done,' Taz said, through a mouthful of egg and cress.

Todd seemed to realise the darker implications. 'So either they'll believe Sherree doesn't know where it's come from – in which case she may find herself in the shit – or they will believe her, and they'll know you've twigged and are therefore all the more dangerous. And she'll still be in the shit. But probably nowhere near as deep as the shit you're in. Oh, Caffy.'

'How did you realise you were being spied on?' Taz asked.

'Sid – the man they'd put in undercover – used a couple of words and phrases I'd used to Paula the previous evening. I thought it might be coincidence at first. Then, although he had the chance to go into the Manor for a look round, he didn't take it. And he seemed so critical of us – well, I lost faith in him.' Him and most of the human race.

Todd put up a hand. 'Did you have the bag with you when you did your recce around Fullers?'

I shook my head. 'I was the butchest dykiest decorator you've ever seen. Far too butch for a bag, anyway.' I did a little impression of myself: they managed to laugh.

'So they've no idea what you found?'

'No, but they may know what I was looking for. I had my bag near me while we were talking about our plans. On the ground. We were at a picnic table in a pub garden.' I willed Taz to say I was probably out of range, but perhaps he was too low in the pecking order ever to have learned about surveillance aids. Perhaps I'd kept cheerful so far on adrenaline: all of a sudden, it subsided, and all my hope and optimism drained.

And then I realised that both my hands were enclosed in warm firm grasps. Todd and Jan were there for me. And if they could pop the steel back into my sagging spine, there was no knowing what they could do for Taz.

With Jan's contacts it didn't take her long to learn whom to phone at Scotland Yard. I supposed I'd dimly suspected that the place only existed in fiction, the sort where local plods are so bewildered by the Murder of one of the Gentry at the Big House that they have to summon aid from the aristocratic brainboxes in London Town. I'd seen the rotating post outside New Scotland Yard often enough on TV to believe in that, of course. We decided not to go mob-handed. Todd and I would hang around while she marched Taz off with her.

'What do you want to do now?' Todd asked.

With Todd I could say things safe in the knowledge I wouldn't shock or disappoint him. 'You see that ice cream seller over there? I can't remember how long it is since I had an ice cream.'

He smiled kindly, adding, as he fished in his pocket for change, 'I warn you – it'll taste of nothing except sweetness. Cold sweetness.'

'What should it taste of then?'

'Well, vanilla or strawberry or whatever. That soft stuff – it's got all the charm of…of wallpaper paste!' he concluded triumphantly.

'I'll give it a miss, then. What I really want,' I said, 'is to get back to work. I'm letting the others down.'

'Or endangering them – which is, as I recall, where we came in.' He grinned. He wasn't blaming me.

I nodded. 'In that case, I want to be at Fullers, getting them out of danger.'

'How do you mean?'

'If I can find that passage, if I can have evidence no one can argue with, then everything can be wrapped up.'

He shook his head. 'Very dangerous.'

'Not as dangerous – for Fullers, that is – as having a load of plods attacking the place with those rams they use to open people's front doors. They wouldn't do Fullers' plaster and woodwork any good at all. And probably not dangerous at all if the police think I'm safe and sound at the hotel. I bet they checked with reception and found I was a dirty stop-out last night.'

'Where did you sleep?'

'Back at my flat. Some obliging soul had cut off my electricity, though I don't recall telling them to.'

He gave me one of his shrewd looks. 'How do you pay?'

'Direct debit.'

'Have you checked your statement?'

Funny, I didn't expect Todd to know about all these day-to-day things: if I'd thought about it, I'd have expected him to have secretaries and accountants and housekeepers to do dull things like paying bills.

'Not yet. There wasn't one – hang on, there was hardly any post, either! You don't suppose – Todd, am I officially dead?'

He pulled a face. 'That might be a good thing. Wasn't that the plan when they blew up the caravan? To prove to Granville that you were dead?'

'Or at least in hospital. You know what, I must have missed the announcement of my own death.' There was what would have been a silence except for the roar of the traffic. After the country, even after dozy little Ashford, it was deafening. Had it been as bad as this in Birmingham? And it wasn't just traffic, it was people. Everyone seemed to be yelling.

'I bet we could find a better ice cream,' Todd said.

While we waited for room service to deliver it, I used Todd's phone again, this time to check with my bank what had happened to my direct debits. They'd all been returned, account not known. Someone had been busy on my behalf. 'Well, don't, whatever anyone says, whatever documentation they have, close down this account,' I said firmly.

'We only do that if we get a death certificate,' the helpful Northern voice told me. Where was she from? Leeds?

'Even if you get a death certificate,' I insisted. 'Do nothing unless I tell you.'

'You can't tell us if you're dead, though,' she said delicately.

'I don't intend to die,' I said. 'Look, if I do, a friend will phone giving you my password. But only then can you close my account. My overdraft, more like.'

The girl didn't laugh.

The ice cream was excellent. Todd watched as if fascinated by the thoroughness with which I cleaned the glass.

'Why didn't you have one?'

'At my age, you have to watch all sorts of boring things like calories and cholesterol. Plus the cold makes my teeth jump.' He grimaced. 'I've been thinking: do you really think you could find the hidden room, passage-way, whatever, at Fullers?'

'If Paula and I couldn't, I don't know who could – unless they knew about it already, of course, or went round with those ram things.'

'I'll have to talk this through with Jan, of course. But if you needed someone to ride shotgun, with a fast getaway car, I'd be game.'

'It doesn't exactly go with watching calories or cholesterol. If you've got a dodgy heart, Todd, it wouldn't be wise.'

He roared with laughter. 'My heart's fine. How old do you think I am, for God's sake? But it was kind of you to think about it,' he added. 'I want to die at a ripe old age, as I hope you do. The other thing we'd have to worry about is muddying the police waters. If only we knew who was doing what to whom!'

'And if we could trust Moffatt when he said he'd involved all those police and other agencies. He certainly got the caravan blown up, and – Todd, I believed him! Or my tum believed him, after that wonderful meal. And the booze, of course.'

'Well, we know the caravan was blown up. The people your Taz notified did that.'

'Not "my Taz".'

'I though you said that dramatic parting was fiction?'

'It was. We seem to have parted a while back – not sure when.'

'So you're footloose and fancy-free?' His face crinkled in a smile.

Jesus, he wasn't going to make a pass at me? Surely not! I hadn't felt a single vibe! I loved him like I'd have liked to love my dad, if you see what I mean.

I waited too long to reply. He looked at me closely. 'I'm sorry. It's none of our business, but Jan and I were just wondering why there wasn't a man in the life of such a pretty young woman, that's all. Pretty until the makeover, at least,' he added, laughing and ruffling my mop.

A man! After all the men who'd flitted through my life, would I ever need another one? Maybe a young and unattached clone of Todd. But what decent man would want to take up an ex-tart, even one who'd been celibate for years? I think Todd knew he wasn't getting the whole answer when I replied blithely, 'Absolutely footloose and fancy-free.'

Todd was just tempting me with full afternoon tea either in their suite or, better still, he said, in the hotel lounge so I could people-watch, when the phone rang.

Picking it up swiftly, he mouthed, 'Jan,' to me, and settled down to listen, his face increasingly stern. 'You're joking! …I don't believe it! … You cannot be serious!' he added in John McEnroe mode. At last he cut the call. 'You may not believe this,' he said, almost grinding his teeth, 'but the man they need to see is in a meeting. And the man below him. And his deputy. All very important! Top brass! All too bloody busy talking about fighting crime to fight crime.'

'Is there no one else – ?'

'I'm quite sure there is,' he said grimly. 'But you don't know Jan like I know Jan. She's going to see the top man if she has to sit there till midnight. And maybe she's right, in the present instance. Maybe only the top guy has the clout to sort all this out. OK. Did you want that afternoon tea or do you want to check dutifully into your hotel and suss out Fullers?'

I blinked. 'What about Jan – don't you want to discuss it with her?'

'The mood she's in now she'd tell us to go and make sure we took a machine gun. Two machine guns. I'll send her a text message. If I can remember how, that is. Jesus, Caffy, remember to take your gingko biloba!'

I smiled vaguely. He wasn't to know a packet of pills like that would consume my entire food budget for a week – and more. He was now fizzing with energy, and no amount of sitting around feeding his face with fine food would calm him. So I said nothing as he bundled us into his Range Rover, delivered to the front door by a young man I wanted to yell at not to be so servile. Valet-parking was a job, for God's sake: if he was doing it well, he should hold his head up.

Todd drove slowly out of London – slowly was the only way – and then pulled over. 'I bet you'd like to drive, would-n't you?'

I risked asking outright. 'How did you know?'

He laughed. 'You'll tackle anything, Caffy. I like to give you a challenge to rise to. Go on, try it! Your excuse is that I need to work out how we get you into the hotel without them seeing me and get you out again without them seeing you, and I can't think while I drive.'

'I've been thinking about nothing else while you drove,' I admitted. 'But the first's easy. You drop me somewhere off-camera if they've got any, that is, and I walk. But we'll need to find a thick hedge – since that's what they'll be expecting, I'll change back into my working gear.' I patted the carrier bag on my lap.

'I wondered what was in there. OK. It won't be so bad walking in those trainers. But what about escaping?'

'That's probably not too hard either. There's a kitchen lad whose bike I should be able to borrow. I can meet you at Fullers.'

'That's a hell of a way to cycle. There must be a lay-by where I can wait.'

'There is. I'll point it out.'

'You'll still have to drive. I've got to text Jan, remember.'

I quite enjoyed it. No, I really enjoyed it. He was a bit surprised when I pulled up at Ashford's big B&Q, but was happy to fork out for a tool belt and a couple of items to hang from it.

The helpful young pseudo-Frenchman who'd pointed out I was booked in for five nights was on duty, smiling. In a genuine Frenchman, it would have been the sort of smile that tells me he knows I didn't come home the previous night and that he hoped the sex had been good. As it was, it just looked seedy. 'And will you be requiring a reservation for dinner this evening, Madame?'

'I'm not sure.' I flicked a glance at my watch. 'I've got a shocking headache. I may just lie down with an aspirin.'

It didn't take me long to change yet again, this time into clean jeans – goodness knows why – and the least vivid top I could find. Slipping the 'Do Not Disturb' sign on the door-knob as I left, I headed not for the lift but for the stairs. With luck they'd continue beyond the reception floor into some sort of basement. Yes! I made the acquaintance of huge bales of what I presumed was dirty sheets and pressed on. More stairs the far side. These definitely led to the kitchens: someone was cooking something involving garlic, and I nearly dribbled. Maybe I should have had that afternoon tea after all. Hell, the smell was so inviting I'd have dribbled anyway.

There was no way the kitchen would be empty. I'd just have to hope everyone was too busy to notice me. In any case, it dawned on me that provided I looked purposeful enough, it didn't matter if I were seen. Someone had left a wad of paper – yes, laundry lists – on one of the bundles. I stalked through the kitchen reading it so intently I nearly collided with a chef with a mega-knife, the sort I'd have liked, come to think of it, hanging from my belt. There propped against the railing was the bike I'd used before. The little rat had bought not lights but a chain! Arms akimbo, I turned back into the kitchen, still clutching my fistful of paper.

'That bike!' I bawled. 'Whose is it? I said, whose bike is that?'

At last Mal sneaked forward. I pointed with what I hoped looked like authority: outside.

Once there, I held my hand out. 'Well?'

'Well what?' he asked sullenly.

'Keys.'

'It'll cost you – '

'It'll cost you – your job if you cheat on the deal. Fifteen quid you had, to buy lights.'

He threw the keys in the air. 'Seems like a seller's market to me.'

I grabbed them as they fell. 'All's fair in love and keys. Don't worry. You won't have to walk home.'

He came and stood over me as I fumbled with the lock. 'How could you get me the sack?'

Cheat he might be, but he was clearly a few spokes short of a wheel.

'You'll have to wait and see, won't you?'

'Let's draw up some ground-rules,' I said. I probably would-n't have got away with that but Todd had just wrestled the wretched bike into the Range Rover and was a touch breathless. 'The first is that you stay in the car and sound your horn if there's any sign of trouble.'

'And the others?'

Bother. 'I don't take any risks.'

'And you come back and report if you find anything interesting. Promise? But that's not as important as the no risks rule.'

'For either of us,' I conceded. 'What does Jan say?'

'A lot. It'd be an exaggeration to say she gives us her blessing, but I think she understands.'

'I'm sure she does,' I said, ironically. 'I'm sure she loves the idea that her husband is larking round the countryside in the company of an ex-whore hell bent on smashing up her beloved house.'

'But not as violently as the police would,' he said. 'OK. And we're in luck! No police presence!'

'In that case back in – so you can make a quick getaway if they do appear. Which I'll bet they will, somehow. And keep your eyes peeled. And if in doubt – Todd, I really, really mean this – save your own skin. I know the house well enough to hide until you can get help. Unless they try to burn it down,' I added under my breath.

He looked around at the mess left by the explosion, the fire and the removal of the caravan. His face set. He said suddenly, 'We need someone else. Two inside and one out here. I'll call Paula.' His jaw set and his thumb was already pressing buttons.

'OK,' I agreed, buckling the belt. Yes, hammer, long thin screwdriver, a couple of chisels. 'If she wants to join me, she can. But it'll take her — what — forty-five minutes to get here. Assuming she's free, of course. I'm going in now. Just in case anyone's got wind of what we're up to.'

'You really are paranoid, Caffy.'

'Yeah. But that doesn't mean they're not out to get me.' I was just going to let myself in when I looked back. He'd sagged against the driver's door, looking older than I'd ever seen him. Old and worried. I ran back and hugged him. 'It'll be all right. You'll see.'

He kissed the top of my head. 'Of course it will.'

OK, that was two of us who were scared witless. But I really couldn't understand why I was. I was doing the easy bit, after all – simply trying to find a room used years ago to save lives. Persecuted folk, like me. I didn't know much about the religious ins and outs – school and I hadn't been very well acquainted, remember – but I pitied anyone having to hide, knowing that if their hunters caught up with them they'd be roast meat. Literally. OK, eventually – after a show trial and a spot of torture. I didn't see torture as high on Moffatt's list of leisure activities. But then, if he was employed by Granville, he'd do as he was told. Granville had had one go at my tum. There was no doubt he'd enjoy repeating the experience, with the extras he'd promised. I wouldn't. I was sure of that. Dead sure, you might say.

I shook myself, almost literally. First of all I went up to my eyrie, bundling everything up and taking it back to Todd. We both knew I wouldn't be staying in precisely the same circumstances again: if all went well, I could set up a proper room there. If it didn't, well, I didn't want Jan or Todd to have to pick over a pitiful mess of odds and ends, as I'd had to for some of my friends in the past.

Off I set again. This time I tapped and knocked in the library. If there was any decorative embossing, I tweaked and twirled it. If there was a panel out of true, I pressed it. Then I realised I'd missed the obvious. There was a loose bit of skirting. I prised it away, and there it was. A big, empty space. The torch showed me it was big enough for a stout man, assuming he could get in in the first place.

So was that it? Just a large coffin? I'm not given to claustrophobia, but I wouldn't have fancied being stuck in there for long, with nothing for company but a bottle of water and a piss-pot. No, he wouldn't need the piss-pot. He'd got a loo. What was a loo called in those days? A *garde-robe*, that was it, on the grounds that the stench of ammonia was good for your clothes. This was a bit more civilised than the hole in the floor you get in some old castles. It was actually a raised bench with a hole in it, the sort of thing old cottages used to have in their outside privy. This was rather a small hole. How on earth could you sit on it without cracking your skull on the coffin lid?

Answer, you didn't sit. You shoved your hand in the hole, and pulled up the whole seat. And it was a good job I hadn't been tempted to take a quick leak, because underneath there wasn't any plumbing, but a staircase – crude, uneven, but a staircase.

I was heading down when I remembered my promise to Todd. Backing reluctantly out of the hole, I sprinted to the front door. He'd love to see it!

He would indeed, but it was clear he wasn't going to get a

chance for some time. He was being manhandled by a load
of roughnecks into a police car. What if some of their colleagues took it into their heads to check the house?

I was back in that hole before I knew it, blessing the
workmanship of whichever of my predecessors that had provided an easy to grasp handle to pull the skirting back in
place. One satisfying click and I knew I was safe.

Safe-ish, Caffy. Those cops would have all sort of unpleasant ways of prising off skirting if they thought they were on
to something. They might even know what they were on to.
At least the chance beam of my torch had shown me what
someone wanted very much. Polythene bags of what looked
very much to be like cocaine. Big ones. It wasn't me they
wanted, but them.

Possibly.

I was down those stairs faster than was safe. But even as I
scuffed my shins and caught my arms on the rough brick, I
stopped to pull back the loo seat. And then I set off wherever
the beam of that good lantern torch would take me. With
luck they'd be so busy checking those bags they wouldn't
bother with me.

The torch beam took me for what seemed miles. Mostly
the corridor was dry, testimony again to the skill of the early
builders. Once or twice, as I listened to sounds of pursuit, I
had time to run my fingers over the old bricks, the mortar
neat even if they didn't expect anyone ever to see it. Yes, even
Helen, thin scared Helen, was part of that tradition, painting
beautifully parts that could only be seen if you lay on your
back and used binoculars. Helen, who felt like my favourite
niece in this family I'd found. Two families. Not just Paula's

Pots, but the Daweses too. Pray God – yes, it seemed easy to say that, as I hid where old men of God had hidden – that Jan's meeting with whoever had all those deputies would take place soon.

There was still no sound except that of my own breathing, not to mention the relentless thudding of my heart. Come off it, Caffy: you've been reading too many books. You need to have a relentlessly thudding heart. If it stops, that's when you're in the shit.

I paused a while to slow it, at least. Playing the torch beam along the floor, I realised that mine weren't the only feet recently to have come this way. Trainers, boots – a forensic scientist with all his modern gizmos would have a field day.

What if I took my trainers off and went on in my socks?

Daft idea, Caffy. They'd pick up sock fibres, and you'd get sore feet. Bruised toes, too, probably. By now the passage was sloping quite steeply away from the house, steeply enough to have little ridges built into the floor – the sort of things you see on some canal towpaths so horses can climb the suddenly steep gradients of the approaches to bridges. Was it wide and high enough to accommodate horses? I was too much of a city girl to know much about a horse's dimensions, but I'd have thought a donkey might fit more easily through a passage this size. Or perhaps they had smaller horses then.

Speculating about that got me another hundred yards. Whoever built this had been very determined.

As were – yes, I could hear the sounds of angry hammering echoing along the passage – the people now chasing me.

Chapter Twenty-Three

There's nothing like finding yourself at the end of a long, low, narrow corridor with people in pursuit to make you discover whether it's a dead end or not. The wall I was staring at certainly looked pretty permanent, still with the original pointing. The bricks underfoot were beautifully even: they'd not been disturbed since they were laid. Which left, in my book, the roof. Yes. A trapdoor. And someone had oiled the huge bolt securing it so that it opened without as sound as I pulled it back. But it didn't drop down. You had to push it up, which was another matter altogether. I reckon that an escaping priest would have had to be doing regular weight-training to shift it. It was a good job I'd been lugging about ladders and dealing with windows that didn't want to open. But it was tough even for me. And once one last heave had got the trapdoor open, it was damned hard to pull myself up, especially as I had the extra weight of the tool belt to fight against. I thought my arms would come out of their sockets. However much I told myself it was no worse than pulling myself out of the hotel swimming pool if someone had taken away the steps, I knew I was lying. It was far worse than that. Then I realised if I turned towards the end face of the tunnel I could walk myself up. And did.

Better shut the trapdoor.

I'd scarcely enough breath or energy. But I managed. And then, for good measure, I collapsed on top of it to catch my breath. I'd be invisible should anyone be looking – surrounded by gorse or something, whatever it was was really thick and prickly, ready to tear me apart when I crawled through it. Not to mention my jeans and top. And while I could grow new skin…

I wasn't far from the Royal Military Canal where I'd seen – how long ago was it? – that human cargo being loaded into the vans. The canal meant the wide footpath this side and the road other. Should I risk running along the road – OK, struggling along it – or should I stick to the canal bank, using the reeds as cover? Against that, I must balance the risk of slipping and falling in. And it was one thing to manage a few lengths in that shallow little hotel pool, quite another to take a dip in water that might be deep or weed-choked. There was always the canal path, of course, but that was far more exposed and I'd be very vulnerable, not knowing where I should cross the canal if I had to.

OK, decision time.

I chose the road. Despite all the obvious things against it, it was safer underfoot for a tired walker. Dog-tired, and very hungry. I thought fleetingly of those posh afternoon teas. Which brought me to Todd: how was he, dear, innocent, naïve Todd, getting on in the hands of the police? I mustn't think about him, or about anything bad happening to him. No: even though not everyone recognised him, he was still too much of a public figure for anyone to take risks with him. If he kept a cool head he'd be all right. Please God he'd be all right. I couldn't bear the thought of anything bad happening to him. It didn't help to think that he was probably worrying himself sick about Jan and me.

Back to the situation I didn't have to speculate about. My own. So far, so good. At least being in the country meant that there were no nasty kerb-crawlers so far. But what about other cars, police cars in particular? Surely, even if a stray police car picked me up, Jan would have bent someone's ear by now. Chewed it off, more likely. Todd and me – we'd both be safe soon.

For some reason I chose to head north-east, towards Appledore and ultimately Hythe and Folkestone. I don't know why. Rye would have been just as good. Good for what? I'd no idea. I just kept plugging along. Cars passed in both directions. I pretended I was invisible.

Soldiers must have patrolled along here for years, fearing a sight of Napoleon and his Froggie army. Or in my grandparents' lifetime, keeping an eye out in case Mr Hitler wasn't kidding. At least they were protected by cannons or by hand weapons.

I had nothing. No ID. Nothing except my toolbelt, which didn't seem to be doing anyone any good. But it was well made, and I hated waste, so I kept it on, telling myself that joggers bought weights to make them fitter faster. Good for them.

So why weren't there police cars looking out for me? After all that fuss and palaver, I'd have expected a helicopter with a searchlight, the sort that had disturbed my sleep with terrifying regularity back in Brum, or, come to think of it, what I feared most – dogs. A fugitive can outface most things, but not dogs. And here I was, walking unhindered along the road.

Things were beginning to make no sense at all.

At last I could see the lights of Appledore. There were pubs there, two of them. The first with a payphone would get my custom. I knew several phone numbers off by heart,

Taz's and Jan's for starters. One of them would reply. Or there was even Paula's – harsh-tongued, safe Paula, who might already be heading this way anyway, in response to Todd's original phonecall. I needed to warn her fast.

The Black Lion. Perhaps I didn't look as bad as I expected: no one turned to stare at me. At least, not for long. But the payphone did nothing except swallow my change.

The barmaid looked very concerned, refunding it without question. She was less keen on letting me use the bar's phone, though.

'Please. It's a matter of life and death,' I gasped. She took another look at me, eyes widening. 'And I'm happy to pay.' I pressed the coins she'd given me on the bar. That clinched it.

Paula's phone rang and rang. There wasn't much point in leaving a message, was there? Hell. Before I could try Jan's number, the bar phone rang. I stepped back to let the barmaid answer. Rolling her eyes, she passed it back to me.

'Where the hell are you? And where's Todd?' Paula was not in her sunniest mood.

I told her.

'You're joking.' She was very quiet.

'No.'

'Would you like me to come and get you?'

'Could you?'

'We've come this far; we might as well finish.'

The barman – maybe he was the landlord – looked at me oddly. I ordered a tomato juice and a packet of crisps and gestured to the phone again. OK? No reply from Taz. Heart tight, I tried Jan. Nothing. And no wonderful incoming calls, either.

Leaving my drink and crisps on a table, I withdrew to the loos. Hmm. At least they had paper towels, not just a blower: I dabbed away the worst of the blood and more or less returned to the human race. I was only surprised no one had remarked out loud.

The landlord looked much more approving when I returned. 'I had a fall,' I volunteered.

'Will you be wanting to eat?'

One wall was covered with blackboards listing a huge regular menu and a load of mouth-watering specials. Knowing it was a waste of time, I checked my pockets. No: I'd only brought enough for emergency phones, hadn't I?

'I'll see what my friend says, thanks.'

Other people didn't have my problem. A waitress ferried plates piled high. I don't think I've ever smelt better chips. I ate my crisps slowly and wondered where Paula was.

I was just re-reading the blackboards for the fifth time, planning an ideal menu, when the door opened. It was hard not to throw myself into her arms. But she wasn't touchy-feely at the best of times, and now she looked ready to repel all comers.

'I ditch my date, drive hell for leather to Fullers, and find – nothing! What the hell's going on?'

Paula, swearing!

'When you say nothing, do you mean nothing? No one? No cars? Nothing?'

'Zilch. Zero. Big round nought. Since we're in spitting distance of France, rien. OK?' She sat down, helping herself to my crisps.

'No sign of anything,' I repeated, but to myself. 'So where

did everyone go? You see, Todd was anxious about my going priest hole hunting on my own. I said he'd be better keeping obbo. That's why he called you, to come with me.'

'Not to sit in the warm and dry with him? Shame. Meg would never have forgiven me, of course. Then I might have had to look for yet another painter.' She sighed.

'I'd buy you a drink, but all my money's back at the hotel.'

'Well, we could have a drink on the police if we went there. You might have to change first,' she added. 'You look as if you've been dragged through the proverbial hedge.'

'Real bush, anyway.' I started on a resume of my evening.

Halfway through, she raised a hand. 'Hang on. It sounds as if I'd better have my drink here.'

It took her a few minutes to get served. By the time she'd got back I was ready to agree with her.

'You mean you don't think the hotel's safe for me?'

'I meant it sounds as if it's going to be a long story. OK.' She sipped her iced water and listened. At last she said, 'I think you might be right. I think the hotel might not be a safe place. But then, where is? If the police can charge your room to someone else's account, can arrest a pop megastar and chase you down a smuggler's passage … Hang on – did you say you had to push the trapdoor up?'

'Yes.'

'But it was bolted on the inside?'

'Good job for me it wasn't bolted on the outside!'

I might not have spoken.

'Was there a ring or handle or anything on the outside? Caffy, you didn't notice, did you?' I might have spilt a whole can of paint on someone's best carpet, she was so scornful.

I thought, staring at the hands that must have put the trapdoor back. If there hadn't been a handle, I must have held it by the edge opposite the hinge and pulled my fingers away very sharply to let it close. That, or crush my fingertips, and I hadn't done that. But short as I kept my nails, three were broken. 'There was a sort of rebated cut into it,' I said. 'Nothing very obvious at all. And no means of locking it from the outside. I thought I might have to sit on it for a very long time.'

'Sounds as if it was used for getting out, not in,' she mused. 'Or only getting in with the co-operation of someone inside.'

'Where does that get us?'

'I just like to have these things straight in my mind.'

I couldn't argue. But I would have liked to strangle her. 'What do we do now you've sorted it out?'

She lifted an eyebrow, and counted the options on her right hand. 'Go back to the hotel, where we may be met by a police reception committee. Go back to my place, where we may find the same, and which is in any case rather occupied.' Without giving me time to ask who was occupying it – imagine, our Paula with a fellow (or a fellowess; try how we might, none of us had ever managed to suss out that aspect of her) – she continued, 'we could try Fullers, and sleep in your eyrie.'

'That's out. I took all my stuff and put it in Todd's car. Which is now – ' I shrugged.

'Your flat?'

'Someone's cut off the power.'

'Trev?'

'Cold and think of the secondhand paint fumes.'

'You're a proper little ray of sunshine.'

I couldn't deny it. My feet were sore after my trip round Tourist-land in sandals. My legs ached after the tunnel steps. My arms wished they didn't belong to my shoulders. I was still dog-tired and still bloody hungry. Another plate of chips, this one also bearing steak and other wonders, went past. 'What we could do,' I said at last, 'is get on your phone and dial all the numbers we know. We must be able to talk to someone.'

'That could take a long time. And my supper's waiting for me.'

'And your supper date? Oh, Paula, do tell.'

Just as I managed to whip up some enthusiasm she turned to me and said, 'It's none of your business. Not yet,' she added, her face softening a little. 'Early days.'

I nodded. 'There aren't all that many numbers. And it'd be quicker for you if someone could pick me up here and let you scoot off.'

'Instead of the round trip to your hotel – which may or may not be a good idea. OK. Who first?'

'Todd. I want to know that he's all right.'

She dialled, pulled a face and held out the handset. 'You'd better leave a message, then.'

All in one breath, I said, 'Todd, it's me. I'm fine. I hope you are. Can you call on Paula's mobile?'

'I'll try Jan.' Bless her for knowing I'd rather not talk to Taz. She held the handset for another message.

'Sid?'

'Sid!'

'He must have some idea what's going on.'

'But he's on their side, isn't he?'

'Not necessarily. He managed to get into work today and was very worried about you – when he'd got over being pissed off at you for leaving him at the William Harvey.'

'I left his keys. What more did he want?'

'A spot of TLC. I told him you only did TLC for buildings.'

'He may have been worried about me because he'd planted that bug.'

'You know, I never checked this bag. A bit busy.' Then and there she tipped the entire contents on to the table. Paula – lipstick?

But there was nothing more sinister.

'I wonder what shifts that Sherree works,' Paula mused. 'Because she might be a source of information.'

I looked at my watch. 'She was off-site much earlier than this last night. Do you think it's worth a try?'

'What else have we got? There can't be all that many Sherree Wagfords in the phone book.' She cadged one from the landlord, plus more water, tomato juice and crisps. Another, braver man might have suggested she was expecting a lot for very little.

Once more she thrust the phone at me. 'Go on. Your gig.'

The whole conversation would involve very delicate negotiation, I could see that. And to be honest – and when am I ever anything else? – I didn't know how to broach the goings on at the police station.

I'd reckoned without Sherree, however. Hardly taking time to register who I was, she burst into a hectic description of the chaos at the police station. Chaos sounded good.

'What's up, then?' I asked.

'It seems they were after some woman who'd messed up some operation for them, then it seems they shouldn't have been involved in the operation after all, and there's talk of suspensions and arrests and the internal investigation people are coming down and goodness knows what. Who did you say you were?'

'The girl who helped you out with that drunk last night.'

'That nice … why, you must have left your pen in my bag. And that's what's set all this off. Tell you what, there's ever such a lot of people looking for you.'

'Really? And which lot of people do you think I ought to let find me?'

Chapter Twenty-Four

I've never seen Paula move so fast: perhaps she wanted to salvage what very little was left of the evening. She drove her hatchback like Attila the Hun late for an invasion, charging round country lanes as if they were a racetrack – quite unlike her usual sedate self. She plunged us into the middle of Ashford, heading round the back of the police station to the parking spaces by the library. Talk about déjà vu. The police station car park must be full: Todd's Range Rover was parked there too, the bike still in the back, one of the wheels turning idly. No sign of Taz's Ford. There were also a number of unmarked plush cars, which didn't look as though they belonged to librarians.

Paula had obviously meant to drop me off and speed off home – to whoever. But, leaving the engine running, she got out, transferring weight from one leg to another and back again, like a toddler wanting a wee. Goodness knows she deserved a private life, but I'll admit I would have liked some moral support.

We turned to each other. 'Look,' we said, at exactly the same moment. We giggled.

I managed to jump in first. 'Have you still got those photos and the rope fibres safe?'

She nodded.

'Well, go home and sit on them. You never know,' I added, meaning to say it darkly, like in books, meaningfully.

'Know what?'

'How I shall be treated in there. And if there's evidence they don't know exists –'

'Do you want me to bring it back straightaway?' She sounded burdened and put upon but I knew she would if I asked.

'Not unless I phone you. If anything goes really wrong, you may have to take it to the media. And there's that MP, Chris Someone, who investigates miscarriages of justice.' Provided I was still in one piece to experience the miscarriage, of course.

We hugged. Not at all a Paula-ish thing to do. She must be anxious behind that calm smile. Then she flashed an urgent look at her watch, and she was away.

Straightening my back and shoulders – hell, they felt as if I'd been heaving coal – I walked purposefully round to the police station front door.

If it had been chaos during Sherree's shift, it was completely calm now. Not so much calm as deserted. No one at all in the reception area. No Sherree substitute to introduce myself to. Not even a bell to ping to announce my presence. I retired to the seats to read those educational posters all over again.

And again, and again. Where the hell was everybody? Had they abolished crime in Ashford? Or was it all committed behind the locked doors of the administrative area? Ten minutes passed. Paula was only half an hour from whoever and their spoilt supper. I wished I'd asked her to stay.

Domestic violence. Animal passports.

And the outside door flew open to admit –

'Jan!' I flung myself into her arms.

I think she'd rather I hadn't. She wasn't on her own, you see, but followed by a couple of very suave-looking men – the sort who look as if their wives polish them before they go out in the morning. But she hugged me reassuringly before she pushed me away, and introduced me as if the men's names might mean something. Thanks to Meg and her news programmes, one did. He was a long-haired barrister whose sole mission in life seemed to be to irritate the Establishment, so off the wall were the cases he took on. I recognised his face as well as his name. I couldn't place the other, a shorter man with hair cut viciously short as if to disguise the fact it was very thin. But it was he who shook my hand with a friendly smile, not like the other who seemed to be expecting something like a curtsey, for all his left-wing credentials.

I hardly expected them to join me on the plastic chairs, nor did they. Marcus, the one I recognised, was tapping away at his mobile as if his life depended on it; James, the other, held a quick but muttered conversation with Jan. I tried to pick up what they were saying, but failed. I wasn't about to interrupt: I had the strongest suspicion that lawyers wouldn't do gigs like this for free, even for a mate. At their rate per minute, I didn't want Jan picking up an even more enormous tab than she thought vital.

When at last there was a nice little pool of silence to drop my stone in, I said, 'I found about ten kilos of cocaine at Fullers. I don't suppose it was for personal use, Jan?'

Three legal eagles turned as one.

'In a priest hole in the library,' I said. 'I couldn't stay to investigate because the police were just dragging Todd away with them.'

'You let him go?' Jan exploded.

I put a pleading hand on her arm. To her infinite credit, she didn't shake it off. 'Wasn't anything I could do,' I protested.

'And we'd promised each other that if one of us was in danger, the other would save his or her skin. So I escaped down a tunnel and ended up near the Military Canal. And Paula brought me here. No, she couldn't stay – she had to get back to her new squeeze.'

'What's she like?' Jan asked, to my amazement plumping herself down beside me, apparently ready for a comfortable natter. 'Lesbian chic? Or grunge?'

'I've no idea. It may even be a bloke. We've never talked about such things,' I added.

'Nor even speculated?'

'She's my boss and my friend,' I said, writhing with embarrassment and wishing I didn't sound such a prig. I added more loudly, 'and she has another set of the photos Taz gave to Moffatt. And another fibre of rope.'

'Lezzy or not, she's beyond rubies or pearls or whatever,' James said.

'Yes,' I said. 'And she took me on without making a song and dance about my past. I take it Jan's filled you in? Good.' It spared me another repeat of the gory details. Maybe one day I wouldn't mind.

'Todd's still here?' Jan asked, rather late in the day, I thought.

'He may be, his car's still here. Or I suppose they may have taken him to Maidstone, the county police headquarters. Jan, I'm so sorry to have involved you in all this,' I told her quietly, gripping her hand reassuringly. She returned the pressure.

James said, with a serious smile, 'If Fullers is being used for drug-smuggling, Mr and Ms Dawes would have been involved sooner or later, I'd have thought.'

Marcus, meanwhile, had finished his call and was banging hard on the counter. I almost expected him to yell, 'Shop!'

Nothing. Somehow I didn't expect him to settle down to read posters.

He might have had to had the outer door not opened again, this time to reveal a couple of police officers with a great deal of silverware on their uniform considering how young they were. Although Jan got to her feet, holding out her hand and addressing them as Mr Parnell and Mr Gates, they only managed a nod, and ignored the rest of us, marching authoritatively to the door to the admin area. They were confronted, of course, by a touch-button lock. And they didn't know the code.

There was nothing for it but to exchange frosty greetings with Jan's lawyer mates, and ponder the next move.

'Since there's no one front of house,' I said, 'and there hasn't been any sign of anyone for fifteen minutes or more, maybe someone should go round the back and knock on the back door. Or a window. Don't look at me,' I said. 'I do it, I get arrested, and that's the last you see of me. I'd have thought with your insignia you'd be all right.'

Jan flashed me a warning, but what the hell? I was tired, I was hungry, I was getting cold and the salt in the tomato juice had made me thirsty. I'd done all the work and taken all the risks and I wasn't about to be anyone's door monitor.

'You may have to knock hard,' I added, 'to be heard above the noise of the shredders.'

The policemen went off together; after a while, the admin door opened and one reappeared, the one with baby-blond hair and hardly any eyebrows. Parnell? He gestured the lawyers in. 'Hang on, young lady. I'll send someone out to deal with you.'

'I don't want to be dealt with,' I said, already halfway through the door. 'It's my turn to do a bit of dealing.' I wished, as I thought of all that coke, that I'd chosen a different word.

I don't know what I expected to find: a huge room full of people looking like red-robed operatives of the Spanish Inquisition, perhaps. In fact, I found the rabbit-warren of corridors and plain rooms like the one I'd originally been interviewed in. I wasn't the only one at sea, of course: it took one of the policemen – Gates, the mouse-haired one with wide shoulders and a peachy little bum – to stride purposefully thought some double doors I'd not noticed and up a flight of echoing stairs.

Parnell kept us back. Not unpleasantly, but definitely. We heard footsteps and slamming doors. Some shouting.

Gates returned, shadowed by a couple of anxious-looking uniformed officers who looked as if they were already working out their excuses. 'It's chaos up there. You were right about the shredder, young lady. It's going to take weeks to put the evidence back together.'

'Todd?' Jan and I asked as one.

'We're fixing his release now.'

'But why, may one ask, was he arrested in the first place?' Jan was no longer an anxious wife but an authoritative lawyer.

Gates checked a file he'd acquired from somewhere. Eventually he had to admit it, though. 'Some minor traffic infringement.'

'In other words, a trumped-up charge?'

He nodded. 'It seems to me – ' he turned to acknowledge a contingent of uniformed officers storming into the corridor, plain-clothes officers in their wake – 'that you may as well let the Fifth Cavalry here do what they have to do. Go home and we'll talk in the morning.'

Jan and I now shook our heads as one.

I spoke first. 'Todd: you have to get him out of wherever he is. Now.'

'Once someone's been arrested there are procedures –' he began.

A look from Jan, augmented by the expensive smiles and upraised fingers of her colleagues, cut him off short. Parnell took the hint and a spare officer and disappeared.

Nicely in the ascendant, I added, 'Then there's a bike in the back of Todd's Range Rover that has to be got back to its owner in the next hour. Seriously. You come off a tedious twilight shift and your wheels aren't there: it's not funny. The owner's a skinny lad working as a skivvy in the kitchen. His name's Mal.'

The guy's eyebrows told me he needed a better description than that.

I smiled slowly, though my brain felt very noisy. Coins were dropping all over the place. 'In fact, you'll find a lot of skinny folk in the kitchen. But he's the only Western European one. And I've never seen an English face doing any of the service jobs, you know, cleaning and serving in the restaurant.'

'Most hotels depend on overseas staff.'

'They don't usually pretend to be anything else. One of them does, at least. There's a bloke on reception with an excruciating French accent. You know, officer, it might pay you to go in mob-handed when you return that bike – so you can check the papers of all the poor sods working there. And I don't suppose you'll find a legal migrant amongst the lot of

them. Amongst the shreds,' I added, 'you'll probably find
some photos of some tired and miserable young men being
loaded into a van. I was sorry for them, thinking they'd probably got miles to travel. I'm still sorry for them, but I'll bet
their destination was just down the road – the hotel where
Mr Moffatt put me up. He wasn't so much protecting me as
keeping an eye on me, maybe. And charging it to the account
of poor Police Constable Tadeuzs Moscicki.'

He looked across at Jan. 'He's the young man who accom-
panied you when you made your complaint.'

'Yes. I was proud of him, risking his career like that.' She
smiled at me but I didn't respond.

Instead I looked at my watch. 'The bike,' I murmured.

'And Todd,' added Jan.

Eventually, the top lawyers agreed that Jan no longer needed
their support and remembered that they had lucrative court
cases the following day. With courteous farewells all round,
they headed back to London. Meanwhile, Todd, Jan and I
trooped across to the County Hotel, tired out. Todd, who'd
spent a tedious hour in a cell, for God's sake, and Jan were no
spring chickens, after all, and I'd had very little sleep the previous night and a very long, hard day. We scarcely noticed
what accommodation we were offered or the fact the staff
were bent almost double in their anxiety to treat a Celebrity
as he deserved.

Any chance of oversleeping was ruined by Ashford's efficient street-cleaners, who were busy hoovering at about
seven. We had a hearty breakfast, attended by a no doubt specially wakened maitre d' and a team of adoring acolytes.

When Jan started muttering to Todd ominous words about cholesterol and weight, he gave me an enormous wink and her a guilty smile. We soon returned to the police station, to be accorded the best of VIP treatment there, too. Todd soon excused himself, saying he could be more usefully employed elsewhere, but Jan promised to stay with me to make sure I wasn't brow-beaten in any way,

'Brow-beaten?' Gates repeated when she told him. He looked as if he'd worked through the night.

'How about lied to and betrayed?' I suggested. 'Look, wouldn't it save everyone a lot of bother if I just told my story all over again? Starting with the body I found at Crabton Manor and my conversation with your Sergeant Marsh? That'll mean –'

'Body at Crabton Manor? I don't think I know about this.' He sat down at a desk that was until recently someone else's, I suspect, his shoulders looking wider than ever. For the first time I noticed his eyes, so grey they looked as hard as flint. I was glad that fundamentally he was on my side. With him taking notes, I began my story.

'You took photos?' he recapped at last.

'Not of the body, I'm afraid. Of the dents left in the duvet it had been dumped on. And we retrieved some fibres from the rope that had throttled him.'

'"We" will be you and your boss? Paula Farmer?'

'Yes. For some reason she didn't hand all the copies to Taz – the ones that I presume are now destroyed?'

He didn't take the hint.

I added, 'When I got back – after DS Marsh had accused

me of wasting police time – I did search the grounds in case van der Poele had simply buried him. Nothing. But I've not checked recently – he's got these really vicious dogs.'

'Would you excuse me a second?'

Before I could scream that this was what had happened before, he simply picked up the phone and dialled, using the word 'Mispa' to the person the other end. A Missing Persons check, then. He seemed to be transferred a couple of times, but finally got whom he wanted, repeating my description of a heavily built man with a lot of rings on his fingers and marks of strangulation about his neck. 'Ah,' he said at last. 'That sounds very interesting. I'll ask our witness if she'd mind identifying him.'

There was a squawk from the other end. Gates fixed those granite eyes on me. 'She'll cope,' he said, overriding what sounded like a stream of protests. 'Won't you?' He smiled at me.

'You don't have to and you're not going to,' I told Jan firmly, when she wanted to come into the morgue with me. The smell, for a start. Not to mention what I was going to have to look at. I wasn't new to it, my friends having been in the same profession as me, and running the same risks. Some far worse risks, with literally fatal results. A few years back I'd rather thought the next time I was in a morgue I'd be in the starring role, as it were, but thanks to Taz I'd been spared that. So far, at least.

Nothing prepared me for the sight of a corpse that had been in water as long as this, though, and water with crabs in it to boot. Jesus. I was hard put not to deposit all that wonderful English breakfast on the pristine tiles of the floor.

'With so little face left it's hard to tell,' I said, trying to sound judicious. 'Though that does look like a nasty bit of bruising on his neck.' That was about all I could manage. I'd reeled out to the waiting area before my brain clicked in again. 'What about his rings? Great big things?'

The WPC with us grinned. 'Would you rather see the photos?'

'Much rather.'

This time I did judicious much better. 'Yes, I'd say that those were the same rings or very similar. And I'd be prepared to say so in court.'

'Very similar isn't really good enough for a court.'

'You'll have lots of other stuff to ID him, though, won't you? Dental records, DNA – I'm sure you're like the TV cops.'

'Smaller budgets,' she said.

As an expert on small budgets, I didn't argue.

Whether Paula had had a disappointing date, or whether she was being wisely uncooperative, she certainly didn't sound keen on bringing over the photos and rope fibres. Well, who could blame her? Apart from anything else, it was the perfect day for painting, warm and dry but overcast, with hardly a breath of wind. Van der Poele still owed us a lot of money which she could only get out of him when the job was finished. Unless, of course, he was arrested first. Hell, what'd happen to our money if he ended in the clink? The RSPCA would no doubt deal with his pooches – but who'd make sure we got paid? I knew the police could confiscate criminals' money, but would they feel they had to share the spoils?

'How do you know this cop's genuine?' Paula demanded.

'I don't. Except they took me to see the corpse of that stiff I found. Very dead.'

'You're sure it was him?'

'Fairly. Tell me, the bedroom we photographed – has van der Poele stripped it? Or has he left it was it was?'

'He's stripped the bed. But you can tell this latest plod the curtains and carpet are still there.'

'He's not a plod at all, Paula – he's really so bright he's quite scary.' Damn, he came into the room just as I said that. I cut the call, flushing.

'It's OK.' He smiled, rather surprising me how attractive he could look. 'I like being bright and scary when it comes to being part of the Rubber Heel squad. Squashing bent cops,' he explained. 'I like a bit of law and order, Ms Tyler, and I don't like it when people lie and cheat and kill, especially when they're police officers.'

That was one thing we agreed on, anyway.

'I'm afraid my boss doesn't want to hand over her bits and pieces.'

'We can subpoena her if absolutely necessary. But I'd rather convince her we were decent, honest cops.'

'So would I.'

'Any idea how we can regain her trust – and yours, of course?'

'The thing is, Mr Gates, I gave Moffatt and Co a lot of information. They appeared to give me a lot back. Moffatt listed all the people and organisations he'd got on the parcel bomb case. MI5, would you believe? Well, I did at the time. But I'm not sure now. Have you got time to sit down and tell me and Jan what's going on? And I mean truthfully.'

I wonder when the last person spoke to him like that, somebody ordinary like me, not another senior officer or a lawyer. He looked completely taken aback.

After a swift gasp, Jan sat back quietly to await developments.

'I'm still trying to separate fact from fiction,' he said. 'The fact that neither Marsh nor Moffatt has uttered a word since they were cautioned doesn't help. And, of course, we know that there must be other officers involved – a regular chain of command.'

'Or irregular, as the case may be,' I chipped in.

'Actually, yes – I can't imagine they follow the approved police hierarchy, can you?' He flashed an impish smile. I was beginning to like him. 'You listed groups of people that Moffatt told you were involved with your case, one of them being us. Well, he was lying about that, no doubt about it. And about the involvement of the Human Smuggling Unit and Immigration.'

'No National Crime Squad?'

'Only when we bring them in. Which will be pretty soon, I should imagine. The only people who seem to have been the genuine article were the ones who destroyed the letter bomb. We've got a great deal of unravelling still to do, as you can see.'

'At least you have hard evidence in the form of the corpse Caffy identified. And harder, if we can persuade Paula to produce the items she's holding.' Jan sounded very lawyerly.

'There may be something else your SOCO teams could find,' I added. 'We may not have photos of those poor devils being loaded into a bread van, but I can show you where it was parked. And you know the van exists, and the removal lorry that collected them the first time I saw them. The men were walked along the canal bank – they may have dropped fag ends or something as they walked. The reeds may have caught bits of clothing. And you may find some of the workers at the hotel ready to talk.'

For some reason his laugh sounded a bit forced. Ah. I must be slipping: he was probably the sort of man who liked having ideas first.

To be fair, he recovered quickly. 'There should be some preliminary reports from the team out at the Mondiale. Excuse me.' He picked up the phone.

At last, it was clear that what Gates called honest, decent painstaking police work was going to take some time. Someone had to persuade Paula to hand over the photos, and who better than me? But it wasn't just the thought of the dogs that made me reluctant to go back to Crabton Manor. It was one thing playing schoolgirl detectives hunting for clues about van der Poele: it was another to have the theories taken dead seriously – with, of course, a corpse to substantiate them.

Jan agreed.

'Surely you could phone Ms Farmer,' Gates said. 'There's no need for you to see her at all.'

'One, it's a mobile black spot – '

'Ah. So we should have landline records of phone calls.'

'Unless Moffatt got there first.'

'You told him? Don't look like that, Caffy. The whole idea of police officers is that you can trust them.'

I nodded. Then I said slowly, 'Two, I have a living to earn, and Paula has a business to run. Crabton Manor is where I ought to be.'

He shook his head sharply, then paused. 'I suppose it wouldn't hurt to pull in van der Poele for preliminary questioning.'

Jan said sharply, 'So long as you can keep him in. I wouldn't give this much for Caffy's chances if he thought she'd grassed him up.' She snapped her fingers impressively. Years of practice clicking in rhythm with Todd, maybe.

'He wouldn't suspect anything if I was just out there in my dungarees painting away as usual.' I didn't sound very convincing to my own ears.

'Dogs,' Jan said tersely.

I shut up. Briefly. 'What about doing some preparation at Fullers? Goodness knows there's enough to be done.'

Gates managed a chilly laugh. 'Swarming with our people. Genuine ones.'

Jan said sharply, 'It's a listed building, not to mention a very lovely one. I don't want a load of macho lads hunting hidey-holes with axes and rams.'

'Point taken. Now, Caffy, you might be useful there. You and your friend Paula. Looking for further hidden spaces. We'd pay a fee,' he added, before I could say a word. 'For professional services. And we might be a better bet than Mr van der Poele: people of the criminal fraternity don't always pay their debts.'

'It'd bankrupt Paula if she didn't get paid! Or if she had to go through some long legal battle to get money off him while he was in jail.'

'You forget you have a tame legal adviser,' Jan smiled. 'We'll make sure you all get your money somehow or other. James is very good too – '

'But his fee – '

'Would be paid by van der Poele if the court awarded costs – which I'm sure they would,' Gates smiled.

'It mustn't come to that! It's all very well for someone like you with a guaranteed monthly salary to talk about litigation. Paula doesn't have that luxury. We don't have that luxury. Jan, can you make him understand?'

'We'll bankroll you ourselves if needs be.'

'Don't you think I know that? You're the loveliest and best and most generous people on God's earth, but you shouldn't have to, not if this is done properly.' I think I even stamped my foot in frustration.

Gates coughed gently and gave the sort of smile designed to wrap up a meeting. However, I still had one or two other things to ask first. 'We had a sort of minder, who painted with us till he got housemaid's knee. Sid. He dropped a pen in my bag, which turned out to hide a bug. I suppose there's no chance he was a decent undercover cop?'

Gates made a note.

'Last seen at the William Harvey Hospital down the road. I suppose he might have had to give a name and address to them?'

'Which will almost certainly be false. But it's a lead. Thanks.' This time he tidied his desk before standing.

'And Taz – my friend Taz. He won't have to pick up the tab for my stay at the Mondiale, will he? And he won't be disciplined for having dealings with Moffatt?'

This time his face was visibly patient, which meant I'd really irritated him. Still, none of this would have been uncovered but for Paula and me, and Taz had done his best to help too. 'The only thing Constable Moscicki is likely to get is a pat on the back. Tell him that if he finds things on his credit card that shouldn't be there, he should come direct to me.'

I would if I ever saw him again. 'Thanks. Just one tiny thing – sorry, I know you're busy, but when you do a job like mine you think of details – you'll send an unmarked car for Paula, won't you? After all, it's not just her and me at risk if van der Poele gets nasty, it's Meg and Helen too. And they've done nothing except work long hours for little pay.'

He held up his hands in surrender, crow's feet dancing round his eyes.

I grinned, a big matey grin. 'Yes, I know I'm a bossy boots. My…my pimp used to tell me I'd make a wonderful dominatrix.'

'There has to be another way from here,' Paula said, squatting beside the gaping priest hole in the library, 'not just down to the canal but also up to your eyrie.'

'That's what we reckon,' said a young woman my age and build wearing a paper suit. 'But we can't investigate further from this end till we've finished our examination of the tunnel.' She gestured at lighting cables and polythene bags and all the things my TV watching demanded.

I nodded. 'Let's think their way. If you know about the priest hole, you're going to make sure you exploit all its possibilities. Those men we assume were illegal immigrants – I suppose they couldn't have come up to the house before Jan and Todd bought it? It'd be easier to collect them from a house than from the roadside. You never know, the builders who did the roof and other structural repairs might have seen something.' I'd ask Jan to look out their names and addresses for the police – always assuming they hadn't thought of that already.

'So we'd better go up to the eyrie,' Paula said, leading the way via the intervening landing, the end wall of which looked and sounded unremittingly solid. But she'd stopped in the entrance hall to pick up her rucksack, now bulging more than it usually did. Only then had she headed for the stairs, running her hand up that lovely banister as Todd and I had done. Which brought me by a very strange association of ideas to her date the previous evening.

'It was fine, thanks,' she said, dumping the rucksack and opening it.

She must have heard the clunk of my brain cells as I worked on a gender-free way of expressing what I really wanted to ask. 'The late meal didn't pose too many problems?'

She smiled as she shook her head. 'Leslie was very understanding.' Or did she say, Lesley? He or she? Before I could ask, she continued, thrusting a paper suit at me. 'Here, no reason why we should contaminate a possible scene of crime just because the police forget to equip us properly. The girls send their love, by the way. I reckon they should finish today, weather permitting. Be nice to have it all done and dusted before the weekend. I've got the bill all ready to plonk in his little hot hand.'

'You've got that far even without me and Sid?'

'Well, he chipped in. But I hope his knees play him up for weeks.'

'And may all his toenails grow in,' I added with venom.

We'd drawn a blank before, of course, but I for one was determined that my eyrie's secrets should be revealed. Without any damage, of course. We tapped and pressed the woodwork, like refugees from a children's storybook. Perhaps the idea had always been that someone could escape up here from below, not the other way round. But it seemed such a waste.

'Let's try the roof-space above here, shall we?' I said at last.

'Thought you'd never ask. Come on!'

However used to it you'd think we'd get to sizing up spaces, it took us a moment to orientate ourselves. Picking our way to the area we eventually settled on, we peered carefully round. It would be easier to reach it on our hands and knees, because the roof, with its profusion of beams, sloped so much, not to mention the fact that the spaces between the joists weren't uniform.

'A chimney? Where did that spring from?' Paula demanded. 'I don't remember one down below.'

'You wouldn't. The one from there comes up over there. This is a little fake, I'll bet.' Saying it was one thing, proving it another. Eventually we discovered that the bricks the furthest side had hardly been mortared. A quick wiggle or two, and they came away in our hands.

'Looks like an ordinary chimney down there. It's even sooty.' Paula showed a blackened palm.

'Even so, I reckon there's room to get down there.'

'Only for a child. OK, OK, I know you're skinny. But I tell you, you're very tall for a child!'

'All the more for the Fire Brigade to get hold of if I get stuck.'

For a few long minutes it was touch and go. But then my feet round metal rungs driven into the wall, and – provided my shoulders would squeeze a bit smaller – yes! I could climb down.

'Torch!' I yelled.

Nothing happened. No torch. No voice. Nothing.

'A phonecall! What sort of excuse is that!' I demanded when I'd let myself out of the space in my eyrie. It wasn't difficult. The rungs stopped at exactly the right level, and as I turned to steady myself my hand rested naturally on a smooth round knob. I didn't need to do anything – it slid gently down, there was a click, and a panel tipped towards me.

'I'm sorry.' It was clear she wasn't. She looked like one of those Halloween pumpkin faces, all lit up from inside. Lesley or Leslie, no doubt.

'Well, now you've got your date for tonight sorted, let's have a proper look, shall we? If you're up to passing me the torch, that is?'

This time it was part of the floor we had to move, not easy in a confined space. It didn't lift, either, but slid, as easily as if it had been oiled, no mean feat in a house where every old timber was slightly out of true. Steep steps descended presumably to the library. But we couldn't use them. Someone had decided they worked well as shelves. Stacked on each were more bags of what I was sure was cocaine, plus a few packs of what was almost certainly heroin. As I played the torch, we gasped as one. Trussed like a Christmas turkey with blue rope, the sort of rope we used, the sort of rope that had throttled van der Poele's guest, was a stiff.

We said it as one. 'Mr Granville, I presume.'

The young woman from SOCO was one of the first on the scene. 'You talked about intelligent use of available space, didn't you? That looks pretty intelligent to me. Except you found him. I suppose the smell would have given him away sooner or later.'

Another bit of a play crept up on me, something about nosing someone as you go up the stairs into the lobby. It wasn't the best bit of the speech, as I recalled – that was where the baddie was told that the victim was in heaven. 'If your messenger find him not there, seek him in the other place yourself,' I murmured.

'But who is yourself?' asked a voice behind me. Gates.

'I'd like it to be Moffatt. Or van der Poele, of course. Or both, aided and abetted by Marsh. But I've no idea why.'

'It'd would be a nice clean sweep. Unlike you, I have to say!' The grey eyes twinkled. 'But we've no idea why, either. Well, we shall see. Meanwhile this further bit of hard evidence should prove useful. By the way, your cycling friend Mal sends his thanks. As you observed, he was about the only native English speaker in the place. And one or two of his overseas colleagues are singing quite happily. Well done,

Caffy. We shall be inviting forensic accountants to look at the Mondiale's books. I think they might make illuminating reading. Money laundering,' he added, as I looked blank. 'Drugs money has to be made respectable – and how better than in a hotel, especially one offering bureau de change facilities?' He smiled again.

I got a vibe. Not an unpleasant one. And one I was reciprocating, if you can reciprocate a vibe. Imagine me fancying a bloke after all this time. Half-fancying. I'd never wholly fancy a man whose eyes could be as cold as his.

'I wonder if you'd do another quite unpleasant thing for me, Caffy. We shall have to leave our friend down there for some time while he's photographed and so on. But we shall need someone to identify him, if not formally. Would you do the honours?'

'Of course,' I said briskly.

'But this time – no argument – you'll have someone with you. OK?' came Todd's voice. 'Meanwhile, I don't know what your officers do about breaks, Gates, but it's pretty well lunchtime. We could knock up a few sandwiches if you don't mind an al fresco meal.'

That ought to have prepared me but it didn't. Todd had certainly had a productive morning. If I'd thought about it I'd have expected him to replace the blown up mobile home with its twin.

He'd done that all right. And added another twin for good measure. A matched pair stood on the site of the first.

Chapter Twenty-Six

Paula was to be driven back to Crabton Manor after lunch, which wasn't quite the social success I think Todd had hoped it would be. Apart from a lot of police comings and goings, there was a good deal of quiet shop-talk from the SOCOs, and Paula had snubbed Jan's gossipy interest in her new significant other. Todd himself was more subdued than I'd known him, rather edgy and anxious. He did something I'd never seen him do before – he kept glancing at his watch. But when I asked, he insisted he was fine.

Before Paula left, I spoke to Gates again: 'I suppose the bloke driving Paula couldn't hang round a bit at Crabton Manor – you know, just in case.' I wondered how I could wangle myself a lift there – I had a yen to see van der Poele's face when he was handed the bill.

'He'll do better than that. He'll get her to find him some overalls and he can help pack all your gear. Before you ask, he's promised not to get housemaid's knee. Would you prefer to see Granville before or after he's sanitised?'

Todd was by my side. Did he have radar ears or something? 'In the surroundings that'll most convince her that he's dead. Haven't you noticed, she'd not stopped shaking since you asked her to ID him? This is a man who's done her permanent lasting harm. Ineradicable.' He was willing me to show my scars, wasn't he?

I ignored him.

But however much I insisted I was fine, I knew I wasn't. I didn't even want to see him taken away lest he suddenly sat up and pointed to me. Once he was on a slab, it should be all right. Should be. In the meantime, furious that I could let a corpse do this to me, I ran – well, stumbled – after Paula and her escort. 'I'm coming too,' I said. 'I want to see the fun when Paula asks van der Poele for her money.'

There turned out to be two blokes driving Paula and me, neither inclined to chat. So I simply looked out of the window at the countryside I was coming to love – why, on a day like this, I could almost believe I was a holidaymaker admiring the view. Windmills; sheep; houses even more attractive than Fullers concealing goodness knows what or whom. Like Sid looking at the sea defences, I found myself shivering again. But I must pull myself together. Those damned dogs would smell my fear a hundred yards away. They wouldn't know it wasn't them that had scared me.

Paula inspected every single square inch of painting before nodding solemnly that we could stow everything in Trev. If I'd hoped to have a ringside seat when she spoke to van der Poele I was to be disappointed. We were all there to pull our weight. We would even check around and under the van so make sure we'd dropped no litter – with our non-smoking team, there'd be no butts, at least. Only one of the policemen helped. The other sat back in the car as if he were half asleep. But he hadn't done as Paula asked and pulled out of sight. And I had an idea he was very far from asleep. Paula nodded, as if to reassure herself, and, her clipboard like a shield across her chest, marched up to the door. We could hear that knock from the van. So could the dogs.

And so, of course, could van der Poele. But he seemed to have quite a pleasant smile on his face, and we could hear him laughing. Paula said something quite sharply, and he laughed again. We could do with Sid's little bug, couldn't we? There was a long pause: he seemed to be showing her something.

Then they shook hands, and Paula returned slowly, still with her clipboard but now with a Tesco carrier bag. I won't say it was bulging, but it certainly looked both full and heavy.

'He's only been and paid us in cash,' she announced. 'In the van, girls, before he changes his mind.'

I hovered. Did she mean me too, or would the uncommunicative policemen return me to Fullers? I looked hopefully at the one stripping off his overalls. 'Best go with them, Miss,' he said. 'Now it's our turn to have a little talk to Mr van der Poele. Sharpish, please, Miss,' he added, to Paula.

Sharpish meant me starting and driving. I reversed neatly, waiting only for a couple of cars hurtling up the lane. And then another. And another. Seizing my chance, I pulled out quickly. Too quickly. I stalled. All the swear words I knew – and there were more than enough to offend Meg – wouldn't make the bloody van start. There we were, stuck in this highly conspicuous vehicle in the middle of what was quickly turning out to be a police raid. An armed raid. Paula said, 'Everyone out this side. Now!' We obeyed. Seeing what had happened, a policewoman waved us over to their version of Trev and bundled us in.

'Keep down,' she urged.

We kept. Paula huddled over the bag as if it were a newborn baby.

There weren't many shots, and those that were fired

seemed to be almost at random. No. Whoever it was was aiming at the police vehicles. They were reinforced. Ours wasn't. And though it's hard to make diesel burn, bottles of paint thinners go up like a dream. And did.

I wouldn't quite have expected Paula to dash up and try to beat out the flames with her bare hands, but I wouldn't have expected her to watch our old friend's funeral pyre as calmly as she did. She watched till the bitter end, as we all did, her face almost impassive. But not quite. It was as if – no, she couldn't have the same pumpkin look as when she thought about her new date. Could she?

When all the fireworks were over, she got up cautiously, grimacing as she straightened her knees. She sat down on one of the seats; we were to do the same. Only when she had our full attention did she open the carrier bag and start to remove its contents, wad by wad. Wad by wad of fivers, to be precise. She counted them out, and then, I'm afraid, counted them back in again. 'He paid in cash,' she said simply. 'At first he asked for a discount. When I said that wasn't part of our terms, he just rolled over like one of his dogs. The whole lot. In cash. I suppose,' she said to the WPC, 'now everything's quiet here, you couldn't run me to a bank, could you?'

The young woman shook her head sadly. 'I think I'd better run you to the police station in Ashford,' she said. 'Chief Superintendent Gates's orders. I'm afraid that may be stolen cash.'

'Laundered, not stolen,' Gates said calmly. 'I'm sorry about the mix-up. I think it ought to be impounded but–'

'If you impound it, these women can't eat or pay their rent this week. I can't buy paint for the next job.'

'A bank loan?' he ventured. So my impassioned lecture had been in vain.

'I can't afford a bank loan. So it looks as if another small business will bite the dust.' Paula might have spoken slowly and calmly, but she stood over him like an avenging Fury.

He stood too: they were eyeball to eyeball. At last I twigged. He was winding her up. He'd promised me she'd not suffer. So why trouble? Because he liked his power, that's why. What a good job I hadn't let myself forget those cold grey eyes and started fancying him. 'My superiors – '

'Bollocks,' I said. 'Stop messing us about, Gates. It's been a long hard day and we need to get to the supermarket for our weekend's shop. Unless your superiors would like to push our trolleys and pay?'

It wasn't the supermarket that I went to, of course. It was the morgue. Fortunately I was so fired up with Gates I forgot to be anxious. And I wouldn't give him the satisfaction of asking why someone at his level, a man surely more used to pushing papers than accompanying young women on routine visits to stiffs, was driving me himself – surely not just because Todd told him to?

I chose my moment – he was just manoeuvring into a tight parking space. 'So who killed Granville? And why?'

He pulled on the handbrake before he replied. 'We're almost certain – on the forensic evidence, of course – that it was van der Poele. Until we've talked to him we can't be sure.'

'Come now, he's not going to lie there on his hospital bed and confess, is he?'

'You never know.'

'I do. Van der Poele wouldn't confess to living and breathing if he wasn't "persuaded" to. And I'm sure you people aren't supposed to "persuade", are you?'

'Not unless you're on the wrong side of the law, and you're trying to "persuade" an apparently friendless young woman. It seems it's open season for anything, then.' He gave an apologetic smile.

Which I didn't return. 'Van der Poele. Were he and Granville in the same business? Or rivals? Or was it needle going way back?'

'You never give up, do you? Van der Poele made a lot of money from drugs.'

'So did Granville. So was it a turf war?'

'More likely, according to our sources, who I'm not about to reveal even to you, Caffy, they'd become partners in this illegal immigration scam – van der Poele had premises he could stow a few people in if needs be. Granville had managed to find those hidey-holes at Fullers. A nice deal. He'd have liked to own Fullers legally, I suspect, but your friend Todd Dawes outbid him and moved Paula's Pots in before he could clear everything out. Everything including a lot of drugs. And the drug-dealing hadn't been part of the deal.'

I nodded. It sounded feasible. If you didn't ask why they hadn't shifted them when the builders were sorting out the outside. Which I did.

'We'd better check out the builders: one of them must have been involved. Maybe one found the cache and offered information about further hiding places – like the staircase from the false chimney.' He seemed to think that had ended the conversation.

It hadn't. 'But what about "my" body – the one on the bed at Crabton Manor?'

'According to the folk at the hotel, one man got stroppy about the conditions he was supposed to work in. So he was taken to work somewhere else: Crabton Manor. They assumed he'd got a nice soft billet there.'

'Soft, yes. On top of that duvet.'

'And now I'm afraid we've got to look at another of "your" bodies, Caffy.' He laid a hand on my wrist. 'Are you sure you're up to this?'

Death hadn't been kind to the cruelly handsome man that had been Clive Granville. Which was fair, I suppose, given how kind he'd been to me.

'Is it Clive Granville?' Gates pressed.

I couldn't reply. Swallowing, I asked, 'Can you leave me alone with him for a minute? I want to say goodbye.'

'Goodbye to that bastard?'

I nodded.

He backed away.

I looked at the lips pulled back in one last grimace, the clenched fists. Standing in the sightline of those now blind eyes, I pulled up my T-shirt. 'You did that to me, you bastard. You made me live with this forever. But at least I'm alive. Get that? And now you can't touch me. Not here on the outside or here on the inside. Ever, ever again.'

Chapter Twenty-Seven

What I needed after all that emotion was a duvet to dive under and a kind hand pressing a mug of creamy drinking chocolate into mine. What I got was a policeman in a dead faint.

Gates. Yes, Gates. Apparently he'd wanted to keep an eye on me – was afraid I might launch an attack on Granville's corpse, maybe. Anyway, there he was, his face as grey as his eyes, spark out on the tiled floor. Yelling for help, I loosened his tie and raised his feet. Yes, he was coming round nicely before the morgue first aider arrived. I'd have thought they were used to fainters: perhaps they were, but not Chief Superintendent fainters.

'Your stomach,' Gates whispered. 'He did that to your stomach?'

'I told you he wasn't a nice guy,' I said mildly, not wishing to upset the sick.

Time for him to be the strong man again. He struggled on to one elbow. 'You've made a claim to the Criminal Injuries Compensation Authority?' Obviously it was easier for him to deal with facts than emotions.

I shook my head, holding out my hand for his car keys. I'd heard of it, of course, I explained as I backed out, but had never wanted to risk asking for money in case some bright civil servant took it into his head to call Granville as a witness.

'No, it doesn't work that way,' Gates explained.

After the van, his Rover was a dream. We positively bowled along to the police station.

'Talk to your friend Jan. She'll be able to tell you all about it. You'll probably have to be seen by a shrink and a plastic surgeon and they'll ask for your notes from the hospital where you were treated. After that, it's a simple matter of telling three old guys about your pain and suffering and holding out your hand for several thousand quid.'

I didn't like the idea of a shrink, and had no intention of enduring plastic surgery, but I didn't argue. People like me can't turn their noses up at the sort of payout he was talking about. Yes, I'd talk to Jan.

His phone rang. I concentrated on my driving, of course, but strained to hear all the same. Van der Poele. They were discussing van der Poele!

'So he'll be fit to stand trial? Excellent. I want him trans-ferred to a different hospital as soon as he's fit to travel. An armed guard at all times. No, two officers.'

I hummed a little tune; Gates took the hint.

'Yes, he's still alive. It'd take more than a bullet to finish him off, I'm afraid.'

'Wouldn't it be better if he'd died? It'd save us tax payers an awful lot of money – his trial, and then providing him with board and lodging.' Whatever had happened to the open-minded, justice-seeking Caffy?

'Possibly. But it'd mean the officer who shot him would have to be investigated, which can be very unpleasant –'

'Even if the bugger was taking pot shots at him?'

'Oh, yes. I know your experience of the service hasn't been ideal, but I can promise you that most of us are dedicat-ed to seeing justice done – and if an officer shoots anyone, even in self-defence, there has to be a full investigation.'

'And the poor guy would have a death on his conscience for the rest of his life,' I mused. 'OK. A trial, then. But what will you charge him with? Apart from money-laundering?'

'Murder. Involvement in people trafficking. Drugs. All the things we spoke about earlier. A lot more maybe when Moffatt and Marsh hear he's off the streets and it's safer for them to turn Queen's Evidence than not. We could throw in trespass and anything else we find. Corrupting police officers, for instance – we've found a young constable out here in Moffatt's pocket and thus his.'

'Would that be one with white eyelashes? He was really nasty when I wanted to wash Arthur the Postie's blood off my hands. Or was it Simon something or other? He was out guarding Fullers.'

'Yes, the one who "arrested" Dawes.'

I sighed. 'Apart from White Lashes there was a nice black sergeant in Streatham. Taylor. I do hope he was just a dupe.'

'We'll find out.' He made a note. 'You're right, of course: the taxpayer will have to look after van der Poele – for the rest of his natural life, I'd say.'

I drove on in silence. I might have scars but I had my life and I had my freedom. And maybe, yes, maybe I'd have a bit of compensation to buy a car. Now that would make things easier for the Pots. Obviously Paula's insurance would come up with a new van, but another set of wheels would mean less trouble for everyone. Maybe she should ask that brother of hers. He might do a family discount. Me, with my own car!

'…when this is all over,' Gates was saying.

'I'm sorry?'

'I said, I was wondering if you might join me for dinner one evening when this is all over,' he said in a rush.

Why not? He'd given me my first frisson since Taz. But then, there was still the small business of Taz to clear up once and for all.

'I'm a bit messed up at the moment,' I said. And I wasn't just referring to my hair and clothes. 'But tell you what, ask me again when it is all over. I shall know what to say then.' I parked neatly and handed him the keys.

'Thanks. I will.' He leant across and kissed me lightly on the cheek.

Why the hell hadn't I said, Sweep me off my feet tonight and I'm yours? Because I still hankered after that kind hand passing me drinking chocolate, I suppose. And I'd no idea what duvet I'd sleep under or where. The obvious place to head was back to Fullers and those twin caravans.

The site was still seething with the police, some of them armed. But when I was delivered there in a police-car, courtesy Gates, now safely back at his desk, I was welcomed politely and handed an envelope. It was already dusk, so someone obligingly passed me a torch, not that I needed one for Jan's huge scrawl. Mine was the right hand van, she said. She and Todd had nipped out for a meal and might be back late, but I was to make myself at home.

Odd. I couldn't imagine them not including me in their meal. They'd know I'd want a bit of looking after. I felt quite let down.

And then extremely guilty. The key the officer handed me opened the door to the nicest pad I'd ever had. All this was mine! Well, mine until I had to hand it back. In the meantime, there were all the little features that had endeared their first caravan to me. And they'd had it kitted out, too – two of everything. There was a picnic hamper on the kitchen surface, champagne and wine in the fridge. In the bedroom area hung all the clothes someone had retrieved from the hotel. My bedroll from the eyrie was neatly stowed too. The bed was made up, with fresh towels nestling on it. *Dubliners* and *Evelina* lay on the bedside table.

Back in the living room were a TV, a sound system and a whole row of the books I'd given to Jan for safekeeping what seemed like weeks ago.

And the buggers weren't here to thank! Perhaps they were right. They knew I'd have a damned good howl, and they'd prefer to hug me when I'd calmed down.

But no. Even as I had my first sniff, there was a knock at the door. I bounded over to open it, holding out my arms to – to Taz?

'What are you doing here?' I asked stupidly.

He shifted from one foot to another, looking as embarrassed as any man might carrying a bouquet as big as a baby.

No point in waiting for an answer, then. 'Come on in.'

So in this fairy grotto now stood a handsome prince. Pity Cinderella hadn't had time to transform herself from a hot, sweaty, scruffy lump desperately in need of not just a new hairdo but also new hair. Still, I'd been attractive enough for Gates to kiss.

Jan – or was it Todd – had even provided a vase for the flowers. They'd set this all up, hadn't they? Popping out for supper, indeed. Making sure the coast was clear and that we both knew it. All we had to do to oblige them was fall into a passionate clinch and become an item.

If only we could.

'Look,' I began, 'you couldn't go and have a natter with your police mates, could you? Just for five minutes? Just till I've sluiced off the day's dust.' Then, trying to sound less practical and sensible, I added, winsomely, seductively, 'If there were a bath we could share it, but – '

He didn't like winsome and seductive, that was for sure. He bolted, almost falling over himself in his efforts to escape. So much for the filmy negligee I found tucked under one of the pillows. I showered in next to no time and slipped into the nice skirt and top I'd bought for my London visit. And tried to tame my hair. And applied discreet make-up and a dab of a perfume sample Meg had once passed on. And unpacked the hamper and laid the table and wondered where the hell he'd got to.

I could hardly go looking for him, could I? Shrugging, I sat on the bed and started on *Dubliners: After the Race*. I'd just got to the bit where the naïve young man thinks he's living the high life just because two men are dancing together when there was another tap at the door. Damn.

'This is like the one that got blown up, isn't it?' he said, stepping inside.

'Yes, it's very kind of them to get me my own place. I don't know how I shall ever repay them. Which reminds me, you won't have to pay for my hotel, will you?'

'I shall be reimbursed, don't worry.'

And that was about as romantic as it got. We broached the champagne, largely because I thought I deserved it, to celebrate a satisfactory conclusion to the case. It went straight to my head. So we had to have some of the picnic. And more booze.

Romance? All I wanted to do was sleep. This was fine, because although booze is supposed to provoke the desire (OK, and take away the performance) the only desire it provoked in Taz was to yawn – and not the sort of yawn shy young men give when they want to be invited into a bed.

Retiring to the bedroom, I emerged not in the negligee but with the bedroll. 'The sofa turns into a bed,' I said. 'Why don't you see to it while I tidy away here?' I couldn't bear to leave the pretty place slovenly with unwashed plates.

He did as he was told.

'I'm sorry, Caffy,' he said, spreading his hands helplessly. 'I really like you. You're a great girl. But I can't – I can't face …'

It was the scars, was it? Maybe I should think about that plastic surgeon.

'I can't face having sex,' he said with a rush, 'with someone who's made love with so many other men.'

I looked at him blankly. 'You don't understand, do you? Lots of men have had sex with me. I don't deny that. That's sex. But – can't you see? – sex isn't love. Taz, I've never made love to anyone, I promise you.'

When I woke up the following morning, he'd gone.

Chapter Twenty-Eight

It was the sort of day when decorators thank God for an indoor contract. Grey? I don't think it had ever got light, and when it tried to, the rain that had simply been threatening started to sluice down. There was a poem about it, wasn't there? Something about no dawn and no dusk, and finishing up with the single word, November.

Yes, I'd moved on to poetry, something I'd never thought anyone like me would read. I'd been to see a couple of plays, too, when Jan and Todd had thought there was something interesting in London or Brighton – and loved them both. I'd managed to identify that bit about seeking the villain in hell: it was from *Hamlet*. Todd kept on at me to do what he'd done – an Open University course – but I was still putting off applying. He pointed out that I'd done well in my residential course in August, learning all sorts of techniques I was now applying in our renovation of Fullers. But I insisted there was a huge difference between practical stuff I already knew the basics of and real, abstract learning. I'd enjoyed that course, actually, and made several good contacts, two of whom were now working here at Fullers.

Yes, there'd been a number of changes in Paula's Pots. There'd had to be. Todd and Jan had been so obviously torn between their desire to let us do the work and a quite reasonable and equally strong desire to be able to move in sometime in the next decade. It wasn't just a matter of people slapping on paint and hanging wallpaper; the whole thing had to be co-ordinated. So they'd asked Paula to become their Clerk of Works, chasing and supervising and generally doing all the things Paula does to perfection.

'It's an offer I can't refuse,' she'd confessed over a drink to celebrate the completion of our work on that pensioner's bungalow, the one we'd done at cost, largely using the paint Meg had spilt. Paula had been right: Mr Green had been happy to use van der Poele's leavings. 'So what I'm going to suggest is this: that Meg takes over chasing new business and costing it, the work I used to do. I know that Fullers will take ages to finish, but we've got to keep other things ticking over too. That's if Caffy and Helen don't mind her being promoted.'

Helen wriggled. 'I'm afraid I shan't be around all that much. You see, I've decided to go for that college course. Get my qualifications.'

There was a huge cheer, a lot of hugging, and a bit of a weep, too. Was this spelling the end of Paula's Pots? From the expression on Paula's face, it might.

'This leaves Caffy as the labourer.' Paula looked uncomfortable, as well she might. We'd always been more a co-operative than a conventional firm. She'd been irritable for a couple of days, but this felt personal.

Meg was already shaking her head. 'You know we've got to expand. And if we take on those women from Caffy's course we'll have to pay them a proper rate. Todd doesn't want sweated labour anyway.' These days she managed to talk about him without blushing.

'Well, I wasn't suggesting we should pay her less than the others.'

'I propose we promote her to forewoman,' Meg said. 'And

since we wouldn't have the Fullers' work at all if it wasn't for her, I reckon she deserves a rise to match.'

I could breathe again. So I could afford to be generous. 'I shan't need it. Not if I'm going to get compensation for Granville's scars.'

Meg shook her head firmly. 'The law takes forever. And we agreed right at the start, a fair day's pay for a fair day's work. And now you're the most skilled of all of us.'

Paula nodded. 'Yes, she is. I suppose the business can afford a bit of a rise.'

'Paula, just because you've broken up with whoever it was, there's no need to take it out on us,' Helen said, fingering a spot on her nose. 'You should be grateful to Caffy, not bad-tempered. And you've got a nice new title – why shouldn't she?'

That was the problem, wasn't it? Paula always liked to come first. When she'd settled into her new role, she'd be sweetness and light itself.

And it was light we could do with this November day. Paula was in Leeds chasing a last marble fireplace, Meg was off meeting a friend of Todd's who'd seen our transformation of Fullers and now wanted his country pad titivated, Helen was busy studying and I'd just told our new colleagues to knock off for the day. I'd stay a little longer. I liked being on my own in the place, wandering round rooms now glowing in the paint I'd helped apply and promising the same treatment to the few still scruffy ones. Nearly the same. Jan had long since decided that as the house evolved over so many periods, each room would be decorated in the style most appropriate to it. The kitchen might be as hi-tech as they came, Aga and refectory table apart, and the central heating might be state of the art, but she'd found some framed stump-work panels for a dark, Jacobean room, and elegant chinoiserie tables for the regency salon. The hall now had a particularly fine mirror in place. The silvering was past its best, but it reflected kindly back to me a young woman now with well-cut blonde hair and blue eyes.

Some evenings, after supper, I'd start work again. This area didn't really offer much in the way of entertainment for a young woman on her own, even one with an elderly Fiesta courtesy of an even more elderly lady who'd been told she could no long drive the three hundred miles a year she'd managed till she was ninety-one. Paula and I were again on good terms, and she'd twisted her brother's arm to come up with bargain wheels for me. But I didn't use them much more than the old lady. Sometimes my fellow Pots shook their heads, fearing loudly that I was going to turn into a dried-up old spinster living only through her books.

Although Todd and Jan always welcomed me as a beloved daughter into their caravan, they weren't there all that much now the weather had changed. Who could blame them, when the Caribbean called? Not me, any more than I'd have blamed my real parents. Real? Blood parents was nearer the term. Todd and Jan, with their unqualified, undemanding love, were my real parents now. I'd tried to ask them why they'd taken me so unquestioningly under their wing. They'd never come up with any sort of rational explanation, any more than I could have done. Love at first sight, I suppose, and not at all in the romantic sense. We'd just walked into one another's lives and found it the best place to be. Sometimes I was uncomfortable when I considered the extent of their generosity. But it made them unhappy if I tried to refuse things they knew I needed. I had a terrible suspicion that my Christmas gift might be a replacement for the Fiesta, simply because they wanted me to have the latest in in-car protection. Mine for them? Well. The best-painted house I could manage. The most loving restoration. The warmest welcome.

When Christmas came, and all the rooms had had their last vacuum and polish, it'd be as perfect as I could have made it. They were planning a housewarming party, a huge one: they'd already told us we must bring our friends too. Apart from anything else, Jan was desperate to see whom Paula would bring. For old times' sake, I could always invite Taz, I suppose, but I didn't want to embarrass him and his new girlfriend. Gates? No, he'd never asked me out again, nor had I really wanted him to. I didn't want a man who could only do emotion when he was shocked into it and preferred to be in control the rest of the time. Think about those cold, grey eyes. Maybe we'd have lunch or dinner when the trial of Moffatt, Marsh, van der Poele and their police minions was over, but I wouldn't hold my breath. Perhaps the Pots had been more accurate in their predictions for my future than I cared to admit. It would take a very special man to deal with my past, always assuming I ever thoroughly dealt with it myself. Maybe the therapy a friend of Jan's had organised would help. Maybe the plastic surgery, but that was still some way down the line.

I went down to lock the door behind the two women and

stood listening to the building breathe as the old timbers settled. Like a chatelaine, I walked solemnly from room to room, making sure the shutters were fast. At least I didn't have to worry about the tunnel any more. After the building archaeologists had photographed it from all angles, it was sealed. First of all a big steel plate was fastened under the trap door. Anyone on the canal-side managing to find and lift it would be met by something as impenetrable as a safe. Then it had been bricked up. Todd had insisted on the belt and braces, although he'd caused a purist eyebrow or two to lift.

There was the sound of a car outside. Yes, Jan and Todd's Range Rover. And they gave their familiar triple toot, so I'd know it was them. The security lights, promised when the troubles began, came on in greeting.

There were their voices now.

So, as if I owned the place, I flung open the big front door, opening my arms wide.

'Welcome home,' I said.